The Raging Sands—

Some change in the failing light must have woken him. For a moment it was impossible to believe that he was not still dreaming; he could only sit and stare, paralyzed with sheer astonishment. No longer was he looking out across a flat, almost featureless landscape meeting the deep blue of the sky at the far horizon. Desert and horizon had both vanished; in their place towered a range of crimson mountains, reaching north and south as far as the eye could follow.

For long seconds the splendor of the scene robbed it of all reality and hence all menace. Then Gibson awoke from his trance, realizing in one dreadful instant that they were flying far too low to clear those Himalayan peaks.

The Sands of Mars

by

ARTHUR C. CLARKE

A SIGNET BOOK
NEW AMERICAN LIBRARY
TIMES MIRROR

This is an authorized reprint of a hardcover edition published by Harcourt Brace Jovanovich, Inc.

SIGNET TRADEMARK REG. U.S. PAT. OFF. AND FOREIGN COUNTRIES
REGISTERED TRADEMARK—MARCA REGISTRADA
HECHO EN CHICAGO, U.S.A.

SIGNET, SIGNET CLASSICS, MENTOR, PLUME, MERIDIAN AND NAL BOOKS *are published by The New American Library, Inc., 1633 Broadway, New York, New York 10019*

FIRST SIGNET PRINTING, JANUARY, 1974

9 10 11 12 13 14 15 16

PRINTED IN THE UNITED STATES OF AMERICA

FOREWORD

The Sands of Mars, my first full-length novel, was written in the late 1940's—when Mars seemed very much farther away than it is today. Reading it again after a lapse of many years, I am agreeably surprised to find how little it has been dated by the explosive developments of the Space Age. True, there are a few technical concepts which are slightly outmoded (readers may get some amusement trying to spot them); and there is perhaps rather more explanation of fundamentals than is strictly necessary in these enlightened times. But there is very little indeed that I would change if I were writing this story today.

It was one of the first science-fiction novels about Mars to abandon the romantic fantasies of Percival Lowell, Edgar Rice Burroughs, C. S. Lewis, and Ray Bradbury (four gentlemen I admire greatly, though not necessarily for the same reasons). By the 1940's, it was already certain that the planet's atmosphere was far too thin to support higher animals of the terrestrial type—and what little there was of it contained no oxygen. There could be no Martian princesses, alas; and when human beings reached the red planet, they would not be able to walk on its surface without breathing aids. The chief problem I faced in writing this novel was, therefore, that of making Mars interesting and exciting despite these limitations. Or, if possible, *because* of them.

The brilliantly successful Mariner IV mission has shown that the atmospheric pressure on Mars is even lower than had been generally assumed; we may need space suits there, not merely breathing masks. Apart from this—and the unexpected (by everyone except Clyde Tombaugh) discovery of extensive cratering—there has been no major change in our picture of the planet.

Above all, the question of Martian life is still entirely open. In their well-known paper "A Search for Life on

Earth at Kilometer Resolution," Carl Sagan and his colleagues used meteorological satellite photographs to show that Mariner IV could not possibly have detected life even on the well-populated Earth. Still less could it do so on Mars, where we do not know what we are looking for. We will have to land before we can tell whether there is anyone at home next door.

And even then we may not be sure for quite a long time. One space scientist has already quoted this book to make precisely this point. The land area of Mars is greater than that of Asia, Africa, and the Americas combined; its exploration will take decades, if not centuries.

Nevertheless, many of the mysteries that have tantalized generations of men are now rushing toward their solution. Before this story is twice its present age, we will have robot explorers dotted all over Mars.

And a little while later, men will be preparing to join them.

ARTHUR C. CLARKE

London, August 1966

1

"So this is the first time you've been upstairs?" said the pilot, leaning back idly in his seat so that it rocked to and fro in the gimbals. He clasped his hands behind his neck in a nonchalant manner that did nothing to reassure his passenger.

"Yes," said Martin Gibson, never taking his eyes from the chronometer as it ticked away the seconds.

"I thought so. You never got it quite right in your stories—all that nonsense about fainting under the acceleration. Why must people write such stuff? It's bad for business."

"I'm sorry," Gibson replied. "But I think you must be referring to my earlier stories. Space-travel hadn't got started then, and I had to use my imagination."

"Maybe," said the pilot grudgingly. (He wasn't paying the slightest attention to the instruments, and take-off was only two minutes away.) "It must be funny, I suppose, for this to be happening to you, after writing about it so often."

The adjective, thought Gibson, was hardly the one he would have used himself, but he saw the other's point of view. Dozens of his heroes—and villains—had gazed hypnotised by remorseless second-hands, waiting for the rockets to hurl them into infinity. And now—as it always did if one waited long enough—the reality had caught up with the fiction. The same moment lay only ninety seconds in his own future. Yes, it *was* funny, a beautiful case of poetic justice.

The pilot glanced at him, read his feelings, and grinned cheerfully.

"Don't let your own stories scare you. Why, I once took off standing up, just for a bet, though it was a damn silly thing to do."

"I'm not scared," Gibson replied with unnecessary emphasis.

"Hmmm," said the pilot, condescending to glance at the

clock. The second-hand had one more circuit to go. "Then I shouldn't hold on to the seat like that. It's only beryl-manganese; you might bend it."

Sheepishly, Gibson relaxed. He knew that he was building up synthetic responses to the situation, but they seemed none the less real for all that.

"Of course," said the pilot, still at ease but now, Gibson noticed, keeping his eyes fixed on the instrument panel, "it wouldn't be very comfortable if it lasted more than a few minutes—ah, there go the fuel pumps. Don't worry when the vertical starts doing funny things, but let the seat swing where it likes. Shut your eyes if that helps at all. (Hear the igniter jets start then?) We take about ten seconds to build up to full thrust—there's really nothing to it, apart from the noise. You just have to put up with that. I SAID, YOU JUST HAVE TO PUT UP WITH THAT!"

But Martin Gibson was doing nothing of the sort. He had already slipped gracefully into unconsciousness at an acceleration that had not yet exceeded that of a high-speed elevator.

He revived a few minutes and a thousand kilometres* later, feeling quite ashamed of himself. A beam of sunlight was shining full on his face, and he realised that the protective shutter on the outer hull must have slid aside. Although brilliant, the light was not as intolerably fierce as he would have expected; then he saw that only a fraction of the full intensity was filtering through the deeply tinted glass.

He looked at the pilot, hunched over his instrument board and busily writing up the log. Everything was very quiet, but from time to time there would come curiously muffled reports—almost miniature explosions—that Gibson found disconcerting. He coughed gently to announce his return to consciousness, and asked the pilot what they were.

"Thermal contraction in the motors," he replied briefly. "They've been running round five thousand degrees and cool mighty fast. You feeling all right now?"

* The metric system is used throughout this account of space-travel. This decimal system is based upon the metre equalling 39.37 inches. Thus a kilometre would be slightly over one-half mile (0:62 mi.).

"I'm fine," Gibson answered, and meant it. "Shall I get up?"

Psychologically, he had hit the bottom and bounced back. It was a very unstable position, though he did not realise it.

"If you like," said the pilot doubtfully. "But be careful —hang on to something solid."

Gibson felt a wonderful sense of exhilaration. The moment he had waited for all his life had come. He was in space! It was too bad that he'd missed the take-off, but he'd gloss that part over when he wrote it up.

From a thousand kilometres away, Earth was still very large—and something of a disappointment. The reason was quickly obvious. He had seen so many hundreds of rocket photographs and films that the surprise had been spoilt; he knew exactly what to expect. There were the inevitable moving bands of cloud on their slow march round the world. At the centre of the disc, the divisions between land and sea were sharply defined, and an infinite amount of minute detail was visible, but towards the horizon everything was lost in the thickening haze. Even in the cone of clear vision vertically beneath him, most of the features were unrecognisable and therefore meaningless. No doubt a meteorologist would have gone into transports of delight at the animated weather-map displayed below—but most of the meteorologists were up in the space stations, anyway, where they had an even better view. Gibson soon grew tired of searching for cities and other works of man. It was chastening to think that all the thousands of years of human civilisation had produced no appreciable change in the panorama below.

Then Gibson began to look for the stars, and met his second disappointment. They were there, hundreds of them, but pale and wan, mere ghosts of the blinding myriads he had expected to find. The dark glass of the port was to blame; in subduing the sun, it had robbed the stars of all their glory.

Gibson felt a vague annoyance. Only one thing had turned out quite as expected. The sensation of floating in mid-air, of being able to propel oneself from wall to wall at the touch of a finger, was just as delightful as he had hoped—though the quarters were too cramped for any ambitious experiments. Weightlessness was an enchanting, a fairy-like state, now that there were drugs to immobilise the balance organs and space-sickness was a thing of the past. He was glad of that. How his heroes had suffered! (His heroines too, presumably, but one never mentioned that.) He remembered Robin Blake's first flight, in the original version of "Martian Dust." When he'd written that, he had been heavily under the influence of D. H. Lawrence. (It would be interesting, one day, to make a list of the authors who *hadn't* influenced him at one time or another.)

There was no doubt that Lawrence was magnificent at describing physical sensations, and quite deliberately Gibson had set out to defeat him on his own ground. He had devoted a whole chapter to space-sickness, describing every symptom from the queasy premonitions that could sometimes be willed aside, the subterranean upheavals that even the most optimistic could no longer ignore, the volcanic cataclysms of the final stages and the ultimate, merciful exhaustion.

The chapter had been a masterpiece of stark realism. It was too bad that his publishers, with an eye on a squeamish Book-of-the-Month Club, had insisted on removing it. He had put a lot of work into that chapter; while he was writing it, he had really *lived* those sensations. Even now—

"It's very puzzling," said the M.O. thoughtfully as the now quiescent author was propelled through the airlock. "He's passed his medical tests O.K., and of course he'll have had the usual injections before leaving Earth. It must be psychosomatic."

"I don't care what it is," complained the pilot bitterly, as he followed the cortege into the heart of Space Station One. "All I want to know is—who's going to clean up my ship?"

No one seemed inclined to answer this heart-felt question, least of all Martin Gibson, who was only vaguely conscious of white walls drifting by his field of vision. Then, slowly, there was a sensation of increasing weight, and a warm, caressing glow began to steal through his limbs. Presently he became fully aware of his surroundings. He was in a hospital ward, and a battery of infrared lamps was bathing him with a glorious, enervating warmth, that sank through his flesh to the very bones.

"Well?" said the medical officer presently.

Gibson grinned feebly.

"I'm sorry about this. Is it going to happen again?"

"I don't know how it happened the first time. It's very unusual; the drugs we have now are supposed to be infallible."

"I think it was my own fault," said Gibson apologetically. "You see, I've got a rather powerful imagination, and I started thinking about the symptoms of space-sickness—in quite an objective sort of way, of course—but before I knew what had happened——"

"Well, just stop it!" ordered the doctor sharply. "Or we'll have to send you right back to Earth. You can't do this sort of thing if you're going to Mars. There wouldn't be much left of you after three months."

A shudder passed through Gibson's tortured frame. But he was rapidly recovering, and already the nightmare of the last hour was fading into the past.

"I'll be O.K.," he said. "Let me out of this muffle-furnace before I cook."

A little unsteadily, he got to his feet. It seemed strange, here in space, to have normal weight again. Then he remembered that Station One was spinning on its axis, and the living quarters were built around the outer walls so that centrifugal force could give the illusion of gravity.

The great adventure, he thought ruefully, hadn't started at all well. But he was determined not to be sent home in disgrace. It was not merely a question of his own pride: the effect on his public and his reputation would be deplorable. He winced as he visualised the headlines: "GIBSON GROUNDED! SPACE-SICKNESS ROUTS AUTHOR-ASTRONAUT." Even the staid literary weeklies would pull his leg, and as for "Time"—no, it was unthinkable!

"It's lucky," said the M.O., "that we've got twelve hours before the ship leaves. I'll take you into the zero-gravity section and see how you manage there, before I give you a clean bill of health."

Gibson also thought that was a good idea. He had always regarded himself as fairly fit, and until now it had never seriously occurred to him that this journey might be not merely uncomfortable but actually dangerous. You could laugh at space-sickness—when you'd never experienced it yourself. Afterwards, it seemed a very different matter.

The Inner Station—"Space Station One," as it was

usually called—was just over two thousand kilometres from Earth, circling the planet every two hours. It had been Man's first stepping-stone to the stars, and though it was no longer technically necessary for spaceflight, its presence had a profound effect on the economics of interplanetary travel. All journeys to the Moon or the planets started from here; the unwieldy atomic ships floated alongside this outpost of Earth while the cargoes from the parent world were loaded into their holds. A ferry service of chemically fuelled rockets linked the station to the planet beneath, for by law no atomic drive unit was allowed to operate within a thousand kilometres of the Earth's surface. Even this safety margin was felt by many to be inadequate, for the radioactive blast of a nuclear propulsion unit could cover that distance in less than a minute.

Space Station One had grown with the passing years, by a process of accretion, until its original designers would never have recognised it. Around the central spherical core had accumulated observatories, communications labs with fantastic aerial systems, and mazes of scientific equipment which only a specialist could identify. But despite all these additions, the main function of the artificial moon was still that of refuelling the little ships with which Man was challenging the immense loneliness of the Solar System.

"Quite sure you're feeling O.K. now?" asked the doctor as Gibson experimented with his feet.

"I think so," he replied, unwilling to commit himself.

"Then come along to the reception room and we'll get you a drink—a nice hot drink," he added, to prevent any misunderstanding. "You can sit there and read the paper for half an hour before we decide what to do with you."

It seemed to Gibson that anticlimax was being piled on anticlimax. He was two thousand kilometres from Earth, with the stars all around him; yet here he was forced to sit sipping sweet tea—tea!—in what might have been an ordinary dentist's waiting-room. There were no windows, presumably because the sight of the rapidly revolving heavens might have undone the good work of the medical staff. The only way of passing the time was to skim through piles of magazines which he'd already seen, and which were difficult to handle as they were ultra-lightweight editions apparently printed on cigarette paper. Fortunately he found a very old copy of "Argosy" containing a story he had written so long ago that he had completely forgotten the ending, and this kept him happy until the doctor returned.

"Your pulse seems normal," said the M.O. grudgingly. "We'll take you along to the zero-gravity chamber. Just follow me and don't be surprised at anything that happens."

With this cryptic remark he led Gibson out into a wide, brightly lit corridor that seemed to curve upwards in both directions away from the point at which he was standing. Gibson had no time to examine this phenomenon, for the doctor slid open a side door and started up a flight of metal stairs. Gibson followed automatically for a few paces, then realised just what lay ahead of him and stopped with an involuntary cry of amazement.

Immediately beneath his feet, the slope of the stairway was a reasonable forty-five degrees, but it rapidly became steeper until only a dozen metres ahead the steps were rising vertically. Thereafter—and it was a sight that might have unnerved anyone coming across it for the first time—the increase of gradient continued remorselessly until the steps began to overhang and at last passed out of sight above and *behind* him.

Hearing his exclamation, the doctor looked back and gave a reassuring laugh.

"You mustn't always believe your eyes," he said. "Come along and see how easy it is."

Reluctantly Gibson followed, and as he did so he became aware that two very peculiar things were happening. In the first place he was gradually becoming lighter; in the second, despite the obvious steepening of the stairway, the slope beneath his feet remained at a constant forty-five degrees. The vertical direction itself, in fact, was slowly tilting as he moved forward, so that despite its increasing curvature the gradient of the stairway never altered.

It did not take Gibson long to arrive at the explanation. All the apparent gravity was due to the centrifugal force produced as the station spun slowly on its axis, and as he approached the centre the force was diminishing to zero. The stairway itself was winding in towards the axis along some sort of spiral—once he'd have known its mathematical name—so that despite the radial gravity field the slope underfoot remained constant. It was the sort of thing that people who lived in space stations must get accustomed to quickly enough; presumably when they returned to Earth the sight of a normal stairway would be equally unsettling.

At the end of the stairs there was no longer any real sense of "up" or "down." They were in a long cylindrical room, criss-crossed with ropes but otherwise empty, and at its far end a shaft of sunlight came blasting through an observation port. As Gibson watched, the beam moved steadily across the metal walls like a questing searchlight, was momentarily eclipsed, then blazed out again from another window. It was the first indication Gibson's senses had given him of the fact that the station was really spinning on its axis, and he timed the rotation roughly by noting how long the sunlight took to return to its original position. The "day" of this little artificial world was less than ten seconds; that was sufficient to give a sensation of normal gravity at its outer walls.

Gibson felt rather like a spider in its web as he followed the doctor hand-over-hand along the guide ropes, towing himself effortlessly through the air until they came to the observation post. They were, he saw, at the end of a sort of chimney jutting out along the axis of the station, so that they were well clear of its equipment and apparatus and had an almost unrestricted view of the stars.

"I'll leave you here for a while," said the doctor. "There's plenty to look at, and you should be quite happy. If not—well, remember there's normal gravity at the bottom of those stairs!"

Yes, thought Gibson; *and* a return trip to Earth by the next rocket as well. But he was determined to pass the test and to get a clean bill of health.

It was quite impossible to realise that the space station itself was rotating, and not the framework of sun and stars: to believe otherwise required an act of faith, a conscious effort of will. The stars were moving so quickly that only the brighter ones were cleary visible and the sun, when Gibson allowed himself to glance at it out of the corner of his eye, was a golden comet that crossed the sky every five seconds. With this fantastic speeding up of the natural order of events, it was easy to see how ancient man had refused to believe that his own solid earth was rotating, and had attributed all movement to the turning celestial sphere.

Partly occulted by the bulk of the station, the Earth was a great crescent spanning half the sky. It was slowly waxing as the station raced along on its globe-encircling orbit; in some forty minutes it would be full, and an hour after that would be totally invisible, a black shield eclipsing the sun while the station passed through its cone of shadow. The Earth would go through all its phases—from new to full and back again—in just two hours. The sense of time became distorted as one thought of these things; the familiar divisions of day and night, of months and seasons, had no meaning here.

About a kilometre from the station, moving with it in its orbit but not at the moment connected to it in any way, were the three spaceships that happened to be "in dock" at the moment. One was the tiny arrowhead of the rocket that had brought him, at such expense and such discomfort, up from Earth an hour ago. The second was a lunar-bound freighter of, he guessed, about a thousand tons gross. And the third, of course, was the *Ares*, almost dazzling in the splendour of her new aluminium paint.

Gibson had never become reconciled to the loss of the sleek, steamlined spaceships which had been the dream of the early twentieth century. The glittering dumb-bell hanging against the stars was not *his* idea of a space-liner; though the world had accepted it, he had not. Of course, he knew the familiar arguments—there was no need for streamlining in a ship that never entered an atmosphere, and therefore the design was dictated purely by structural and power-plant considerations. Since the violently radioactive drive-unit had to be as far away from the crew quarters as possible, the double-sphere and long connecting tube was the simplest solution.

It was also, Gibson thought, the ugliest; but that hardly mattered since the *Ares* would spend practically all her life in deep space where the only spectators were the stars. Presumably she was already fuelled and merely waiting for the precisely calculated moment when her motors would burst into life, and she would pull away out of the orbit in which she was circling and had hitherto spent all her existence, to swing into the long hyperbola that led to Mars.

When that happened, he would be aboard, launched at last upon the adventure he had never really believed would come to him.

2

The captain's office aboard the *Ares* was not designed to hold more than three men when gravity was acting, but there was plenty of room for six while the ship was in a free orbit and one could stand on walls or ceiling according to taste. All except one of the group clustered at surrealist angles around Captain Norden had been in space before and knew what was expected of them, but this was no ordinary briefing. The maiden flight of a new spaceship is always an occasion and the *Ares* was the first of her line—the first, indeed, of all spaceships ever to be built primarily for passengers and not for freight. When she was fully commissioned, she would carry a crew of thirty and a hundred and fifty passengers in somewhat spartan comfort. On her first voyage, however, the proportions were almost reversed and at the moment her crew of six was waiting for the single passenger to come aboard.

"I'm still not quite clear," said Owen Bradley, the electronics officer, "what we are supposed to do with the fellow when we've got him. Whose bright idea was this, anyway?"

"I was coming to that," said Captain Norden, running his hands over where his magnificent blond hair had been only a few days before. (Spaceships seldom carry professional barbers, and though there are always plenty of eager amateurs one prefers to put off the evil day as long as possible.) "You all know of Mr. Gibson, of course."

This remark produced a chorus of replies, not all of them respectful.

"I think his stories stink," said Dr. Scott. "The later ones, anyway. 'Martian Dust' wasn't bad, but of course it's completely dated now."

"Nonsense!" snorted astrogator Mackay. "The last stories are much the best, now that Gibson's got interested in fundamentals and has cut out the blood and thunder."

This outburst from the mild little Scott was most uncharacteristic. Before anyone else could join in, Captain Norden interrupted.

"We're not here to discuss literary criticism, if you don't mind. There'll be plenty of time for that later. But there are one or two points the Corporation wants me to make clear before we begin. Mr. Gibson is a very important man—a distinguished guest—and he's been invited to come on this trip so that he can write a book about it later. It's not just a publicity stunt." ("Of course not!" interjected Bradley, with heavy sarcasm.) "But naturally the Corporation hopes that future clients won't be—er discouraged by what they read. Apart from that, we *are* making history; our maiden voyage ought to be recorded properly. So try and behave like gentlemen for a while; Gibson's book will probably sell half a million copies, and your future reputations may depend on your behaviour these next three months!"

"That sounds dangerously like blackmail to me," said Bradley.

"Take it that way if you please," continued Norden cheerfully. "Of course, I'll explain to Gibson that he can't expect the service that will be provided later when we've got stewards and cooks and Lord knows what. He'll understand that, and won't expect breakfast in bed every morning."

"Will he help with the washing-up?" asked someone with a practical turn of mind.

Before Norden could deal with this problem in social etiquette a sudden buzzing came from the communications panel, and a voice began to call from the speaker grille.

"Station One calling *Ares*—your passenger's coming over."

Norden flipped a switch and replied, "O.K.—we're ready." Then he turned to the crew.

"With all these hair-cuts around, the poor chap will think it's graduation day at Alcatraz. Go and meet him, Jimmy, and help him through the airlock when the tender couples up."

Martin Gibson was still feeling somewhat exhilarated at having surmounted his first major obstacle—the M.O. at Space Station One. The loss of gravity on leaving the station and crossing to the *Ares* in the tiny, compressed-air driven tender had scarcely bothered him at all, but the sight that met his eyes when he entered Captain Norden's cabin caused him a momentary relapse. Even when there was no gravity, one liked to pretend that *some* direction was "down," and it seemed natural to assume that the surface on which chairs and table were bolted was the floor. Unfortunately the majority decision seemed otherwise, for two members of the crew were hanging like stalactites from the "ceiling," while two more were relaxed at quite arbitrary angles in mid-air. Only the Captain was, according to Gibson's ideas, the right way up. To make matters worse, their shaven heads gave these normally quite presentable men a faintly sinister appearance, so that the whole tableau looked like a family reunion at Castle Dracula.

There was a brief pause while the crew analysed Gibson. They all recognised the novelist at once; his face had been familiar to the public ever since his first best-seller, *Thunder in the Dawn,* had appeared nearly twenty years ago. He was a chubby yet sharp-featured little man, still on the right side of forty-five, and when he spoke his voice was surprisingly deep and resonant.

"This," said Captain Norden, working round the cabin from left to right, "is my engineer, Lieutenant Hilton. This is Dr. Mackay, our navigator—only a Ph.D., not a *real* doctor, like Dr. Scott here. Lieutenant Bradley is Electronics Officer, and Jimmy Spencer, who met you at the airlock, is our supernumerary and hopes to be Captain when he grows up."

Gibson looked round the little group with some surprise. There were so few of them—five men and a boy! His face must have revealed his thoughts, for Captain Norden laughed and continued.

"Not many of us, are there? But you must remember that this ship is almost automatic—and besides, nothing ever happens in space. When we start the regular passenger run, there'll be a crew of thirty. On this trip, we're making up the weight in cargo, so we're really travelling as a fast freighter."

Gibson looked carefully at the men who would be his only companions for the next three months. His first reaction (he always distrusted first reactions, but was at pains to note them) was one of astonishment that they seemed so ordinary—when one made allowance for such superficial matters as their odd attitudes and temporary baldness. There was no way of guessing that they belonged to a profession more romantic than any that the world had known since the last cowboys traded in their broncos for helicopters.

At a signal which Gibson did not intercept, the others took their leave by launching themselves with fascinatingly effortless precision through the open doorway. Captain Norden settled down in his seat again and offered Gibson a cigarette. The author accepted it doubtfully.

"You don't mind smoking?" he asked. "Doesn't it waste oxygen?"

"There'd be a mutiny," laughed Norden, "if I had to ban smoking for three months. In any case, the oxygen consumption's negligible."

Captain Norden, thought Gibson a little ruefully, was not fitting at all well into the expected pattern. The skipper of a space-liner, according to the best—or at least the most popular—literary tradition, should be a grizzled, keen-eyed veteran who had spent half his life in the ether and could navigate across the Solar System by the seat of his pants, thanks to his uncanny knowledge of the spaceways. He must also be a martinet; when he gave orders, his officers must jump to attention (not an easy thing under zero gravity), salute smartly, and depart at the double.

Instead, the captain of the *Ares* was certainly less than forty, and might have been taken for a successful business executive. As for being a martinet—so far Gibson had detected no signs of discipline whatsoever. This impression, he realised later, was not strictly accurate. The only discipline aboard the *Ares* was entirely self-imposed; that was the only form possible among the type of men who composed her crew.

"So you've never been in space before," said Norden, looking thoughtfully at his passenger.

"I'm afraid not. I made several attempts to get on the lunar run, but it's absolutely impossible unless you're on official business. It's a pity that space-travel's still so infernally expensive."

Norden smiled.

"We hope the *Ares* will do something to change that. I must say," he added, "that you seem to have managed to write quite a lot about the subject with ah—the mimimum of practical experience.

"Oh, that!" said Gibson airily, with what he hoped was a light laugh. "It's a common delusion that authors must have experienced everything they describe in their books. I read all I could about space-travel when I was younger and did my best to get the local colour right. Don't forget that all my interplanetary novels were written in the early days—I've hardly touched the subject in the last few years. It's rather surprising that people still associate my name with it."

Norden wondered how much of this modesty was assumed. Gibson must know perfectly well that it was his space-travel novels that had made him famous—and had prompted the Corporation to invite him on this trip. The whole situation, Norden realised, had some highly entertaining possibilities. But they would have to wait; in the meantime he must explain to this landlubber the routine of life aboard the private world of the *Ares*.

"We keep normal Earth-time—Greenwich Meridian—aboard the ship and everything shuts down at 'night.' There are no watches, as there used to be in the old days; the instruments can take over when we're sleeping, so we aren't on continuous duty. That's one reason why we can manage with such a small crew. On this trip, as there's plenty of space, we've all got separate cabins. Yours is a regular passenger stateroom; the only one that's fitted up, as it happens. I think you'll find it comfortable. Is all your cargo aboard? How much did they let you take?"

"A hundred kilos. It's in the airlock."

"A hundred kilos?" Norden managed to repress his amazement. The fellow must be emigrating—taking all his family heirlooms with him. Norden had the true astronaut's horror of surplus mass, and did not doubt that Gibson was carrying a lot of unnecessary rubbish. However, if the Corporation had O.K.'d it, and the authorised load wasn't exceeded, he had nothing to complain about.

"I'll get Jimmy to take you to your room. He's our odd-job man for this trip, working his passage and learning something about spaceflight. Most of us start that way, signing up for the lunar run during college vacations. Jimmy's quite a bright lad—he's already got his Bachelor's degree."

By now Gibson was beginning to take it quite for granted that the cabin-boy would be a college graduate. He followed Jimmy—who seemed somewhat overawed by his presence—to the passengers' quarters.

The stateroom was small, but beautifully planned and designed in excellent taste. Ingenious lighting and mirror-faced walls made it seem much larger than it really was, and the pivoted bed could be reversed during the "day" to act as a table. There were very few reminders of the absence of gravity; everything had been done to make the traveller feel at home.

For the next hour Gibson sorted out his belongings and experimented with the room's gadgets and controls. The device that pleased him most was a shaving mirror which, when a button was pressed, transformed itself into a porthole looking out on the stars. He wondered just how it was done.

At last everything was stowed away where he could find it; there was absolutely nothing else for him to do. He lay down on the bed and buckled the elastic belts around his chest and thighs. The illusion of weight was not very convincing, but it was better than nothing and did give some sense of a vertical direction.

Lying at peace in the bright little room that would be his world for the next hundred days, he could forget the disappointments and petty annoyances that had marred his departure from Earth. There was nothing to worry about now; for the first time in almost as long as he could remember, he had given his future entirely into the keeping of others. Engagements, lecture appointments, deadlines—all these things he had left behind on Earth. The sense of blissful relaxation was too good to last, but he would let his mind savour it while he could.

A series of apologetic knocks on the cabin door roused Gibson from sleep an indeterminate time later. For a moment he did not realise where he was; then full consciousness came back; he unclipped the retaining straps and thrust himself off the bed. As his movements were still poorly co-ordinated he had to make a carom off the nominal ceiling before reaching the door.

Jimmy Spencer stood there, slightly out of breath.

"Captain's compliments, sir, and would you like to come and see the take-off?"

"I certainly would," said Gibson. "Wait until I get my camera."

He reappeared a moment later carrying a brand-new

Leica XXA, at which Jimmy stared with undisguised envy, and festooned with auxiliary lenses and exposure meters. Despite these handicaps, they quickly reached the observation gallery, which ran like a circular belt around the body of the *Ares.*

For the first time Gibson saw the stars in their full glory, no longer dimmed either by atmosphere or by darkened glass, for he was on the night side of the ship and the sun-filters had been drawn aside. The *Ares,* unlike the space-station, was not turning on her axis but was held in the rigid reference system of her gyroscopes so that the stars were fixed and motionless in her skies.

As he gazed on the glory he had so often, and so vainly, tried to describe in his books, Gibson found it very hard to analyse his emotions—and he hated to waste an emotion that might profitably be employed in print. Oddly enough neither the brightness nor the sheer numbers of the stars made the greatest impression on his mind. He had seen skies little inferior to this from the tops of mountains on Earth, or from the observation decks of stratoliners; but never before had he felt so vividly the sense that the stars were all around him, down to the horizon he no longer possessed, and even below, under his very feet.

Space Station One was a complicated, brightly polished toy floating in nothingness a few metres beyond the port. There was no way in which its distance or size could be judged, for there was nothing familiar about its shape, and the sense of perspective seemed to have failed. Earth and Sun were both invisible, hidden behind the body of the ship.

Startlingly close, a disembodied voice came suddenly from a hidden speaker.

"One hundred seconds to firing. Please take your positions."

Gibson automatically tensed himself and turned to Jimmy for advice. Before he could frame any questions, his guide said hastily, "I must get back on duty," and disappeared in a graceful power-dive, leaving Gibson alone with his thoughts.

The next minute and a half passed with remarkable slowness, punctuated though it was with frequent time-checks from the speakers. Gibson wondered who the announcer was; it did not sound like Norden's voice, and probably it was merely a recording, operated by the automatic circuit which must now have taken over control of the ship.

"Twenty seconds to go. Thrust will take about ten seconds to build up."

"Ten seconds to go."

"Five seconds, four, three, two, one——"

Very gently, something took hold of Gibson and slid him down the curving side of the porthole-studded wall on to what had suddenly become the floor. It was hard to realise that up and down had returned once more, harder still to connect their reappearance with that distant, attenuated thunder that had broken in upon the silence of the ship. Far away in the second sphere that was the other half of the *Ares,* in that mysterious, forbidden world of dying atoms and automatic machines which no man could ever enter and live, the forces that powered the stars themselves were being unleashed. Yet there was none of that sense of mounting, pitiless acceleration that always accompanies the take-off of a chemically propelled rocket. The *Ares* had unlimited space in which to manœuvre; she could take as long as she pleased to break free from her present orbit and crawl slowly out into the transfer hyperbola that would lead her to Mars. In any case, the utmost power of the atomic drive could move her two-thousand-ton mass with an acceleration of only a tenth of a gravity; at the moment it was throttled back to less than half of this small value.

It did not take Gibson long to re-orientate himself. The ship's acceleration was so low—it gave him, he calculated, an effective weight of less than four kilogrammes—that his movements were still practically unrestricted. Space Station One had not moved from its apparent position, and he had to wait almost a minute before he could detect that the *Ares* was, in fact, slowly drawing away from it. Then he belatedly remembered his camera, and began to record the departure. When he had finally settled (he hoped) the tricky problem of the right exposure to give a small, brilliantly lit object against a jet-black background, the station was already appreciably more distant. In less than ten minutes, it had dwindled to a distant point of light that was hard to distinguish from the stars.

When Space Station One had vanished completely, Gibson went round to the day side of the ship to take some photographs of the receding Earth. It was a huge, thin crescent when he first saw it, far too large for the eye to take in at a single glance. As he watched, he could see that it was slowly waxing, for the *Ares* must make at least one more circuit before she could break away and spiral out towards Mars. It would be a good hour before the Earth was appreciably smaller and in that time it would pass again from new to full.

Well, this is it, thought Gibson. Down there is all my past life, and the lives of all my ancestors back to the first blob of jelly in the first primeval sea. No colonist or explorer setting sail from his native land ever left so much behind as I am leaving now. Down beneath those clouds lies the whole of human history; soon I shall be able to eclipse with my little finger what was, until a lifetime ago, all of Man's dominion and everything that his art had saved from time.

This inexorable drawing away from the known into the unknown had almost the finality of death. Thus must the naked soul, leaving all its treasures behind it, go out at last into the darkness and the night.

Gibson was still watching at the observation post when, more than an hour later, the *Ares* finally reached escape velocity and was free from Earth. There was no way of telling that this moment had come and passed, for Earth still dominated the sky and the motors still maintained their muffled, distant thunder. Another ten hours of continuous operation would be needed before they had completed their task and could be closed down for the rest of the voyage.

Gibson was sleeping when that moment came. The sudden silence, the complete loss of even the slight gravity the ship had enjoyed these last few hours, brought him back to a twilight sense of awareness. He looked dreamily around the darkened room until his eye found the little pattern of stars framed in the porthole. They were, of course, utterly motionless. It was impossible to believe that the *Ares* was now racing out from the Earth's orbit at a speed so great that even the Sun could never hold her back.

Sleepily, he tightened the fastenings of his bedclothes to prevent himself drifting out into the room. It would be nearly a hundred days before he had any sense of weight again.

3

The same pattern of stars filled the porthole when a series of bell-like notes tolling from the ship's public address system woke Gibson from a comparatively dreamless sleep. He dressed in some haste and hurried out to the observation deck, wondering what had happened to Earth overnight.

It is very disconcerting, at least to an inhabitant of Earth, to see two moons in the sky at once. But there they were, side by side, both in their first quarter, and one about twice as large as the other. It was several seconds before Gibson realised that he was looking at Moon and Earth together—and several seconds more before he finally grasped the fact that the smaller and more distant crescent was his own world.

The *Ares* was not, unfortunately, passing very close to the Moon, but even so it was more than ten times as large as Gibson had ever seen it from the Earth. The interlocking chains of crater-rings were clearly visible along the ragged line separating day from night, and the still unilluminated disc could be faintly seen by the reflected earthlight falling upon it. And surely—Gibson bent suddenly forward, wondering if his eyes had tricked him. Yet there was no doubt of it: down in the midst of that cold and faintly gleaming land, waiting for the dawn that was still many days away, minute sparks of light were burning like fireflies in the dusk. They had not been there fifty years ago; they were the lights of the first lunar cities, telling the stars that life had come at last to the Moon after a billion years of waiting.

A discreet cough from nowhere in particular interrupted Gibson's reverie. Then a slightly overamplified voice remarked in a conversational tone:

"If Mr. Gibson will kindly come to the mess-room, he will find some tepid coffee and a few flakes of cereal still left on the table."

He glanced hurriedly at his watch. He had completely

forgotten about breakfast—an unprecedented phenomenon. No doubt someone had gone to look for him in his cabin and, failing to find him there, was paging him through the ship's public address system.

When he burst apologetically into the mess-room he found the crew engaged in technical controversy concerning the merits of various types of spaceships.

While he ate, Gibson watched the little group of arguing men, fixing them in his mind and noting their behaviour and characteristics. Norden's introduction had merely served to give them labels; as yet they were not definite personalities to him. It was curious to think that before the voyage had ended, he would probably know every one of them better than most of his acquaintances back on Earth. There could be no secrets and no masks aboard the tiny world of the *Ares*.

At the moment, Dr. Scott was talking. (Later, Gibson would realise that there was nothing very unusual about this.) He seemed a somewhat excitable character, inclined to lay down the law at a moment's provocation on subjects about which he could not possibly be qualified to speak. His most successful interrupter was Bradley, the electronics and communications expert—a dryly cynical person who seemed to take a sardonic pleasure in verbal sabotage. From time to time he would throw a small bombshell into the conversation which would halt Scott for a moment, though never for long. Mackay, the little Scots mathematician, also entered the battle from time to time, speaking rather quickly in a precise, almost pedantic fashion. He would, Gibson thought, have been more at home in a university common-room than on a spaceship.

Captain Norden appeared to be acting as a not entirely disinterested umpire, supporting first one side and then the other in an effort to prevent any conclusive victory. Young Spencer was already at work, and Hilton, the only remaining member of the crew, had taken no part in the discussion. The engineer was sitting quietly watching the others with a detached amusement, and his face was hauntingly familiar to Gibson. Where had they met before? Why, of course—what a fool he was not to have realised it!—this was *the* Hilton. Gibson swung round in his chair so that he could see the other more clearly. His half-finished meal was forgotten as he looked with awe and envy at the man who had brought the *Arcturus* back to Mars after the greatest adventure in the history of spaceflight. Only six men had ever reached Saturn; and only three of them were still alive. Hilton had stood, with his lost companions, on those far-off moons whose very names were magic—Titan, Encladus, Tethys, Rhea, Dione . . . He had seen the incomparable splendour of the great rings spanning the sky in symmetry that seemed too perfect for nature's contriving. He had been into that Ultima Thule in which circled the cold outer giants of the Sun's scattered family, and he had returned again to the light and warmth of the inner worlds. Yes, thought Gibson, there are a good many things I want to talk to you about before this trip's over.

The discussion group was breaking up as the various officers drifted—literally—away to their posts, but Gibson's thoughts were still circling Saturn as Captain Norden came across to him and broke into his reverie.

"I don't know what sort of schedule you've planned," he said, "but I suppose you'd like to look over our ship. After all, that's what usually happens around this stage in one of your stories."

Gibson smiled, somewhat mechanically. He feared it was going to be some time before he lived down his past.

"I'm afraid you're quite right there. It's the easiest way, of course, of letting the reader know how things work, and sketching in the *locale* of the plot. Luckily it's not so important now that everyone knows exactly what a spaceship is like inside. One can take the technical details for granted, and get on with the story. But when I started writing about astronautics, back in the '60's, one had to hold up the plot for thousands of words to explain how the spacesuits worked, how the atomic drive operated, and clear up anything else that might come into the story."

"Then I can take it," said Norden, with the most disarming of smiles, "that there's not a great deal we can teach you about the *Ares*."

Gibson managed to summon up a blush.

"I'd appreciate it very much if you'd show me round—whether you do it according to the standard literary pattern or not."

"Very well," grinned Norden. "We'll start at the control room. Come along."

For the next two hours they floated along the labyrinth of corridors that crossed and criss-crossed like arteries in the spherical body of the *Ares*. Soon, Gibson knew, the interior of the ship would be so familiar to him that he could find his way blindfold from one end to the other; but he had already lost his way once and would do so again before he had learned his way around.

As the ship was spherical, it had been divided into zones of latitude like the Earth. The resulting nomenclature was very useful, since it at once gave a mental picture of the liner's geography. To go "North" meant that one was heading for the control cabin and the crew's quarters. A trip to the Equator suggested that one was visiting either the great dining-hall occupying most of the central plane of the ship, or the observation gallery which completely encircled the liner. The Southern hemisphere was almost entirely fuel tank, with a few storage holds and miscellaneous machinery. Now that the *Ares* was no longer using her motors, she had been swung round in space so that the Northern Hemisphere was in perpetual sunlight and the "uninhabited" Southern one in darkness. At the South Pole itself was a small metal door bearing a set of impressive official seals and the notice: "To be Opened only under the Express Orders of the Captain or his Deputy." Behind it lay the long, narrow tube connecting the main body of the ship with the smaller sphere, a hundred metres away, which held the power plant and drive units. Gibson wondered what was the point of having a door at all if no one could ever go through it; then he remembered that there must be some provision to enable the servicing robots of the Atomic Energy Commission to reach their work.

Strangely enough, Gibson received one of his strongest impressions not from the scientific and technical wonders of the ship, which he had expected to see in any case, but from the empty passenger quarters—a honeycomb of closely packed cells that occupied most of the North Temperate Zone. The impression was rather a disagreeable one. A house so new that no one has ever lived in it can be more lonely than an old, deserted ruin that has once known life and may still be peopled by ghosts. The sense of desolate emptiness was very strong here in the echoing, brightly lit corridors which would one day be crowded with life, but which now lay bleak and lonely in the sunlight piped through the walls—a sunlight much bluer than on Earth and therefore hard and cold.

Gibson was quite exhausted, mentally and physically, when he got back to his room. Norden had been an altogether too conscientious guide, and Gibson suspected that he had been getting some of his own back, and thoroughly enjoying it. He wondered exactly what his companions thought of his literary activities; probably he would not be left in ignorance for long.

He was lying in his bunk, sorting out his impressions, when there came a modest knock on the door.

"Damn," said Gibson, quietly. "Who's that?" he continued, a little louder.

"It's Jim—Spencer, Mr. Gibson. I've got a radiogram for you."

Young Jimmy floated into the room, bearing an envelope with the Signals Officer's stamp. It was sealed, but Gibson surmised that he was the only person on the ship who didn't know its contents. He had a shrewd idea of what they would be, and groaned inwardly. There was really no way of escape from Earth; it could catch you wherever you went.

The message was brief and contained only one redundant word:

NEW YORKER, REVUE DES QUATRE MONDES, LIFE INTERPLANETARY WANT FIVE THOUSAND WORDS EACH. PLEASE RADIO BY NEXT SUNDAY. LOVE. RUTH.

Gibson sighed. He had left Earth in such a rush that there had been no time for a final consultation with his agent, Ruth Goldstein, apart from a hurried phone-call half-way around the world. But he'd told her quite clearly that he wanted to be left alone for a fortnight. It never made any difference, of course. Ruth always went happily ahead, confident that he would deliver the goods on time. Well, for once he wouldn't be bullied and she could darned well wait; he'd earned this holiday.

He grabbed his scribbling pad and, while Jimmy gazed ostentatiously elsewhere, wrote quickly:

SORRY. EXCLUSIVE RIGHTS ALREADY PROMISED TO SOUTH ALABAMA PIG KEEPER AND POULTRY FANCIER. WILL SEND DETAILS ANY MONTH NOW. WHEN ARE YOU GOING TO POISON HARRY? LOVE. MART.

Harry was the literary, as opposed to the business, half of Goldstein and Co. He had been happily married to Ruth for over twenty years, during the last fifteen of which Gibson had never ceased to remind them both that they were getting in a rut and needed a change and that the whole thing couldn't possibly last much longer.

Goggling slightly, Jimmy Spencer disappeared with this unusual message, leaving Gibson alone with his thoughts. Of course, he would have to start work some time, but meanwhile his typewriter was buried down in the hold where he couldn't see it. He had even felt like attaching one of those "NOT WANTED IN SPACE—MAY BE STOWED IN VACUUM" labels, but had manfully resisted the temptation. Like most writers who had never had to rely solely on their literary earnings, Gibson hated *starting* to write. Once he had begun, it was different . . . sometimes.

His holiday lasted a full week. At the end of that time, Earth was merely the most brilliant of the stars and would soon be lost in the glare of the Sun. It was hard to believe that he had ever known any life but that of the little, self-contained universe that was the *Ares.* And its crew no longer consisted of Norden, Hilton, Mackay, Bradley, and Scott—but of John, Fred, Angus, Owen, and Bob.

He had grown to know them all, though Hilton and Bradley had a curious reserve that he had been unable to penetrate. Each man was a definite and sharply contrasted character; almost the only thing they had in common was intelligence. Gibson doubted if any of them had an I.Q. of less than 120, and he sometimes wriggled with embarrassment as he remembered the crews he had imagined for some of his fictional spaceships. He recalled Master Pilot Graham, from "Five Moons Too Many"—still one of his favourite characters. Graham had been tough (had he not once survived half a minute in vacuum before being able to get to his spacesuit?) and he regularly disposed of a bottle of whisky a day. He was a distinct contrast to Dr. Angus Mackay, Ph.D. (Astron.), F.R.A.S., who was now sitting quietly in a corner reading a much annotated copy of "The Canterbury Tales" and taking an occasional squirt from a bulbful of milk.

The mistake that Gibson had made, along with so many other writers back in the '50's and '60's, was the assumption that there would be no fundamental difference between ships of space and ships of the sea—or between the men who manned them. There were parallels, it was true, but they were far outnumbered by the contrasts. The reason was purely technical, and should have been foreseen, but the popular writers of the mid-century had taken the lazy course and had tried to use the traditions of Herman Melville and Frank Dana in a medium for which they were grotesquely unfitted.

A ship of space was much more like a stratosphere liner than anything that had ever moved on the face of the ocean, and the technical training of its crew was at much higher level even than that required in aviation. A man like Norden had spent five years at college, three years in space, and another two back at college on advanced astronautical theory before qualifying for his present position.

Gibson was having a quiet game of darts with Dr. Scott when the first excitement of the voyage burst unexpectedly upon them. There are not many games of skill that can be played in space; for a long time cards and chess had been the classical stand-bys, until some ingenious Englishman had decided that a flight of darts would perform very well in the absence of gravity. The distance between thrower and board had been increased to ten metres, but otherwise the game still obeyed the rules that had been formulated over the centuries amid an atmosphere of beer and tobacco smoke in English pubs.

Gibson had been delighted to find that he was quite good at the game. He almost always managed to beat Scott, despite—or because of—the other's elaborate technique. This consisted of placing the "arrow" carefully in mid-air, and then going back a couple of metres to squint along it before smacking it smartly on its way.

Scott was optimistically aiming for a treble twenty when Bradley drifted into the room bearing a signals form in his hand.

"Don't look now," he said in his soft, carefully modulated voice, "but we're being followed."

Everyone gaped at him as he relaxed in the doorway. Mackay was the first to recover.

"Please elucidate," he said primly.

"There's a Mark III carrier missile coming after us hell for leather. It's just been launched from the Outer Station and should pass us in four days. They want me to catch it with our radio control as it goes by, but with the dispersion it will have at this range that's asking a lot. I doubt if it will go within a hundred thousand kilometres of us."

"What's it in aid of? Someone left their toothbrush behind?"

"It seems to be carrying urgent medical supplies. Here, Doc, you have a look."

Dr. Scott examined the message carefully.

"This *is* interesting. They think they've got an antidote for Martian fever. It's a serum of some kind; the Pasteur Institute's made it. They must be pretty sure of the stuff if they've gone to all this trouble to catch us."

"What, for heaven's sake, is a Mark III missile—not to mention Martian fever?" exploded Gibson at last.

Dr. Scott answered before anyone else could get a word in.

"Martian fever isn't really a Martian disease. It seems to be caused by a terrestrial organism that we carried there and which liked the new climate more than the old one. It has the same sort of effect as malaria: people aren't often killed by it, but its economic effects are very serious. In any one year the percentage of man-hours lost——"

"Thank you very much. I remember all about it now. And the missile?"

Hilton slid smoothly into the conversation.

"That's simply a little automatic rocket with radio control and a very high terminal speed. It's used to carry cargoes between the space-stations, or to chase after spaceships when they've left anything behind. When it gets into radio range it will pick up our transmitter and home on to us. Hey, Bob," he said suddenly, turning to Scott, "why haven't they sent it direct to Mars? It could get there long before we do."

"Because its little passengers wouldn't like it. I'll have to fix up some cultures for them to live in, and look after them like a nursemaid. Not my usual line of business, but I think I can remember some of the stuff I did at St. Thomas's."

"Wouldn't it be appropriate," said Mackay with one of his rare attempts at humour, "if someone went and painted the Red Cross outside?"

Gibson was thinking deeply.

"I was under the impression," he said after a pause, "that life on Mars was very healthy, both physically and psychologically."

"You mustn't believe all you read in books," drawled Bradley. "Why anyone should ever want to go to Mars I can't imagine. It's flat, it's cold, and it's full of miserable half-starved plants looking like something out of Edgar Allan Poe. We've sunk millions into the place and haven't got a penny back. Anyone who goes there of his own free will should have his head examined. Meaning no offence, of course."

Gibson only smiled amicably. He had learned to discount Bradley's cynicism by about ninety per cent; but he was never quite sure how far the other was only *pretending* to be insulting. For once, however, Captain Norden asserted his authority; not merely to stop Bradley from getting away with it, but to prevent such alarm and despondency from spreading into print. He gave his electronics officer an angry glare.

"I ought to tell you, Martin," he said, "that although Mr. Bradley doesn't like Mars, he takes an equally poor view of Earth and Venus. So don't let his opinions depress you."

"I won't," laughed Gibson. "But there's one thing I'd like to ask."

"What's that?" said Norden anxiously.

"Does Mr. Bradley take as 'poor a view,' as you put it, of Mr. Bradley as he does of everything else?"

"Oddly enough, he does," admitted Norden. "That shows that one at least of his judgments is accurate."

"Touché," murmured Bradley, for once at a loss. "I will retire in high dudgeon and compose a suitable reply. Meanwhile, Mac, will you get the missile's co-ordinates and let me know when it should come into range?"

"All right," said Mackay absently. He was deep in Chaucer again.

4

During the next few days Gibson was too busy with his own affairs to take much part in the somewhat limited social life of the *Ares*. His conscience had smitten him, as it always did when he rested for more than a week, and he was hard at work again.

The typewriter had been disentangled from his belongings and now occupied the place of honour in the little cabin. Sheets of manuscript lay everywhere—Gibson was an untidy worker—and had to be prevented from escaping by elastic bands. There had been a lot of trouble with the flimsy carbon paper, which had a habit of getting into the airflow and glueing itself against the ventilator, but Gibson had now mastered the minor techniques of life under zero gravity. It was amazing how quickly one learned them, and how soon they became a part of everyday life.

Gibson had found it very hard to get his impressions of space down on paper; one could not very well say "space is awfully big" and leave it at that. The take-off from Earth had taxed his skill to the utmost. He had not actually lied, but anyone who read his dramatic description of the Earth falling away beneath the blast of the rocket would certainly never get the impression that the writer had then been in a state of blissful unconsciousness, swiftly followed by a state of far from blissful consciousness.

As soon as he had produced a couple of articles which would keep Ruth happy for a while (she had meanwhile sent three further radiograms of increasing asperity) he went Northwards to the Signals Office. Bradley received the sheets of MSS. with marked lack of enthusiasm.

"I suppose this is going to happen every day from now on," he said glumly.

"I hope so—but I'm afraid not. It depends on my inspiration."

"There's a split infinitive right here on the top of page 2."

"Excellent; nothing like 'em."

"You've put 'centrifugal' on page 3 where you mean 'centripetal.' "

"Since I get paid by the word, don't you think it's generous of me to use such long ones?"

"There are two successive sentences on page 4 beginning with 'And.' "

"Look here, are you going to send the damned stuff, or do I have to do it myself?"

Bradley grinned.

"I'd like to see you try. Seriously, though, I should have warned you to use a black ribbon. Contrast isn't so good with blue, and though the facsimile sender will be able to handle it all right at this range, when we get farther away from Earth it's important to have a nice, clean signal."

As he spoke, Bradley was slipping the quarto sheets into the tray of the automatic transmitter. Gibson watched, fascinated, as they disappeared one by one into the maw of the machine and emerged five seconds later into the wire collecting-basket. It was strange to think that his words were now racing out through space in a continuous stream, getting a million kilometres farther away every three seconds.

He was just collecting his MSS. sheets again when a buzzer sounded somewhere in the jungle of dials, switches and meter panels that covered practically the entire wall of the little office. Bradley shot across to one of his receivers and proceeded to do incomprehensible things with great rapidity. A piercing whistle started to come from a loudspeaker.

"The carrier's in range at last," said Bradley, "but it's a long way off—at a guess I'd say it will miss us by a hundred thousand kilometres."

"What can we do about that?"

"Very little. I've got our own beacon switched on, and if it picks up our signals it will home on to us automatically and navigate itself to within a few kilometres of us."

"And if it *doesn't* pick us up?"

"Then it will just go shooting on out of the Solar System. It's travelling fast enough to escape from the Sun; so are we, for that matter."

"That's a cheeful thought. How long would it take us?"

"To do what?"

"To leave the system."

"A couple of years, perhaps. Better ask Mackay. I don't know *all* the answers—I'm not like one of the characters in your books!"

"You may be one yet," said Gibson darkly, and withdrew.

The approach of the missile had added an unexpected —and welcome—element of excitement to life aboard the *Ares*. Once the first fine careless rapture had worn off, space-travel could become exceedingly monotonous. It would be different in future days, when the liner was crowded with life, but there were times when her present loneliness could be very depressing.

The missile sweepstake had been organised by Dr. Scott, but the prizes were held firmly by Captain Norden. Some calculations of Mackay's indicated that the projectile would miss the *Ares* by a hundred and twenty-five thousand kilometres, with an uncertainty of plus or minus thirty thousand. Most of the bets had been placed near the most probable value, but some pessimists, mistrusting Mackay completely, had gone out to a quarter of a million kilometres. The bets weren't in cash, but in far more useful commodities such as cigarettes, candies, and other luxuries. Since the crew's personal weight allowance was strictly limited, these were far more valuable than pieces of paper with marks on them. Mackay had even thrown a half-bottle of whisky into the pool, and had thereby staked a claim to a volume of space about twenty thousand kilometres across. He never drank the stuff himself, he explained, but was taking some to a compatriot on Mars, who couldn't get the genuine article and was unable to afford the passage back to Scotland. No one believed him, which, as the story was more or less true, was a little unfair.

"Jimmy!"

"Yes, Captain Norden."

"Have you finished checking the oxygen gauges?"

"Yes, sir. All O.K."

"What about that automatic recording gear those physicists have put in the hold? Does it look as if it's still working?"

"Well, it's making the same sort of noises as it did when we started."

"Good. You've cleaned up that mess in the kitchen where Mr. Hilton let the milk boil over?"

"Yes, Captain."

"Then you've really finished everything?"

"I suppose so, but I was hoping——"

"That's fine. I've got a rather interesting job for you—something quite out of the usual run of things. Mr. Gibson wants to start polishing up his astronautics. Of course, any of us could tell him all he wants to know, but—er—you're the last one to come from college and maybe you could put things across better. You've not forgotten the beginner's difficulties—*we'd* tend to take too much for granted. It won't take much of your time—just go along when he asks and deal with his questions. I'm sure you can manage."

Exit Jimmy, glumly.

"Come in," said Gibson, without bothering to look up from his typewriter. The door opened behind him and Jimmy Spencer came floating into the room.

"Here's the book, Mr. Gibson. I think it will give you everything you want. It's Richardson's 'Elements of Astronautics,' special light-weight edition."

He laid the volume in front of Gibson, who turned over the thin sheets with an interest that rapidly evaporated as he saw how quickly the proportion of words per page diminished. He finally gave up halfway through the book after coming across a page where the only sentence was "Substituting for the value of perihelion distance from Equation 15.3, we obtain . . ." All else was mathematics.

"Are you *quite* sure this is the most elementary book in the ship?" he asked doubtfully, not wishing to disappoint Jimmy. He had been a little surprised when Spencer had been appointed as his unofficial tutor, but had been shrewd enough to guess the reason. Whenever there was a job that no one else wanted to do, it had a curious tendency to devolve upon Jimmy.

"Oh yes, it really *is* elementary. It manages without vector notation and doesn't touch perturbation theory. You should see some of the books Mackay has in his room. Each equation takes a couple of pages of print."

"Well, thanks anyway. I'll give you a shout when I get

stuck. It's about twenty years since I did any maths, though I used to be quite hot at it once. Let me know when you want the book back."

"There's no hurry, Mr. Gibson. I don't very often use it now I've got on to the advanced stuff."

"Oh, before you go, maybe you can answer a point that's just cropped up. A lot of people are still worried about meteors, it seems, and I've been asked to give the latest information on the subject. Just how dangerous are they?"

Jimmy pondered for a moment.

"I could tell you, roughly," he said, "but if I were you I'd see Mr. Mackay. He's got tables giving the exact figures."

"Right, I'll do that."

Gibson could quite easily have rung Mackay but any excuse to leave his work was too good to be missed. He found the little astrogator playing tunes on the big electronic calculating machine.

"Meteors?" said Mackay. "Ah, yes, a very interesting subject. I'm afraid, though, that a great deal of highly misleading information has been published about them. It wasn't so long ago that people believed a spaceship would be riddled as soon as it left atmosphere."

"Some of them still do," replied Gibson. "At least, they think that large-scale passenger travel won't be safe."

Mackay gave a snort of disgust.

"Meteors are considerably less dangerous than lightning and the biggest normal one is a lot smaller than a pea."

"But, after all, one ship has been damaged by them!"

"You mean the *Star Queen?* One serious accident in the last five years is quite a satisfactory record. No ship has ever actually been *lost* through meteors."

"What about the *Palls?*"

"No one knows what happened to her. That's only the popular theory. It's not at all popular among the experts."

"So I can tell the public to forget all about the matter?"

"Yes. Of course, there *is* the question of dust. . . ."

"Dust?"

"Well, if by meteors you mean fairly large particles, from a couple of millimetres upwards, you needn't worry. But dust is a nuisance, particularly on space-stations. Every few years someone has to go over the skin to locate the punctures. They're usually far too small to be visible to the eye, but a bit of dust moving at fifty kilometres a second can get through a surprising thickness of metal."

This sounded faintly alarming to Gibson, and Mackay hastened to reassure him.

"There really isn't the slightest need to worry," he repeated. "There's always a certain hull leakage taking place; the air supply simply takes it in its stride."

However busy Gibson might be, or pretend to be, he always found time to wander restlessly around the echoing labyrinths of the ship, or to sit looking at the stars from the equatorial observation galley. He had formed a habit of going there during the daily concert. At 15.00 hours precisely the ship's public address system would burst into life and for an hour the music of Earth would whisper or roar through the empty passageways of the *Ares*. Every day a different person would choose the programmes, so one never knew what was coming—though after a while it was easy to guess the identity of the arranger. Norden played light classics and opera; Hilton practically nothing but Beethoven and Tchaikovsky. They were regarded as hopeless lowbrows by Mackay and Bradley, who indulged in astringent chamber music and atonal cacophonies of which no one else could make head or tail, or indeed particularly desired to. The ship's micro-library of books and music was so extensive that it would outlast a lifetime in space. It held, in fact, the equivalent of a quarter of a million books and some thousands of orchestral works, all recorded in electronic patterns, awaiting the orders that would bring them into life.

Gibson was sitting in the observation gallery, trying to see how many of the Pleiades he could resolve with the naked eye, when a small projectile whispered past his ear and attached itself with a "thwack!" to the glass of the port, where it hung vibrating like an arrow. At first sight, indeed, this seemed exactly what it was and for a moment Gibson wondered if the Cherokee were on the warpath again. Then he saw that a large rubber sucker had replaced the head, while from the base, just behind the feathers, a long, thin thread trailed away into the distance. At the end of the thread was Dr. Robert Scott, M.D., hauling himself briskly along like an energetic spider.

Gibson was still composing some suitably pungent remark when, as usual, the doctor got there first.

"Don't you think it's cute?" he said. "It's got a range of twenty metres—only weighs half a kilo, and I'm going to patent it as soon as I get back to Earth."

"Why?" said Gibson, in tones of resignation.

"Good gracious, can't you see? Suppose you want to get from one place to another inside a space-station where there's no rotational gravity. All you've got to do is to fire at any flat surface near your destination, and reel in the cord. It gives you a perfect anchor until you release the sucker."

"And just what's wrong with the usual way of getting around?"

"When you've been in space as long as *I* have," said Scott smugly, "you'll know what's wrong. There are plenty of handholds for you to grab in a ship like this. But suppose you want to go over to a blank wall at the other side of a room, and you launch yourself through the air from wherever you're standing. What happens? Well, you've got to break your fall somehow, usually with your hands, unless you can twist round on the way. Incidentally, do you know the commonest complaint a spaceship M.O. has to deal with? It's sprained wrists, and *that's* why. Anyway, even when you get to your target you'll bounce back unless you can grab hold of something. You might even get stranded in mid-air. I did that once in Space Station Three, in one of the big hangars. The nearest wall was fifteen metres away and I couldn't reach it."

"Couldn't you spit your way towards it?" said Gibson solemnly. "I thought that was the approved way out of the difficulty."

"You try it someday and see how far it gets you. Anyway, it's not hygienic. Do you know what I had to do? It was most embarrassing. I was only wearing shorts and vest, as usual, and I calculated that they had about a hundredth of my mass. If I could throw them away at thirty metres a second, I could reach the wall in about a minute."

"And did you?"

"Yes. But the Director was showing his wife round the Station that afternoon, so now you know why I'm reduced to earning my living on an old hulk like this, working my way from port to port when I'm not running a shady surgery down by the docks."

"I think you've missed your vocation," said Gibson admiringly. "You should be in my line of business."

"I don't think you believe me," complained Scott bitterly.

"That's putting it mildly. Let's look at your toy."

Scott handed it over. It was a modified air pistol, with a spring-loaded reel of nylon thread attached to the butt.

"It looks like——"

"If you say it's like a ray-gun I'll certify you as infectious. Three people have made that crack already."

"Then it's a good job you interrupted me," said Gibson, handing the weapon back to the proud inventor. "By the way, how's Owen getting on? Has he contacted that missile yet?"

"No, and it doesn't look as if he's going to. Mac says it will pass about a hundred and forty-five thousand kilometres away—certainly out of range. It's a damn shame; there's not another ship going to Mars for months, which is why they were so anxious to catch us."

"Owen's a queer bird, isn't he?" said Gibson with some inconsequence.

"Oh, he's not so bad when you get to know him. It's quite untrue what they say about him poisoning his wife. She drank herself to death of her own free will," replied Scott with relish.

Owen Bradley, Ph.D., M.I.E.E., M.I.R.E., was very annoyed with life. Like every man aboard the *Ares*, he took his job with a passionate seriousness, however much he might pretend to joke about it. For the last twelve hours he had scarcely left the communications cabin, hoping that the continuous carrier wave from the missile would break into the modulation that would tell him it was receiving his signals and would begin to steer itself towards the *Ares*. But it was completely indifferent, and he had no right to expect otherwise. The little auxiliary beacon which was intended to call such projectiles had a reliable range of only twenty thousand kilometres; though that was ample for all normal purposes, it was quite inadequate now.

Bradley dialled the astrogation office on the ship's intercom, and Mackay answered almost at once.

"What's the latest, Mac?"

"It won't come much closer. I've just reduced the last bearing and smoothed out the errors. It's now a hundred and fifty thousand kilometres away, travelling on an almost parallel course. Nearest point will be a hundred and forty-four thousand, in about three hours. So I've lost the sweep—and I suppose we lose the missile."

"Looks like it, I'm afraid," grunted Bradley, "but we'll see. I'm going down to the workshop."

"Whatever for?"

"To make a one-man rocket and go after the blasted thing, of course. That wouldn't take more than half an hour in one of Martin's stories. Come down and help me."

Mackay was nearer the ship's equator than Bradley; consequently he had reached the workshop at the South Pole first and was waiting in mild perplexity when Bradley arrived, festooned with lengths of coaxial cable he had collected from stores. He outlined his plan briefly.

"I should have done this before, but it will make rather a mess and I'm one of those people who always go on hoping till the last moment. The trouble with our beacon is that it radiates in all directions—it has to, of course, since we never know where a carrier's coming from. I'm going to build a beam array and squirt *all* the power I've got after our runaway."

He produced a rough sketch of a simple Yagi aerial and explained it swiftly to Mackay.

"This dipole's the actual radiator—the others are directors and reflectors. Antique, but it's easy to make and it should do the job. Call Hilton if you want any help. How long will it take?"

Mackay, who for a man of his tastes and interests had a positively atavistic skill with his hands, glanced at the drawings and the little pile of materials Bradley had gathered.

"About an hour," he said, already at work. "Where are you going now?"

"I've got to go out on the hull and disconnect the plumbing from the beacon transmitter. Bring the array round to the airlock when you're ready, will you?"

Mackay knew little about radio, but he understood clearly enough what Bradley was trying to do. At the moment the tiny beacon on the *Ares* was broadcasting its power over the entire sphere of space. Bradley was about to disconnect it from its present aerial system and aim its whole output accurately towards the fleeing projectile, thus increasing its range many-fold.

It was about an hour later that Gibson met Mackay hurrying through the ship behind a flimsy structure of parallel wires, spaced apart by plastic rods. He gaped at it in amazement as he followed Mackay to the lock, where Bradley was already waiting impatiently in his cumbersome spacesuit, the helmet open beside him.

"What's the nearest star to the missile?" Bradley asked.

Mackay thought rapidly.

"It's nowhere near the ecliptic now," he mused. "The last figures I got were—let's see—declination fifteen something north, right ascension about fourteen hours. I suppose that will be—I never can remember these things!—somewhere in Böotes. Oh yes—it won't be far from Arcturus: not more than ten degrees away, I'd say at a guess. I'll work out the exact figures in a minute."

"That's good enough to start with. I'll swing the beam around, anyway. Who's in the Signals Cabin now?"

"The Skipper and Fred. I've rung them up and they're listening to the monitor. I'll keep in touch with you through the hull transmitter."

Bradley snapped the helmet shut and disappeared through the airlock. Gibson watched him go with some envy. He had always wanted to wear a spacesuit, but though he had raised the matter on several occasions Norden had told him it was strictly against the rules. Spacesuits were very complex mechanisms and he might make a mistake in one—and then there would be hell to pay and perhaps a funeral to be arranged under rather novel circumstances.

Bradley wasted no time admiring the stars once he had launched himself through the outer door. He jetted slowly over the gleaming expanse of hull with his reaction units until he came to the section of plating he had already removed. Underneath it a network of cables and wires lay nakedly exposed to the blinding sunlight, and one of the cables had already been cut. He made a quick temporary connection, shaking his head sadly at the horrible mismatch that would certainly reflect half the power right back to the transmitter. Then he found Arcturus and aimed the beam towards it. After waving it around hopefully for a while, he switched on his suit radio.

"Any luck?" he asked anxiously.

Mackay's despondent voice came through the loudspeaker.

"Nothing at all. I'll switch you through to communications."

Norden confirmed the news.

"The signal's still coming in, but it hasn't acknowledged us yet."

Bradley was taken aback. He had been quite sure that this would do the trick; at the very least, he must have increased the beacon's range by a factor of ten in this one direction. He waved the beam around for a few more minutes, then gave it up. Already he could visualise the little missile with its strange but precious cargo slipping silently out of his grasp, out towards the unknown limits of the Solar System—and beyond.

He called Mackay again.

"Listen, Mac," he said urgently, "I want you to check those co-ordinates again and then come out here and have a shot yourself. I'm going in to doctor the transmitter."

When Mackay had relieved him, Bradley hurried back to his cabin. He found Gibson and the rest of the crew gathered glumly round the monitor receiver from which the unbroken whistle from the distant, and now receding, missile was coming with a maddening indifference.

There were very few traces of his normally languid, almost feline movements as Bradley pulled out circuit diagrams by the dozen and tore into the communications rack. It took him only a moment to run a pair of wires into the heart of the beacon transmitter. As he worked, he fired a series of questions at Hilton.

"You know something about these carrier missiles. How long must it receive our signal to give it time to home accurately on to us?"

"That depends, of course, on its relative speed and several other factors. In this case, since it's a low-acceleration job, a good ten minutes, I should say."

"And then it doesn't matter even if our beacon fails?"

"No. As soon as the carrier's vectored itself towards you, you can go off the air again. Of course, you'll have to send it another signal when it passes right by you, but that should be easy."

"How long will it take to get here if I *do* catch it?"

"A couple of days, maybe less. What are you trying out now?"

"The power amplifiers of this transmitter run at seven

hundred and fifty volts. I'm taking a thousand-volt line from another supply, that's all. It will be a short life and a merry one, but we'll double or treble the output while the tubes last."

He switched on the intercom and called Mackay, who, not knowing the transmitter had been switched off for some time, was still carefully holding the array lined up on Arcturus, like an armour-plated William Tell aiming a crossbow.

"Hello, Mac, you all set?"

"I am practically ossified," said Mackay with dignity. "How much longer——"

"We're just starting now. Here goes."

Bradley threw the switch. Gibson, who had been expecting sparks to start flying, was disappointed. Everything seemed exactly as before; but Bradley, who knew better, looked at his meters and bit his lips savagely.

It would take radio waves only half a second to bridge the gap to that tiny, far-off rocket with its wonderful automatic mechanisms that must remain forever lifeless unless this signal could reach them. The half-second passed, and the next. There had been time for the reply, but still that maddening heterodyne whistle came unbroken from the speaker. Then, suddenly, it stopped. For an age there was absolute silence. A hundred and fifty thousand kilometres away, the robot was investigating this new phenomenon. It took perhaps five seconds to make up its mind—and the carrier wave broke through again, but now modulated into an endless string of "beep-beep-beeps."

Bradley checked the enthusiasm in the cabin.

"We're not out of the wood yet," he said. "Remember it's got to hold our signal for ten minutes before it can complete its course alterations." He looked anxiously at his meters and wondered how long it would be before the output tubes gave up the unequal battle.

They lasted seven minutes, but Bradley had spares ready and was on the air again in twenty seconds. The replacements were still operating when the missile carrier wave changed its modulation once more, and with a sigh of relief Bradley shut down the maltreated beacon.

"You can come indoors now, Mac," he called into the microphone. "We made it."

"Thank heavens for that. I've nearly got sunstroke, as

well as calcification of the joints, doing this Cupid's bow act out here."

"When you've finished celebrating," complained Gibson, who had been an interested but baffled spectator, "perhaps you'll tell me in a few short, well-chosen phrases just how you managed to pull this particular rabbit out of the hat."

"By beaming our beacon signal and then overloading the transmitter, of course."

"Yes, I know that. What I don't understand is why you've switched it off again."

"The controlling gear in the missile has done its job," explained Bradley, with the air of a professor of philosophy talking to a mentally retarded child. "That first signal indicated that it had detected our wave; we knew then that it was automatically vectoring on to us. That took it several minutes, and when it had finished it shut off its motors and sent us the second signal. It's still at almost the same distance, of course, but it's heading towards us now and should be passing in a couple of days. I'll have the beacon running again then. That will bring it to within a kilometre or less."

There was a gentle cough at the back of the room.

"I hate to remind you, sir . . ." began Jimmy.

Norden laughed.

"O.K.—I'll pay up. Here are the keys—locker 26. What are you going to do with that bottle of whisky?"

"I was thinking of selling it back to Dr. Mackay."

"Surely," said Scott, looking severely at Jimmy, "this moment demands a general celebration, at which a toast . . ."

But Jimmy didn't stop to hear the rest. He had fled to collect his loot.

5

"An hour ago we had only one passenger," said Dr. Scott, nursing the long metal case delicately through the airlock. "Now we've got several billion."

"How do you think they've stood the journey?" asked Gibson.

"The thermostats seemed to be working well, so they should be all right. I'll transfer them to the cultures I've got ready, and then they should be quite happy until we get to Mars, gorging themselves to their little hearts' content."

Gibson moved over to the nearest observation post. He could see the stubby, white-painted shape of the missile lying alongside the airlock, with the slack mooring cables drifting away from it like the tentacles of some deep-sea creature. When the rocket had been brought almost to rest a few kilometres away by its automatic radio equipment, its final capture had been achieved by much less sophisticated techniques. Hilton and Bradley had gone out with cables and lassoed the missile as it slowly drifted by. Then the electric winches on the *Ares* had hauled it in.

"What's going to happen to the carrier now?" Gibson asked Captain Norden, who was also watching the proceedings.

"We'll salvage the drive and control assembly and leave the carcase in space. It wouldn't be worth the fuel to carry it all back to Mars. So until we start accelerating again, we'll have a little moon of our own."

"Like the dog in Jules Verne's story."

"What, 'From the Earth to the Moon'? I've never read it. At least, I tried once, but couldn't be bothered. That's the trouble with all those old stories. Nothing is deader than yesterday's science-fiction—and Verne belongs to the day before yesterday."

Gibson felt it necessary to defend his profession.

"So you don't consider that science-fiction can ever have any permanent literary value?"

"I don't think so. It may sometimes have a *social* value when it's written, but to the next generation it must always seem quaint and archaic. Just look what happened, for example, to the space-travel story."

"Go on. Don't mind my feelings—as if you would."

Norden was clearly warming to the subject, a fact which did not surprise Gibson in the least. If one of his companions had suddenly been revealed as an expert on reafforestation, Sanskrit, or bimetallism, Gibson would now have taken it in his stride. In any case, he knew that science-fiction was widely—sometimes hilariously—popular among professional astronauts.

"Very well," said Norden. "Let's see what happened there. Up to 1960—maybe 1970—people were still writing stories about the first journey to the Moon. They're all quite unreadable now. When the Moon was reached, it was safe to write about Mars and Venus for another few years. Now *those* stories are dead too; no one would read them except to get a laugh. I suppose the outer planets will be a good investment for another generation; but the interplanetary romances our grandfathers knew really came to an end in the late 1970's."

"But the theme of space-travel is still as popular as ever."

"Yes, but it's no longer science-fiction. It's either purely factual—the sort of thing you are beaming back to Earth now—or else it's pure fantasy. The stories have to go right outside the Solar System and so they might just as well be fairy tales. Which is all that most of them are."

Norden had been speaking with great seriousness, but there was a mischievous twinkle in his eye.

"I contest your argument on two points," said Gibson. "First of all people—lots of people—still read Wells' yarns, though they're a century old. And, to come from the sublime to the ridiculous, they still read *my* early books, like 'Martian Dust,' although facts have caught up with them and left them a long way in the rear."

"Wells wrote literature," answered Norden, "but even so, I think I can prove my point. Which of his stories are most popular? Why, the straight novels like 'Kipps' and 'Mr. Polly.' When the fantasies are read at all, it's in spite of their hopelessly dated prophecies, not because of them. Only 'The Time Machine' is still at all popular, simply because it's set so far in the future that it's not outmoded—and because it contains Wells' best writing."

There was a slight pause. Gibson wondered if Norden was going to take up his second point. Finally he said:

"When did you write 'Martian Dust'?"

Gibson did some rapid mental arithmetic.

"In '73 or '74."

"I didn't know it was as early as that. But that's part of the explanation. Space-travel was just about to begin then, and everybody knew it. You had already begun to make a name with conventional fiction, and 'Martian Dust' caught the rising tide very nicely."

"That only explains why it sold *then*. It doesn't answer my other point. It's still quite popular, and I believe the Martian colony has taken several copies, despite the fact that it describes a Mars that never existed outside my imagination."

"I attribute that to the unscrupulous advertising of your publisher, the careful way you've managed to keep in the public eye, and—just possibly—to the fact that it was the best thing you ever wrote. Moreover, as Mac would say, it managed to capture the *Zeitgeist* of the '70's, and that gives it a curiosity value now."

"Hmm," said Gibson, thinking matters over.

He remained silent for a moment; then his face creased into a smile and he began to laugh.

"Well, share the joke. What's so funny?"

"Our earlier conversation. I was just wondering what H. G. Wells would have thought if he'd known that one day a couple of men would be discussing his stories, half-way between Earth and Mars."

"Don't exaggerate," grinned Norden. "We're only a third of the way so far."

It was long after midnight when Gibson suddenly awoke from a dreamless sleep. Something had disturbed him—some noise like a distant explosion, far away in the bowels of the ship. He sat up in the darkness, tensing against the broad elastic bands that held him to his bed. Only a glimmer of starlight came from the porthole-mirror, for his cabin was on the night side of the liner. He listened, mouth half opened, checking his breath to catch the faintest murmur of sound.

There were many voices in the *Ares* at night, and Gibson knew them all. The ship was alive, and silence would have meant the death of all aboard her. Infinitely reassuring was the unresting, unhurried suspiration of the air-pumps, driving the man-made trade winds of this tiny planet. Against that faint but continuous background were other intermittent noises: the occasional "whirr" of hidden motors carrying out some mysterious and automatic task, the "tick," every thirty seconds precisely, of the electric clock, and sometimes the sound of water racing through the pressurised plumbing system. Certainly none of these could have roused him, for they were as familiar as the beating of his own heart.

Still only half awake, Gibson went to the cabin door and listened for a while in the corridor. Everything was perfectly normal; he knew that he must be the only man awake. For a moment he wondered if he should call Norden, then thought better of it. He might only have been dreaming, or the noise might have been produced by some equipment that had not gone into action before.

He was already back in bed when a thought suddenly occurred to him. Had the noise, after all, been so far away? That was merely his first impression; it might have been quite near. Anyway, he was tired, and it didn't matter. Gibson had a complete and touching faith in the ship's instrumentation. If anything had really gone wrong, the automatic alarms would have alerted everyone. They had been tested several times on the voyage, and were enough to awaken the dead. He could go to sleep, confident that they were watching over him with unresting vigilance.

He was perfectly correct, though he was never to know it; and by the morning he had forgotten the whole affair.

The camera swept out of the stricken council chamber, following the funeral cortege up the endlessly twining stairs, and on to the windy battlements above the sea. The music sobbed into silence; for a moment, the lonely figures with their tragic burden were silhouetted against the setting sun, motionless upon the ramparts of Elsinore. "Good night, sweet prince . . ." The play was ended.

The lights in the tiny theatre came on abruptly, and the State of Denmark was four centuries and fifty million kilometres away. Reluctantly, Gibson brought his mind back to the present, tearing himself free from the magic that had held him captive. What, he wondered, would Shakespeare have made of this interpretation, already a lifetime old, yet as untouched by time as the still older splendours of the immortal poetry? And what, above all, would he have made of this fantastic theatre, with its latticework of seats floating precariously in mid-air with the flimsiest of supports?

"It's rather a pity," said Dr. Scott, as the audience of six drifted out into the corridor, "that we'll never have as fine a collection of films with us on our later runs. This batch is for the Central Martian Library, and we won't be able to hang on to it."

"What's the next programme going to be?" asked Gibson.

"We haven't decided. It may be a current musical, or we may carry on with the classics and screen 'Gone With the Wind.' "

"My grandfather used to rave about that; I'd like to see it now we have the chance," said Jimmy Spencer eagerly.

"Very well," replied Scott. "I'll put the matter to the Entertainments Committee and see if it can be arranged." Since this Committee consisted of Scott and no one else, these negotiations would presumably be successful.

Norden, who had remained sunk in thought since the end of the film, came up behind Gibson and gave a nervous little cough.

"By the way, Martin," he said. "You remember you were badgering me to let you go out in a spacesuit?"

"Yes. You said it was strictly against the rules."

Norden seemed embarrassed, which was somewhat unlike him.

"Well, it *is* in a way, but this isn't a normal trip and you aren't technically a passenger. I think we can manage it after all."

Gibson was delighted. He had always wondered what it was like to wear a spacesuit, and to stand in nothingness with the stars all around one. It never even occurred to him to ask Norden why he had changed his mind, and for this Norden was very thankful.

The plot had been brewing for about a week. Every morning a little ritual took place in Norden's room when Hilton arrived with the daily maintenance schedules, summarising the ship's performance and the behaviour of all its multitudinous machines during the past twenty-four hours. Usually there was nothing of any importance, and Norden signed the reports and filed them away with the log book. Variety was the last thing he wanted here, but sometimes he got it.

"Listen, Johnnie," said Hilton (he was the only one who called Norden by his first name; to the rest of the crew he was always "Skipper"). "It's quite definite now about our air-pressure. The drop's practically constant; in about ten days we'll be outside tolerance limits."

"Confound it! That means we'll have to do something. I was hoping it wouldn't matter till we dock."

"I'm afraid we can't wait until then; the records have to be turned over to the Space Safety Commission when we get home, and some nervous old woman is sure to start yelling if pressure drops below limits."

"Where do you think the trouble is?"

"In the hull, almost certainly."

"That pet leak of yours up round the North Pole?"

"I doubt it; this is too sudden. I think we've been holed again."

Norden looked mildly annoyed. Punctures due to meteoric dust happened two or three times a year on a ship of this size. One usually let them accumulate until they were worth bothering about, but this one seemed a little too big to be ignored.

"How long will it take to find the leak?"

"That's the trouble," said Hilton in tones of some disgust. "We've only one leak detector, and fifty thousand square metres of hull. It may take a couple of days to go over it. Now if it had only been a nice big hole, the automatic bulkheads would have gone into operation and located it for us."

"I'm mighty glad they didn't!" grinned Norden. "That would have taken some explaining away!"

Jimmy Spencer, who as usual got the job that no one else wanted to do, found the puncture three days later, after only a dozen circuits of the ship. The blurred little crater was scarcely visible to the eye, but the supersensitive leak detector had registered the fact that the vacuum near this part of the hull was not as perfect as it should have been. Jimmy had marked the place with chalk and gone thankfully back into the airlock.

Norden dug out the ship's plans and located the approximate position from Jimmy's report. Then he whistled softly and his eyebrows climbed towards the ceiling.

"Jimmy," he said, "does Mr. Gibson know what you've been up to?"

"No," said Jimmy. "I've not missed giving him his astronautics classes, though it's been quite a job to manage it as well as——"

"All right, all right! You don't think anyone else would have told him about the leak?"

"I don't know, but I think he'd have mentioned it if they had."

"Well, listen carefully. This blasted puncture is smack in the middle of his cabin wall, and if you breathe a word about it to him, I'll skin you. Understand?"

"Yes," gulped Jimmy, and fled precipitately.

"Now what?" said Hilton, in tones of resignation.

"We've got to get Martin out of the way on some pretext and plug the hole as quickly as we can."

"It's funny he never noticed the impact. It would have made quite a din."

"He was probably out at the time. *I'm* surprised he never noticed the air current; it must be fairly considerable."

"Probably masked by the normal circulation. But anyway, why all the fuss? Why not come clean about it and explain what's happened to Martin? There's no need for all this melodrama."

"Oh, isn't there? Suppose Martin tells his public that a 12th magnitude meteor has holed the ship—and then goes on to say that this sort of thing happens every other voyage? How many of his readers will understand not only that it's no real danger, but that we don't usually bother to do anything even when it does happen? I'll tell you what the popular reaction would be: 'If it was a little one, it might just as well be a big 'un.' The public's never trusted statistics. And can't you see the headlines: '*Ares* Holed by Meteor!' That *would* be bad for trade!"

"Then why not simply tell Martin and ask him to keep quiet?"

"It wouldn't be fair on the poor chap. He's had no news to hang his articles on to for weeks. It would be kinder to say nothing."

"O.K.," sighed Hilton. "It's your idea. Don't blame me if it backfires."

"It won't. I think I've got a watertight plan."

"I don't give a damn if it's watertight. Is it airtight?"

All his life Gibson had been fascinated by gadgets, and the spacesuit was yet another to add to the collection of mechanisms he had investigated and mastered. Bradley had been detailed to make sure that he understood the drill correctly, to take him out into space, and to see that he didn't get lost.

Gibson had forgotten that the suits on the *Ares* had no legs, and that one simply sat inside them. That was sensible enough, since they were built for use under zero gravity, and not for walking on airless planets. The absence of flexible leg-joints greatly simplified the designs of the suits, which were nothing more than perspex-topped cylinders sprouting articulated arms at their upper ends. Along the sides were mysterious flutings and bulges concerned with the air conditioning, radio, heat regulators, and the low-powered propulsion system. There was considerable freedom of movement inside them: one could withdraw one's arms to get at the internal controls, and even take a meal without too many acrobatics.

Bradley had spent almost an hour in the airlock, making certain that Gibson understood all the main controls and catechising him on their operation. Gibson appreciated his thoroughness, but began to get a little impatient when the lesson showed no sign of ending. He eventually mutinied when Bradley started to explain the suit's primitive sanitary arrangements.

"Hang it all!" he protested, "we aren't going to be outside *that* long!"

Bradley grinned.

"You'd be surprised," he said darkly, "just how many people make that mistake."

He opened a compartment in the airlock wall and took out two spools of line, for all the world like fishermen's reels. They locked firmly into mountings on the suits so that they could not be accidentally dislodged.

"Number One safety precaution," he said. "Always have a lifeline anchoring you to the ship. Rules are made to be broken—but not this one. To make doubly sure, I'll tie your suit to mine with another ten metres of cord. Now we're ready to ascend the Matterhorn."

The outer door slid aside. Gibson felt the last trace of

air tugging at him as it escaped. The feeble impulse set him moving towards the exit, and he drifted slowly out into the stars.

The slowness of motion and the utter silence combined to make the moment deeply impressive. The *Ares* was receding behind him with a terrifying inevitability. He was plunging into space—at last—his only link with safety that tenuous thread unreeling at his side. Yet the experience, though so novel, awoke faint echoes of familiarity in his mind.

His brain must have been working with unusual swiftness, for he recalled the parallel almost immediately. This was like the moment in his childhood—a moment, he could have sworn until now, forgotten beyond recall—when he had been taught to swim by being dropped into ten metres of water. Once again he was plunging headlong into a new and unknown element.

The friction of the reel had checked his momentum when the cord attaching him to Bradley gave a jerk. He had almost forgotten his companion, who was now blasting away from the ship with the little gas jets at the base of his suit, towing Gibson behind him.

Gibson was quite startled when the other's voice, echoing metallically from the speaker in his suit, shattered the silence.

"Don't use your jets unless I tell you. We don't want to build up too much speed, and we must be careful not to get our lines tangled."

"All right," said Gibson, vaguely annoyed at the intrusion into his privacy. He looked back at the ship. It was already several hundred metres away, and shrinking rapidly.

"How much line have we got?" he asked anxiously. There was no reply, and he had a moment of mild panic before remembering to press the "TRANSMIT" switch.

"About a kilometre," Bradley answered when he repeated the question. "That's enough to make one feel nice and lonely."

"Suppose it broke?" asked Gibson, only half joking.

"It won't. It could support your full weight, back on Earth. Even if it did, we could get back perfectly easily with our jets."

"And if they ran out?"

"This is a very cheerful conversation. I can't imagine that happening except through gross carelessness or about three simultaneous mechanical failures. Remember, there's a spare propulsion unit for just such emergencies—*and* you've got warning indicators in the suit which let you know well before the main tank's empty."

"But just *supposing,*" insisted Gibson.

"In that case the only thing to do would be to switch on the suit's S.O.S. beacon and wait until someone came out to haul you back. I doubt if they'd hurry, in such circumstances. Anyone who got himself in a mess like that wouldn't receive much sympathy."

There was a sudden jerk; they had come to the end of the line. Bradley killed the rebound with his jets.

"We're a long way from home now," he said quietly.

It took Gibson several seconds to locate the *Ares.* They were on the night side of the ship so that it was almost wholly in shadow; the two spheres were thin, distant crescents that might easily have been taken for Earth and Moon, seen from perhaps a million kilometres away. There was no real sense of contact: the ship was too small and frail a thing to be regarded as a sanctuary any more. Gibson was alone with the stars at last.

He was always grateful that Bradley left him in silence and did not intrude upon his thoughts. Perhaps the other was equally overwhelmed by the splendid solemnity of the moment. The stars were so brilliant and so numerous that at first Gibson could not locate even the most familiar constellations. Then he found Mars, the brightest object in the sky next to the Sun itself, and so determined the plane of the ecliptic. Very gently, with cautious bursts from his gas jets, he swung the suit round so that his head pointed roughly towards the Pole Star. He was "the right way up" again, and the star patterns were recognisable once more.

Slowly he made his way along the Zodiac, wondering how many other men in history had so far shared this experience. (Soon, of course, it would be common enough, and the magic would be dimmed by familiarity.) Presently he found Jupiter, and later Saturn—or so he imagined. The planets could no longer be distinguished from the stars by the steady, unwinking light that was such a useful, though sometimes treacherous, guide to amateur astronomers. Gibson did not search for Earth or Venus, for the glare of the sun would have dazzled him in a moment if he had turned his eyes in that direction.

A pale band of light welding the two hemispheres of the sky together, the whole ring of the Milky Way was visible. Gibson could see quite clearly the vents and tears along its edge, where entire continents of stars seemed trying to break away and go voyaging alone into the abyss. In the Southern Hemisphere, the black chasm of the Coal Sack gaped like a tunnel drilled through the stars into another universe.

The thought made Gibson turn towards Andromeda. There lay the great Nebula—a ghostly lens of light. He could cover it with his thumbnail, yet it was a whole galaxy as vast as the sky-spanning ring of stars in whose heart he was floating now. That misty spectre was a million times farther away than the stars—and *they* were a million times more distant than the planets. How pitiful were all men's voyagings and adventures when seen against this background!

Gibson was looking for Alpha Centauri, among the unknown constellations of the Southern Hemisphere, when he caught sight of something which, for a moment, his mind failed to identify. At an immense distance, a white rectangular object was floating against the stars. That, at least, was Gibson's first impression; then he realised that his sense of perspective was at fault and that, in fact, he was really seeing something quite small, only a few metres away. Even then it was some time before he recognised this interplanetary wanderer for what it was—a perfectly ordinary sheet of quarto manuscript paper, very slowly revolving in space. Nothing could have been more commonplace—or more unexpected here.

Gibson stared at the apparition for some time before he convinced himself that it was no illusion. Then he switched on his transmitter and spoke to Bradley.

The other was not in the least surprised.

"There's nothing very remarkable about that," he replied, rather impatiently. "We've been throwing out waste every day for weeks, and as we haven't any acceleration some of it may still be hanging round. As soon as we start braking, of course, we'll drop back from it and all our junk will go shooting out of the Solar System."

How perfectly obvious, thought Gibson, feeling a little foolish, for nothing is more disconcerting than a mystery which suddenly evaporates. It was probably a rough draft of one of his own articles. If it had been a little closer, it would be amusing to retrieve it as a souvenir, and to see what effects its stay in space had produced. Unfortunately it was just out of reach, and there was no way of capturing it without slipping the cord that linked him with the *Ares*.

When he had been dead for ages, that piece of paper would still be carrying its message out among the stars; and what it was, he would never know.

Norden met them when they returned to the airlock. He seemed rather pleased with himself, though Gibson was in no condition to notice such details. He was still lost among the stars and it would be some time before he returned to normal—before his typewriter began to patter softly as he tried to recapture his emotions.

"You managed the job in time?" asked Bradley, when Gibson was out of hearing.

"Yes, with fifteen minutes to spare. We shut off the ventilators and found the leak right away with the good old smoky-candle technique. A blind rivet and a spot of quick-drying paint did the rest; we can plug the outer hull when we're in dock, if it's worth it. Mac did a pretty neat job—he's wasting his talents as a navigator."

6

For Martin Gibson, the voyage was running smoothly and pleasantly enough. As he always did, he had now managed to organise his surroundings (by which he meant not only his material environment but also the human beings who shared it with him) to his maximum comfort. He had done a satisfactory amount of writing, some of it quite good and most of it passable, though he would not get properly into his stride until he had reached Mars.

The flight was now entering upon its closing weeks, and there was an inevitable sense of anticlimax and slackening interest, which would last until they entered the orbit of Mars. Nothing would happen until then; for the time being all the excitements of the voyage were over.

The last high-light, for Gibson, had been the morning when he finally lost the Earth. Day by day it had come closer to the vast pearly wings of the corona, as though about to immolate all its millions in the funeral pyre of the Sun. One evening it had still been visible through the telescope—a tiny spark glittering bravely against the splendour that was soon to overwhelm it. Gibson had thought it might still be visible in the morning, but overnight some colossal explosion had thrown the corona half a million kilometres farther into space, and Earth was lost against that incandescent curtain. It would be a week before it reappeared, and by then Gibson's world would have changed more than he would have believed possible in so short a time.

If anyone had asked Jimmy Spencer just what he thought of Gibson, that young man would have given rather different replies at various stages of the voyage. At first he had been quite overawed by his distinguished shipmate, but that stage had worn off very quickly. To do Gibson credit, he was completely free from snobbery, and he never made unreasonable use of his privileged position on board the *Ares*. Thus from Jimmy's point of view he was more approachable than the rest of the liner's inhabitants—all of whom were in some degree his superior officers.

When Gibson had started taking a serious interest in astronautics, Jimmy had seen him at close quarters once or twice a week and had made several efforts to weigh him up. This had not been at all easy, for Gibson never seemed to be the same person for very long. There were times when he was considerate and thoughtful and generally good company. Yet there were other occasions when he was so grumpy and morose that he easily qualified as the person on the *Ares* most to be avoided.

What Gibson thought of *him* Jimmy wasn't at all sure. He sometimes had an uncomfortable feeling that the author regarded him purely as raw material that might or might not be of value some day. Most people who knew Gibson slightly had that impression, and most of them were right. Yet as he had tried to pump Jimmy directly, there seemed no real grounds for these suspicions.

Another puzzling thing about Gibson was his technical background. When Jimmy had started his evening classes, as everyone called them, he had assumed that Gibson was merely anxious to avoid glaring errors in the material he radioed back to Earth, and had no very deep interest in astronautics for its own sake. It soon became clear that this was far from being the case. Gibson had an almost pathetic anxiety to master quite abstruse branches of the science, and to demand mathematical proofs, some of which Jimmy was hard put to provide. The older man must once have had a good deal of technical knowledge, fragments of which still remained with him. How he had acquired it he never explained; nor did he give any reason for his almost obsessive attempts, doomed though they were to repeated failures, to come to grips with scientific ideas far too advanced for him. Gibson's disappointment after these failures was so obvious that Jimmy found himself very sorry for him—except on those occasions when his pupil became bad-tempered and showed a tendency to blame his instructor. Then there would be a brief exchange of discourtesies, Jimmy would pack up his books, and the lesson would not be resumed until Gibson had apologised.

Sometimes, on the other hand, Gibson took these setbacks with humorous resignation and simply changed the subject. He would then talk about his experiences in the strange literary jungle in which he lived—a world of weird and often carnivorous beasts whose behaviour Jimmy found quite fascinating. Gibson was a good raconteur, with a fine flair for purveying scandal and undermining reputations. He seemed to do this without any malice, and some of the stories he told Jimmy about the distinguished figures of the day quite shocked that somewhat strait-laced youth. The curious fact was that the people whom Gibson so readily dissected often seemed to be his closest friends. This was something that Jimmy found very hard to understand.

Yet despite all these warnings Jimmy talked readily enough when the time came. One of their lessons had grounded on a reef of integro-differential equations and there was nothing to do but abandon ship. Gibson was in one of his amiable moods, and as he closed his books with a sigh he turned to Jimmy and remarked casually:

"You've never told me anything about yourself, Jimmy. What part of England do you come from, anyway?"

"Cambridge—at least, that's where I was born."

"I used to know it quite well, twenty years ago. But you don't live there now?"

"No; when I was about six, my people moved to Leeds. I've been there ever since."

"What made you take up astronautics?"

"It's rather hard to say. I was always interested in science, and of course spaceflight was the coming thing when I was growing up. So I suppose it was just natural. If I'd been born fifty years before, I guess I'd have gone into aeronautics."

"So you're interested in spaceflight purely as a technical problem, and not as—shall we say—something that might revolutionise human thought, open up new planets, and all that sort of thing?"

Jimmy grinned.

"I suppose that's true enough. Of course, I *am* interested in these ideas, but it's the technical side that really fascinates me. Even if there was nothing on the planets, I'd still want to know how to reach them."

Gibson shook his head in mock distress.

"You're going to grow up into one of those cold-blooded scientists who know everything about nothing. Another good man wasted!"

"I'm glad you think it *will* be a waste," said Jimmy with some spirit. "Anyway, why are you so interested in science?"

Gibson laughed, but there was a trace of annoyance in his voice as he replied:

"I'm only interested in science as a means, not as an end in itself."

That, Jimmy was sure, was quite untrue. But something warned him not to pursue the matter any further, and before he could reply Gibson was questioning him again.

It was all done in such a friendly spirit of apparently genuine interest that Jimmy couldn't avoid feeling flattered, couldn't help talking freely and easily. Somehow it didn't matter if Gibson was indeed studying him as disinterestedly and as clinically as a biologist watching the reactions of one of his laboratory animals. Jimmy felt like talking, and he preferred to give Gibson's motives the benefit of the doubt.

He talked of his childhood and early life, and presently Gibson understood the occasional clouds that sometimes seemed to overlie the lad's normally cheerful disposition. It was an old story—one of the oldest. Jimmy's mother had died when he was a little more than a baby, and his father had left him in the charge of a married sister. Jimmy's aunt had been kind to him, but he had never felt at home among his cousins, had always been an outsider. Nor had his father been a great deal of help, for he was seldom in England, and had died when Jimmy was about ten years old. He appeared to have left very little impression on his son, who, strangely enough, seemed to have clearer memories of the mother whom he could scarcely have known.

Once the barriers were down, Jimmy talked without reticence, as if glad to unburden his mind. Sometimes Gibson asked questions to prompt him, but the questions grew further and further apart and presently came no more.

"I don't think my parents were really very much in love," said Jimmy. "From what Aunt Ellen told me, it was all rather a mistake. There was another man first, but that fell through. My father was the next best thing. Oh, I know this sounds rather heartless, but please remember it all happened such a long time ago, and doesn't mean much to me now."

"I understand," said Gibson quietly; and it seemed as if he really did. "Tell me more about your mother."

"Her father—my granddad, that is—was one of the professors at the university. I think Mother spent all her life in Cambridge. When she was old enough she went to college for her degree—she was studying history. Oh, all this can't possibly interest you!"

"It really does," said Gibson earnestly. "Go on."

So Jimmy talked. Everything he told must have been learned from hearsay, but the picture he gave Gibson was surprisingly clear and detailed. His listener guessed that Aunt Ellen must have been very talkative, and Jimmy a very attentive small boy.

It was one of those innumerable college romances that briefly flower and wither during that handful of years which seems a microcosm of life itself. But this one had been more serious than most. During her last term Jimmy's mother—he still hadn't told Gibson her name—had fallen in love with a young engineering student who was half-way through his college career. It had been a whirlwind romance, and the match was an ideal one despite the fact that the girl was several years older than the boy. Indeed, it had almost reached the stage of an engagement when—Jimmy wasn't quite sure what had happened. The young man had been taken seriously ill, or had had a nervous breakdown, and had never come back to Cambridge.

"My mother never really got over it," said Jimmy, with a grave assumption of wisdom which somehow did not seem completely incongruous. "But another student was very much in love with her, and so she married him. I sometimes feel rather sorry for my father, for he must have known all about the other affair. I never saw much of him because—why, Mr. Gibson, don't you feel well?"

Gibson forced a smile.

"It's nothing—just a touch of space-sickness. I get it now and then—it will pass in a minute."

He only wished that the words were true. All these weeks, in total ignorance and believing himself secure against all the shocks of time and chance, he had been steering a collision course with Fate. And now the moment of impact had come; the twenty years that lay behind had vanished like a dream, and he was face to face once more with the ghosts of his own forgotten past.

"There's something wrong with Martin," said Bradley, signing the signals log with a flourish. "It can't be any news he's had from Earth—I've read it all. Do you suppose he's getting homesick?"

"He's left it a little late in the day, if that's the explanation," replied Norden. "After all, we'll be on Mars in a fortnight. But you do rather fancy yourself as an amateur psychologist, don't you?"

"Well, who doesn't?"

"*I* don't for one," began Norden pontifically. "Prying into other people's affairs isn't one of my——"

An anticipatory gleam in Bradley's eyes warned him just in time, and to the other's evident disappointment he checked himself in mid-sentence. Martin Gibson, complete with notebook and looking like a cub reporter attending his first press conference, had hurried into the office.

"Well, Owen, what was it you wanted to show me?" he asked eagerly.

Bradley moved to the main communication rack.

"It isn't really very impressive," he said, "but it means that we've passed another milestone and always gives me a bit of a kick. Listen to this."

He pressed the speaker switch and slowly brought up the volume control. The room was flooded with the hiss and crackle of radio noise, like the sound of a thousand frying pans at the point of imminent ignition. It was a sound that Gibson had heard often enough in the signals cabin and, for all its unvarying monotony, it never failed to fill him with a sense of wonder. He was listening, he knew, to the voices of the stars and nebulae, to radiations that had set out upon their journey before the birth of Man. And buried far down in the depths of that crackling, whispering chaos there might be—there *must* be—the sounds of alien civilisations talking to one another in the deeps of space. But, alas, their voices were lost beyond recall in the welter of cosmic interference which Nature herself had made.

This, however, was certainly not what Bradley had called him to hear. Very delicately, the signals officer made some vernier adjustments, frowning a little as he did so.

"I had it on the nose a minute ago—hope it hasn't drifted off—ah, here it is!"

At first Gibson could detect no alteration in the barrage of noise. Then he noticed that Bradley was silently marking time with his hand—rather quickly, at the rate of some two beats every second. With this to guide him, Gibson presently detected the infinitely faint undulating whistle that was breaking through the cosmic storm.

"What is it?" he asked, already half guessing the answer.

"It's the radio beacon on Deimos. There's one on Phobos as well, but it's not so powerful and we can't pick it up yet. When we get nearer Mars, we'll be able to fix ourselves within a few hundred kilometres by using them. We're at ten times the usable range now, but it's nice to know."

Yes, thought Gibson, it is nice to know. Of course, these radio aids weren't essential when one could see one's destination all the time, but they simplified some of the navigational problems. As he listened with half-closed eyes to that faint pulsing, sometimes almost drowned by the cosmic barrage, he knew how the mariners of old must have felt when they caught the first glimpse of the harbour lights from far out at sea.

"I think that's enough," said Bradley, switching off the speaker and restoring silence. "Anyway, it should give you something new to write about—things have been pretty quiet lately, haven't they?"

He was watching Gibson intently as he said this, but the author never responded. He merely jotted a few words in his notebook, thanked Bradley with absent-minded and unaccustomed politeness, and departed to his cabin.

"You're quite right," said Norden when he had gone. "Something's certainly happened to Martin. I'd better have a word with Doc."

"I shouldn't bother," replied Bradley. "Whatever it is, I don't think it's anything you can handle with pills. Better leave Martin to work it out his own way."

"Maybe you're right," said Norden grudgingly. "But I hope he doesn't take too long over it!"

He had now taken almost a week. The initial shock of discovering that Jimmy Spencer was Kathleen Morgan's son had already worn off, but the secondary effects were beginning to make themselves felt. Among these was a feeling of resentment that anything like this should have happened to *him*. It was such an outrageous violation of the laws of probability—the sort of thing that would never have happened in one of Gibson's own novels. But life was so inartistic and there was really nothing one could do about it.

This mood of childish petulance was now passing, to be replaced by a deeper sense of discomfort. All the emotions he had thought safely buried beneath twenty years of feverish activity were now rising to the surface again, like deep-sea creatures slain in some submarine eruption. On Earth, he could have escaped by losing himself once more in the crowd, but here he was trapped, with nowhere to flee.

It was useless to pretend that nothing had really changed, to say: "Of course I knew that Kathleen and Gerald had a son: what difference does that make now?" It made a great deal of difference. Every time he saw Jimmy he would be reminded of the past and—what was worse—of the future that might have been. The most urgent problem now was to face the facts squarely, and to come to grips with the new situation. Gibson knew well enough that there was only one way in which this could be done, and the opportunity would arise soon enough.

Jimmy had been down to the Southern Hemisphere and was making his way along the equatorial observation deck when he saw Gibson sitting at one of the windows, staring out into space. For a moment he thought the other had not seen him and had decided not to intrude upon his thoughts when Gibson called out: "Hello, Jimmy. Have you got a moment to spare?"

As it happened, Jimmy was rather busy. But he knew that there had been something wrong with Gibson, and realised that the older man needed his presence. So he came and sat on the bench recessed into the observation port, and presently he knew as much of the truth as Gibson thought good for either of them.

"I'm going to tell you something, Jimmy," Gibson began, "which is known to only a handful of people. Don't interrupt me and don't ask any questions—not until I've finished, at any rate.

"When I was rather younger than you, I wanted to be an engineer. I was quite a bright kid in those days and had no difficulty in getting into college through the usual examinations. As I wasn't sure what I intended to do, I took the five-year course in general engineering physics, which was quite a new thing in those days. In my first year I did fairly well—well enough to encourage me to work harder next time. In my second year I did—not brilliantly, but a lot better than average. And in the third year I fell in love. It wasn't exactly for the first time, but I knew it was the real thing at last.

"Now falling in love while you're at college may or may not be a good thing for you; it all depends on circumstances. If it's only a mild flirtation, it probably doesn't matter one way or the other. But if it's really serious, there are two possibilities.

"It may act as a stimulus—it may make you determined to do your best, to show that you're better than the other fellows. On the other hand, you may get so emotionally involved in the affair that nothing else seems to matter, and your studies go to pieces. That is what happened in my case."

Gibson fell into a brooding silence, and Jimmy stole a glance at him as he sat in the darkness a few feet away. They were on the night side of the ship, and the corridor lights had been dimmed so that the stars could be seen in their unchallenged glory. The constellation of Leo was directly ahead, and there in its heart was the brilliant ruby gem that was their goal. Next to the Sun itself, Mars was by far the brightest of all celestial bodies, and already its disc was just visible to the naked eye. The brilliant crimson light playing full on his face gave Gibson a healthy, even a cheerful appearance quite out of keeping with his feelings.

Was it true, Gibson wondered, that one never really forgot anything? It seemed now as if it might be. He could still see, as clearly as he had twenty years ago, that message pinned on the faculty noticeboard: "The Dean of Engineering wishes to see M. Gibson in his office at 3.00." He had had to wait, of course, until 3.15, and that hadn't helped. Nor would it have been so bad if the Dean had been sarcastic, or icily aloof, or even if he had lost his temper. Gibson could still picture that inhumanly tidy room, with its neat files and careful rows of books, could remember the Dean's secretary padding away on her typewriter in the corner, pretending not to listen.

(Perhaps, now he came to think of it, she wasn't pretending after all. The experience wouldn't have been so novel to her as it was to him.)

Gibson had liked and respected the Dean, for all the old man's finicky ways and meticulous pedantry, and now he had let him down, which made his failure doubly hard to bear. The Dean had rubbed it in with his "more in sorrow than in anger" technique, which had been more effective than he knew or intended. He had given Gibson another chance, but he was never to take it.

What made matters worse, though he was ashamed to admit the fact, was that Kathleen had done fairly well in her own exams. When his results had been published, Gibson had avoided her for several days, and when they met again he had already identified her with the cause of his failure. He could see this so clearly now that it no longer hurt. Had he really been in love if he was prepared to sacrifice Kathleen for the sake of his own self-respect? For that is what it came to; he had tried to shift the blame on to her.

The rest was inevitable. That quarrel on their last long cycle ride together into the country, and their returns by separate routes. The letters that hadn't been opened—above all, the letters that hadn't been written. Their unsuccessful attempt to meet, if only to say good-bye, on his last day in Cambridge. But even this had fallen through; the message hadn't reached Kathleen in time, and though he had waited until the last minute she had never come. The crowded train, packed with cheering students, had drawn noisily out of the station, leaving Cambridge and Kathleen behind. He had never seen either again.

There was no need to tell Jimmy about the dark months that had followed. He need never know what was meant by the simple words: "I had a breakdown and was advised not to return to college." Dr. Evans had made a pretty good job of patching him up, and he'd always be grateful for that. It was Evans who'd persuaded him to take up writing during his convalescence, with results that had surprised them both. (How many people knew that his first novel had been dedicated to his psychoanalyst? Well, if Rachmaninoff could do the same thing with the C Minor Concerto, why shouldn't he?)

Evans had given him a new personality and a vocation through which he could win back his self-confidence. But he couldn't restore the future that had been lost. All his life Gibson would envy the men who had finished what he had only begun—the men who could put after their names the degrees and qualifications he would never possess, and who would find their life's work in fields of which he could be only a spectator.

If the trouble had lain no deeper than this, it might not have mattered greatly. But in salvaging his pride by throwing the blame on to Kathleen he had warped his whole life. She, and through her all women, had become identified with failure and disgrace. Apart from a few attachments which had not been taken very seriously by either partner, Gibson had never fallen in love again, and now he realised that he never would. Knowing the cause of his complaint had helped him not in the least to find a cure.

None of these things, of course, need be mentioned to Jimmy. It was sufficient to give the bare facts, and to leave Jimmy to guess what he could. One day, perhaps, he might tell him more, but that depended on many things.

When Gibson had finished, he was surprised to find how nervously he was waiting for Jimmy's reactions. He felt himself wondering if the boy had read between the lines and apportioned blame where it was due, whether he would be sympathetic, angry—or merely embarrassed. It had suddenly become of the utmost importance to win Jimmy's respect and friendship, more important than anything that had happened to Gibson for a very long time. Only thus could he satisfy his conscience and quieten those accusing voices from the past.

He could not see Jimmy's face, for the other was in shadow and it seemed an age before he broke the silence.

"Why have you told me this?" he asked quietly. His voice was completely neutral—free both from sympathy or reproach.

Gibson hesitated before answering. The pause was natural enough, for, even to himself, he could hardly have explained all his motives.

"I just *had* to tell you," he said earnestly. "I couldn't have been happy until I'd done so. And besides—I felt I might be able to help, somehow."

Again that nerve-racking silence. Then Jimmy rose slowly to his feet.

"I'll have to think about what you've told me," he said, his voice still almost emotionless. "I don't know what to say now."

Then he was gone. He left Gibson in a state of extreme

uncertainty and confusion, wondering whether he had made a fool of himself or not. Jimmy's self-control, his failure to react, had thrown him off balance and left him completely at a loss. Only of one thing was he certain: in telling the facts, he had already done a great deal to relieve his mind.

But there was still much that he had not told Jimmy; indeed there was still much that he did not know himself.

7

"This is completely crazy!" stormed Norden, looking like a berserk Viking chief. "There must be *some* explanation! Good heavens, there aren't any proper docking facilities on Deimos—how do they expect us to unload? I'm going to call the Chief Executive and raise hell!"

"I shouldn't if I were you," drawled Bradley. "Did you notice the signature? This isn't an instruction from Earth, routed through Mars. It originated in the C.E.'s office. The old man may be a Tartar, but he doesn't do things unless he's got a good reason."

"Name just one!"

Bradley shrugged his shoulders.

"*I* don't have to run Mars, so how would I know? We'll find out soon enough." He gave a malicious little chuckle. "I wonder how Mac is going to take it? He'll have to recompute our approach orbit."

Norden leaned across the control panel and threw a switch.

"Hello, Mac—Skipper here. You receiving me?"

There was a short pause; then Hilton's voice came from the speaker.

"Mac's not here at the moment. Any message?"

"All right—you can break it to him. We've had orders from Mars to re-route the ship. They've diverted us from Phobos—no reason given at all. Tell Mac to calculate an orbit to Deimos, and to let me have it as soon as he can."

"I don't understand it. Why, Deimos is just a lot of mountains with no——"

"Yes—we've been through all that! Maybe we'll know the answer when we get there. Tell Mac to contact me as soon as he can, will you?"

Dr. Scott broke the news to Gibson while the author was putting the final touches to one of his weekly articles.

"Heard the latest?" he exclaimed breathlessly. "We've

been diverted to Deimos. Skipper's mad as hell—it may make us a day late."

"Does anyone know why?"

"No; it's a complete mystery. We've asked, but Mars won't tell."

Gibson scratched his head, examining and rejecting half a dozen ideas. He knew that Phobos, the inner moon, had been used as a base ever since the first expedition had reached Mars. Only 6,000 kilometres from the surface of the planet, and with a gravity less than a thousandth of Earth's, it was ideal for this purpose.

The *Ares* was due to dock in less than a week, and already Mars was a small disc showing numerous surface markings even to the naked eye. Gibson had borrowed a large Mercator projection of the planet and had begun to learn the names of its chief features—names that had been given, most of them, more than a century ago by astronomers who had certainly never dreamed that men would one day use them as part of their normal lives. How poetical those old mapmakers had been when they had ransacked mythology! Even to look at those words on the map was to set the blood pounding in the veins—Deucalion, Elysium, Eumenides, Arcadia, Atlantis, Utopia, Eos. . . . Gibson could sit for hours, fondling those wonderful names with his tongue, feeling as if in truth Keats' charm'd magic casements were opening before him. But there were no seas, perilous or otherwise, on Mars—though many of its lands were sufficiently forlorn.

The path of the *Ares* was now cutting steeply across the planet's orbit, and in a few days the motors would be checking the ship's outward speed. The change of velocity needed to deflect the voyage orbit from Phobos to Deimos was trivial, though it had involved Mackay in several hours of computing.

Every meal was devoted to discussing one thing—the crew's plans when Mars was reached. Gibson's could be summed up in one phrase—to see as much as possible. It was, perhaps, a little optimistic to imagine that one could get to know a whole planet in two months, despite Bradley's repeated assurances that two days was quite long enough for Mars.

The excitement of the voyage's approaching end had, to some extent, taken Gibson's mind away from his personal problems. He met Jimmy perhaps half a dozen times a day at meals and during accidental encounters, but they had not reopened their earlier conversation. For a while Gibson suspected that Jimmy was deliberately avoiding him, but he soon realised that this was not altogether the case. Like the rest of the crew, Jimmy was very busy preparing for the end of the voyage. Norden was determined to have the ship in perfect condition when she docked, and a vast amount of checking and servicing was in progress.

Yet despite this activity, Jimmy had given a good deal of thought to what Gibson had told him. At first he had felt bitter and angry towards the man who had been responsible, however unintentionally, for his mother's unhappiness. But after a while, he began to see Gibson's point of view and understood a little of the other's feelings. Jimmy was shrewd enough to guess that Gibson had not only left a good deal untold, but had put his own case as favourably as possible. Even allowing for this, however, it was obvious that Gibson genuinely regretted the past, and was anxious to undo whatever damage he could, even though he was a generation late.

It was strange to feel the sensation of returning weight and to hear the distant roar of the motors once again as the *Ares* reduced her speed to match the far smaller velocity of Mars. The manoeuvring and the final delicate course-corrections took more than twenty-four hours. When it was over, Mars was a dozen times as large as the full moon from Earth, with Phobos and Deimos visible as tiny stars whose movements could be clearly seen after a few minutes of observation.

Gibson had never really realised how red the great deserts were. But the simple word "red" conveyed no idea of the variety of colour on that slowly expanding disc. Some regions were almost scarlet, others yellow-brown, while perhaps the commonest hue was what could best be described as powdered brick.

It was late spring in the southern hemisphere, and the polar cap had dwindled to a few glittering specks of whiteness where the snow still lingered stubbornly on higher ground. The broad belt of vegetation between pole and desert was for the greater part a pale bluish-green, but every imaginable shade of colour could be found somewhere on that mottled disc.

The *Ares* was swimming into the orbit of Deimos at a

relative speed of less than a thousand kilometres an hour. Ahead of the ship, the tiny moon was already showing a visible disc, and as the hours passed it grew until, from a few hundred kilometres away, it looked as large as Mars. But what a contrast it presented! Here were no rich reds and greens, only a dark chaos of jumbled rocks, of mountains which jutted up towards the stars at all angels in this world of practically zero gravity.

Slowly the cruel rocks slid closer and swept past them, as the *Ares* cautiously felt her way down towards the radio beacon which Gibson had heard calling days before. Presently he saw, on an almost level area a few kilometres below, the first signs that man had ever visted this barren world. Two rows of vertical pillars jutted up from the ground, and between them was slung a network of cables. Almost imperceptibly the *Ares* sank towards Deimos; the main rockets had long since been silenced, for the small auxiliary jets had no difficulty in handling the ship's effective weight of a few hundred kilogrammes.

It was impossible to tell the moment of contact; only the sudden silence when the jets were cut off told Gibson that the journey was over, and the *Ares* was now resting in the cradle that had been prepared for her. He was still, of course, twenty thousand kilometres from Mars and would not actually reach the planet itself for another day, in one of the little rockets that was already climbing up to meet them. But as far as the *Ares* was concerned, the voyage was ended.

The tiny cabin that had been his home for so many weeks would soon know him no more.

He left the observation deck and hurried up to the control room, which he had deliberately avoided during the last busy hours. It was no longer so easy to move around inside the *Ares,* for the minute gravitational field of Deimos was just sufficient to upset his instinctive movements and he had to make a conscious allowance for it. He wondered just what it would be like to experience a *real* gravitational field again. It was hard to believe that only three months ago the idea of having no gravity at all had seemed very strange and unsettling, yet now he had come to regard it as normal. How adaptable the human body was!

The entire crew was sitting round the chart table, looking very smug and self-satisfied.

"You're just in time, Martin," said Norden cheerfully. "We're going to have a little celebration. Go and get your camera and take our pictures while we toast the old crate's health."

"Don't drink it all before I come back!" warned Gibson, and departed in search of his Leica. When he re-entered, Dr. Scott was attempting an interesting experiment.

"I'm fed up with squirting my beer out of a bulb," he explained. "I want to pour it properly into a glass now we've got the chance again. Let's see how long it takes."

"It'll be flat before it gets there," warned Mackay. "Let's see—*g's* about half a centimetre a second squared, you're pouring from a height of . . ." He retired into a brown study.

But the experiment was already in progress. Scott was holding the punctured beer-tin about a foot above his glass—and, for the first time in three months, the word "above" had some meaning, even if very little. For, with incredible slowness, the amber liquid oozed out of the tin —so slowly that one might have taken it for syrup. A thin column extended downwards, moving almost imperceptibly at first, but then slowly accelerating. It seemed an age before the glass was reached; then a great cheer went up as contact was made and the level of the liquid began to creep upwards.

". . . I calculate it should take a hundred and twenty seconds to get there," Mackay's voice was heard to announce above the din.

"Then you'd better calculate again," retorted Scott. "That's two minutes, and it's already there!"

"Eh?" said Mackay, startled, and obviously realising for the first time that the experiment was over. He rapidly rechecked his calculations and suddenly brightened at discovering a misplaced decimal point.

"Silly of me! I never was any good at mental arithmetic. I meant twelve seconds, of course."

"And that's the man who got us to Mars!" said someone in shocked amazement. "I'm going to walk back!"

Nobody seemed inclined to repeat Scott's experiment, which, though interesting, was felt to have little practical value. Very soon large amounts of liquid were being squirted out of bulbs in the "normal" manner, and the party began to get steadily more cheerful. Dr. Scott recited the whole of that saga of the spaceways—and a prodigious feat of memory it was—which paying passengers seldom encounter and which begins:

"It was the spaceship *Venus* . . ."

Gibson followed for some time the adventures of this all too appropriately named craft and its ingenious though single-minded crew. Then the atmosphere began to get too close for him and he left to clear his head. Almost automatically, he made his way back to his favourite viewpoint on the observation deck.

He had to anchor himself in it, lest the tiny but persistent pull of Deimos dislodge him. Mars, more than half full and slowly waxing, lay dead ahead. Down there the preparations to greet them would already be under way, and even at this moment the little rockets would be climbing invisibly towards Deimos to ferry them down. Fourteen thousand kilometres below, but still six thousand kilometres above Mars, Phobos was transiting the unlighted face of the planet, shining brilliantly against its star-eclipsing crescent. Just what *was* happening on that little moon, Gibson wondered half-heartedly. Oh, well, he'd find out soon enough. Meanwhile he'd polish up his aerography. Let's see—there was the double fork of the Sinus Meridiani (very convenient, that, smack on the equator and in zero longitude) and over to the east was the Syrtis Major. Working from these two obvious landmarks he could fill in the finer detail. Margaritifer Sinus was showing up nicely today, but there was a lot of cloud over Xanthe, and——

"Mr. Gibson!"

He looked round, startled.

"Why, Jimmy—you had enough too?"

Jimmy was looking rather hot and flushed—obviously another seeker after fresh air. He wavered, a little unsteadily, into the observation seat and for a moment stared silently at Mars as if he'd never seen it before. Then he shook his head disapprovingly.

"It's awfully big," he announced to no one in particular.

"It isn't as big as Earth," Gibson protested. "And in any case your criticism's completely meaningless, unless you state what standards you're applying. Just what size do you think Mars should be, anyway?"

This obviously hadn't occurred to Jimmy and he pondered it deeply for some time.

"I don't know," he said sadly. "But it's still too big. *Everything's* too big."

This conversation was going to get nowhere, Gibson decided. He would have to change the subject.

"What are you going to do when you get down to Mars? You've got a couple of months to play with before the *Ares* goes home."

"Well, I suppose I'll wander round Port Lowell and go out and look at the deserts. I'd like to do a bit of exploring if I can manage it."

Gibson thought this quite an interesting idea, but he knew that to explore Mars on any useful scale was not an easy undertaking and required a good deal of equipment, as well as experienced guides. It was hardly likely that Jimmy could attach himself to one of the scientific parties which left the settlements from time to time.

"I've an idea," he said. "They're supposed to show me everything I want to see. Maybe I can organise some trips out into Hellas or Hesperia, where no one's been yet. Would you like to come? We might meet some Martians!"

That, of course, had been the stock joke about Mars ever since the first ships had returned with the disappointing news that there weren't any Martians after all. Quite a number of people still hoped, against all evidence, that there might be intelligent life somewhere in the many unexplored regions of the planet.

"Yes," said Jimmy, "that would be a great idea. No one can stop me, anyway—my time's my own as soon as we get to Mars. It says so in the contract."

He spoke this rather belligerently, as if for the information of any superior officers who might be listening, and Gibson thought it wisest to remain silent.

The silence lasted for some minutes. Then Jimmy began, very slowly, to drift out of the observation port and to slide down the sloping walls of the ship. Gibson caught him before he had travelled very far and fastened two of the elastic hand-holds to his clothing—on the principle that Jimmy could sleep here just as comfortably as anywhere else. He was certainly much too tired to carry him to his bunk.

Is it true that we only look our true selves when we are asleep? wondered Gibson. Jimmy seemed very peaceful and contented now that he was completely relaxed—although perhaps the ruby light from the great planet above gave him his appearance of well-being. Gibson hoped it was not all illusion. The fact that Jimmy had at last deliberately sought him out was significant. True, Jimmy was not altogether himself, and he might have forgotten the whole incident by morning. But Gibson did not think so. Jimmy had decided, perhaps not yet consciously, to give him another chance.

He was on probation.

Gibson awoke the next day with a most infernal din ringing in his ears. It sounded as if the *Ares* was falling to pieces around him, and he hastily dressed and hurried out into the corridor. The first person he met was Mackay, who didn't stop to explain but shouted after him as he went by. "The rockets are here! The first one's going down in two hours. Better hurry—you're supposed to be on it!"

Gibson scratched his head a little sheepishly.

"Someone ought to have told me," he grumbled. Then he remembered that someone had, so he'd only himself to blame. He hurried back to his cabin and began to throw his property into suitcases. From time to time the *Ares* gave a distinct shudder around him, and he wondered just what was going on.

Norden, looking rather harassed, met him at the airlock. Dr. Scott, also dressed for departure, was with him. He was carrying, with extreme care, a bulky metal case.

"Hope you two have a nice trip down," said Norden. "We'll be seeing you in a couple of days, when we've got the cargo out. So until then—oh, I almost forgot! I'm supposed to get you to sign this."

"What is it?" asked Gibson suspiciously. "I never sign anything until my agent's vetted it."

"Read it and see," grinned Norden. "It's quite an historic document."

The parchment which Norden had handed him bore these words:

THIS IS TO CERTIFY THAT MARTIN M. GIBSON, AUTHOR, WAS THE FIRST PASSENGER TO TRAVEL IN THE LINER ARES, OF EARTH, ON HER MAIDEN VOYAGE FROM EARTH TO MARS.

Then followed the date, and space for the signatures of Gibson and the rest of the crew. Gibson wrote his autograph with a flourish.

"I suppose this will end up in the museum of Astronautics, when they decide where they're going to build it," he remarked.

"So will the *Ares,* I expect," said Scott.

"That's a fine thing to say at the end of her first trip!" protested Norden. "But I guess you're right. Well, I must be off. The others are outside in their suits—shout to them as you go across. See you on Mars!"

For the second time, Gibson climbed into a spacesuit, now feeling quite a veteran at this sort of thing.

"Of course, you'll understand," explained Scott, "that when the service is properly organised the passengers will go across to the ferry through a connecting tube. That will cut out all this business."

"They'll miss a lot of fun," Gibson replied as he quickly checked the gauges on the little panel beneath his chin.

The outer door opened before them, and they jetted themselves slowly out across the surface of Deimos. The *Ares,* supported in the cradle of ropes (which must have been hastily prepared within the last week) looked as if a wrecking party had been at work on her. Gibson understood now the cause of the bangings and thumpings that had awakened him. Most of the plating from the Southern Hemisphere had been removed to get at the hold, and the space-suited members of the crew were bringing out the cargo, which was now being piled on the rocks around the ship. It looked, Gibson thought, a very haphazard sort of operation. He hoped that no one would accidentally give his luggage a push which would send it off irretrievably into space, to become a third and still tinier satellite of Mars.

Lying fifty metres from the *Ares,* and quite dwarfed by her bulk, were the two winged rockets that had come up from Mars during the night. One was already having cargo ferried into it; the other, a much smaller vessel, was obviously intended for passengers only. As Gibson slowly and cautiously followed Scott towards it, he switched over to the general wavelength of his suit and called good-bye to his crewmates. Their envious replies came back promptly, interspersed with much puffing and blowing—for the loads they were shifting, though practically weightless, possessed their normal inertia and so were just as hard to set moving as on Earth.

"That's right!" came Bradley's voice. "Leave us to do all the work!"

"You've one compensation," laughed Gibson. "You must be the highest-paid stevedores in the Solar System!" He could sympathise with Bradley's point of view; this was not the sort of work for which the highly trained technicians of the *Ares* had signed on. But the mysterious diversion of the ship from the tiny though well-equipped port on Phobos had made such improvisations unavoidable.

One couldn't very well make individual good-byes on open circuit with half a dozen people listening, and in any case Gibson would be seeing everyone again in a few days. He would like to have had an extra word with Jimmy, but that would have to wait.

It was quite an experience seeing a new human face again. The rocket pilot came into the airlock to help them with their suits, which were gently deposited back on Deimos for future use simply by opening the outer door again and letting the air current do the rest. Then he led them into the tiny cabin and told them to relax in the padded seats.

"Since you've had no gravity for a couple of months," he said, "I'm taking you down as gently as I can. I won't use more than a normal Earth gravity—but even that may make you feel as if you weigh a ton. Ready?"

"Yes," said Gibson, trying valiantly to forget his last experience of this nature.

There was a gentle, far-away roar and something thrust him firmly down into the depths of his seat. The crags and mountains of Deimos sank swiftly behind; he caught a last glimpse of the *Ares*—a bright silver dumb-bell against that nightmare jumble of rocks.

Only a second's burst of power had liberated them from the tiny moon; they were now floating round Mars in a free orbit. For several minutes the pilot studied his instruments, receiving radio checks from the planet beneath, and swinging the ship round its gyros. Then he punched the firing key again, and the rockets thundered for a few seconds more. The ship had broken free from the orbit of Deimos, and was falling towards Mars. The whole operation was an exact replica, in miniature, of a true interplanetary voyage. Only the times and durations were changed; it would take them three hours, not months, to reach their goal, and they had only thousands instead of millions of kilometres to travel.

"Well," said the pilot, locking his controls and swinging round in his seat. "Had a good trip?"

"Quite pleasant, thanks," said Gibson. "Not much excitement, of course. Everything went very smoothly."

"How's Mars these days?" asked Scott.

"Oh, just the same as usual. All work and not much play. The big thing at the moment is the new dome we're building at Lowell. Three hundred metres clear span—you'll be able to think you're back on Earth. We're wondering if we can arrange clouds and rain inside it."

"What's all this Phobos business?" said Gibson, with a nose for news. "It caused us a lot of trouble."

"Oh, I don't think it's anything important. No one seems to know exactly, but there are quite a lot of people up there building a big lab. My guess is that Phobos is going to be a pure research station, and they don't want liners coming and going—and messing up their instruments with just about every form of radiation known to science."

Gibson felt disappointed at the collapse of several interesting theories. Perhaps if he had not been so intent on the approaching planet he might have considered this explanation a little more critically, but for the moment it satisfied him and he gave the matter no further thought.

When Mars seemed in no great hurry to come closer, Gibson decided to learn all he could about the practical details of life on the planet, now that he had a genuine colonist to question. He had a morbid fear of making a fool of himself, either by ignorance or tactlessness, and for the next couple of hours the pilot was kept busy alternating between Gibson and his instruments.

Mars was less than a thousand kilometres away when Gibson released his victim and devoted his whole attention to the expanding landscape beneath. They were passing swiftly over the equator, coming down into the outer fringes of the planet's extremely deep yet very tenuous atmosphere. Presently—and it was impossible to tell when the moment arrived—Mars ceased to be a planet floating in space, and became instead a landscape far below.. Deserts and oases fled beneath; the Syrtis Major came and passed before Gibson had time to recognise it. They were fifty kilometres up when there came the first hint that the air was thickening around them. A faint and distant sighing, seeming to come from nowhere, began to fill the cabin. The thin air was tugging at their hurtling projectile with feeble fingers, but its strength would grow swiftly—too swiftly, if their navigation had been at fault. Gibson could feel the deceleration mounting as the ship slackened its speed; the whistle of air was now so loud, even through the insulation of the walls, that normal speech would have been difficult.

This seemed to last for a very long time, though it could only have been a few minutes. At last the wail of the wind died slowly away. The rocket had shed all its surplus speed against air resistance; the refractory material of its nose and knife-edged wings would be swiftly cooling from cherry-red. No longer a spaceship now, but simply a high-speed glider, the little ship was racing across the desert at less than a thousand kilometres an hour, riding down the radio beam into Port Lowell.

Gibson first glimpsed the settlement as a tiny white patch on the horizon, against the dark background of the Aurorae Sinus. The pilot swung the ship round in a great whistling arc to the south, losing altitude and shedding his surplus speed. As the rocket banked, Gibson had a momentary picture of half a dozen large, circular domes, clustered closely together. Then the ground was rushing up to meet him, there was a series of gentle bumps, and the machine rolled slowly to a standstill.

He was on Mars. He had reached what to ancient man had been a moving red light among the stars, what to the men of only a century ago had been a mysterious and utterly unattainable world—and what was now the frontier of the human race.

"There's quite a reception committee," remarked the pilot. "All the transport fleet's come out to see us. I didn't know they had so many vehicles serviceable!"

Two small, squat machines with very wide balloon tires had come racing up to meet them. Each had a pressurised driving cab, large enough to hold two people, but a dozen passengers had managed to crowd on to the little vehicles by grabbing convenient hand-holds. Behind them came two large half-tracked buses, also full of spectators. Gibson had not expected quite such a crowd, and began to compose a short speech.

"I don't suppose you know how to use these things

yet," said the pilot, producing two breathing masks. "But you've only got to wear them for a minute while you get over to the Fleas." (The *what?* thought Gibson. Oh, of course, those little vehicles would be the famous Martian "Sand Fleas," the planet's universal transports.) "I'll fix them on for you. Oxygen O.K.? Right—here we go. It may feel a bit queer at first."

The air slowly hissed from the cabin until the pressure inside and out had been equalised. Gibson felt his exposed skin tingling uncomfortably; the atmosphere around him was now thinner than above the peak of Everest. It had taken three months of slow acclimatisation on the *Ares*, and all the resources of modern medical science, to enable him to step out on to the surface of Mars with no more protection than a simple oxygen mask.

It was flattering that so many people had come to meet him. Of course, it wasn't often that Mars could expect so distinguished a visitor, but he knew that the busy little colony had no time for ceremonial.

Dr. Scott emerged beside him, still carrying the large metal case he had nursed so carefully through the whole of the trip. At his appearance a group of the colonists came rushing forward, completely ignored Gibson, and crowded round Scott. Gibson could hear their voices, so distorted in this thin air as to be almost incomprehensible.

"Glad to see you again, Doc! Here—let us carry it!"

"We've got everything ready, and there are ten cases waiting in hospital now. We should know how good it is in a week."

"Come on—get into the bus and talk later!"

Before Gibson had realised what was happening, Scott and his impedimenta had been swept away. There was a shrill whine of a powerful motor and the bus tore off towards Port Lowell, leaving Gibson feeling as foolish as he had ever been in his life.

He had completely forgotten the serum. To Mars, its arrival was of infinitely greater importance than a visit by any novelist, however distinguished he might be on his own planet. It was a lesson he would not forget in a hurry.

Luckily, he had not been completely deserted—the Sand Fleas were still left. One of the passengers disembarked and hurried up to him.

"Mr. Gibson? I'm Westerman of the 'Times'—the 'Martian Times,' that is. Very pleased to meet you. This is——"

"Henderson, in charge of port facilities," interrupted a tall, hatchet-faced man, obviously annoyed that the other had got in first. "I've seen that your luggage will be collected. Jump aboard."

It was quite obvious that Westerman would have much preferred Gibson as his own passenger, but he was forced to submit with as good grace as he could manage. Gibson climbed into Henderson's Flea through the flexible plastic bag that was the vehicle's simple but effective airlock, and the other joined him a minute later in the driving cab. It was a relief to discard the breathing mask; the few minutes he had spent in the open had been quite a strain. He also felt very heavy and sluggish—the exact reverse of the sensation one would have expected on reaching Mars. But for three months he had known no gravity at all, and it would take him some time to grow accustomed to even a third of his terrestrial weight.

The vehicle began to race across the landing strip towards the domes of the Port, a couple of kilometres away. For the first time, Gibson noticed that all around him was the brilliant mottled green of the hardy plants that were the commonest life-form on Mars. Overhead the sky was no longer jet black, but a deep and glorious blue. The sun was not far from the zenith, and its rays struck with surprising warmth through the plastic dome of the cabin.

Gibson peered at the dark vault of the sky, trying to locate the tiny moon on which his companions were still at work. Henderson noticed his gaze, took one hand off the steering wheel, and pointed close to the Sun.

"There she is," he said.

Gibson shielded his eyes and stared into the sky. Then he saw, hanging like a distant electric arc against the blue, a brilliant star a little westwards of the Sun. It was far too small even for Deimos, but it was a moment before Gibson realised that his companion had mistaken the object of his search.

That steady, unwinking light, burning so unexpectedly in the daylight sky, was now, and would remain for many weeks, the morning star of Mars. But it was better known as Earth.

8

"Sorry to have kept you waiting," said Mayor Whittaker, "but you know the way it is—the Chief's been in conference for the last hour. I've only just been able to get hold of him myself to tell him you're here. This way—we'll take the short cut through Records."

It might have been an ordinary office on Earth. The door said, simply enough: "Chief Executive." There was no name; it wasn't necessary. Everyone in the Solar System knew who ran Mars—indeed, it was difficult to think of the planet without thinking of Warren Hadfield at the same time.

Gibson was surprised, when he rose from his desk, to see that the Chief Executive was a good deal shorter than he had imagined. He must have judged the man by his works, and had never guessed that he could give him a couple of inches in height. But the thin, wiry frame and sensitive, rather birdlike head were exactly as he had expected.

The interview began with Gibson somewhat on the defensive, for so much depended on his making a good impression. His way would be infinitely easier if he had the Chief on his side. In fact, if he made an enemy of Hadfield he might just as well go home right away.

"I hope Whittaker's been looking after you," said the Chief when the initial courtesies had been exchanged. "You'll realise that I couldn't see you before—I've only just got back from an inspection. How are you settling down here?"

"Quite well," smiled Gibson. "I'm afraid I've broken a few things by leaving them in mid-air, but I'm getting used to living with gravity again."

"And what do you think of our little city?"

"It's a remarkable achievement. I don't know how you managed to do so much in the time."

Hadfield was eyeing him narrowly.

"Be perfectly frank. It's smaller than you expected, isn't it?"

Gibson hesitated.

"Well, I suppose it is—but then I'm used to the
dards of London and New York. After all, two
sand people would only make a large village bac
Earth. Such a lot of Port Lowell's underground, toc
that makes a difference."

The Chief Executive seemed neither annoyed no
prised.

"Everyone has a disappointment when they see
largest city," he said. "Still, it's going to be a lot big
another week, when the new dome goes up. Tell
just what are your plans now you've got here? I su
you know I wasn't very much in favour of this visit
first place."

"I gathered that on Earth," said Gibson, a little
aback. He had yet to discover that frankness was o
the Chief Executive's major virtues; it was not on
endeared him to many people. "I suppose you were
I'd get in the way."

"Yes. But now you're here, we'll do the best fo
I hope you'll do the same for us."

"In what way?" asked Gibson, stiffening defensively

Hadfield leaned across the table and clasped his
together with an almost feverish intensity.

"We're at war, Mr. Gibson. We're at war with
and all the forces it can bring against us—cold, la
water, lack of air. And we're at war with Earth.
paper war, true, but it's got its victories and defeat
fighting a campaign at the end of a supply line
never less than fifty million kilometres long. The
urgent goods take at least five months to reach me
I only get them if Earth decides I can't manage any
way.

"I suppose you realise what I'm fighting for—m
mary objective, that is? It's self-sufficiency. Rem
that the first expeditions had to bring *everything*
them. Well, we can provide all the basic necessities
now, from our own resources. Our workshops can
almost anything that isn't too complicated—but it's
question of manpower. There are some very spec
goods that simply have to be made on Earth, and
our population's at least ten times as big we can't do
about it. Everyone on Mars is an expert at somet
but there are more skilled trades back on Earth than

are people on this planet, and it's no use arguing with arithmetic.

"You see those graphs over there? I started keeping them five years ago. They show our production index for various key materials. We've reached the self-sufficiency level—that horizontal red line—for about half of them. I hope that in another five years there will be very few things we'll have to import from Earth. Even now our greatest need is manpower, and that's where you may be able to help us."

Gibson looked a little uncomfortable.

"I can't make any promises. Please remember that I'm here purely as a reporter. Emotionally, I'm on your side, but I've got to describe the facts as I see them."

"I appreciate that. But facts aren't everything. What I hope you'll explain to Earth is the things we hope to do, just as much as the things we've done. They're even more important—but we can achieve them only if Earth gives us its support. Not all your predecessors have realised that."

That was perfectly true, thought Gibson. He remembered a critical series of articles in the "Daily Telegraph" about a year before. The facts had been quite accurate, but a similar account of the first settlers' achievements after five years' colonisation of North America would probably have been just as discouraging.

"I think I can see both sides of the question," said Gibson. "You've got to realise that from the point of view of Earth, Mars is a long way away, costs a lot of money, and doesn't offer anything in return. The first glamour of interplanetary exploration has worn off. Now people are asking, 'What do we get out of it?' So far the answer's been, 'Very little.' I'm convinced that your work is important, but in my case it's an act of faith rather than a matter of logic. The average man back on Earth probably thinks the millions you're spending here could be better used improving his own planet—when he thinks of it at all, that is."

"I understand your difficulty; it's a common one. And it isn't easy to answer. Let me put it this way. I suppose most intelligent people would admit the value of a scientific base on Mars, devoted to pure research and investigation?"

"Undoubtedly."

"But they can't see the purpose of building up a self-contained culture, which may eventually become an independent civilisation?"

"That's the trouble, precisely. They don't believe it's possible—or, granted the possibility, don't think it's worth while. You'll often see articles pointing out that Mars will always be a drag on the home planet, because of the tremendous natural difficulties under which you're labouring."

"What about the analogy between Mars and the American colonies?"

"It can't be pressed too far. After all, men could breathe the air and find food to eat when they got to America!"

"That's true, but though the problem of colonising Mars is so much more difficult, we've got enormously greater powers at our control. Given time and material, we can make this a world as good to live on as Earth. Even now, you won't find many of our people who want to go back. They know the importance of what they're doing. Earth may not need Mars yet, but one day it will."

"I wish I could believe that," said Gibson, a little unhappily. He pointed to the rich green tide of vegetation that lapped, like a hungry sea, against the almost invisible dome of the city, at the great plain that hurried so swiftly over the edge of the curiously close horizon, and at the scarlet hills within whose arms the city lay. "Mars is an interesting world, even a beautiful one. But it can never be like Earth."

"Why should it be? And what do you mean by 'Earth,' anyway? Do you mean the South American pampas, the vineyards of France, the coral islands of the Pacific, the Siberian steppes? 'Earth' is every one of those! Wherever men can live, that will be home to someone, some day. And sooner or later men will be able to live on Mars without all this." He waved towards the dome which floated above the city and gave it life.

"Do you really think," protested Gibson, "that men can ever adapt themselves to the atmosphere outside? They won't be men any longer if they do!"

For a moment the Chief Executive did not reply. Then he remarked quietly: "I said nothing about men adapting themselves to Mars. Have you ever considered the possibility of Mars meeting us half-way?"

He left Gibson just sufficient time to absorb the words; then, before his visitor could frame the questions that were leaping to his mind, Hadfield rose to his feet.

"Well, I hope Whittaker looks after you and shows you everything you want to see. You'll understand that the transport situation's rather tight, but we'll get you to all the outposts if you give us time to make the arrangements. Let me know if there's any difficulty."

The dismissal was polite and, at least for the time being, final. The busiest man on Mars had given Gibson a generous portion of his time, and his questions would have to wait until the next opportunity.

"What do you think of the Chief, now you've met him?" said Mayor Whittaker when Gibson had returnd to the outer office.

"He was very pleasant and helpful," replied Gibson cautiously. "Quite an enthusiast about Mars, isn't he?"

Whittaker pursed his lips.

"I'm not sure that's the right word. I think he regards Mars as an enemy to be beaten. So do we all, of course, but the Chief's got better reasons than most. You'd heard about his wife, hadn't you?"

"No."

"She was one of the first people to die of Martian fever, two years after they came here."

"Oh," said Gibson slowly. "I see. I suppose that's one reason why there's been such an effort to find a cure."

"Yes; the Chief's very much set on it. Besides, it's such a drain on our resources. We can't afford to be sick here!"

That last remark, thought Gibson as he crossed Broadway (so called because it was all of fifteen metres wide), almost summed up the position of the colony. He had still not quite recovered from his initial disappointment at finding how small Port Lowell was, and how deficient in all the luxuries to which he was accustomed on Earth. With its rows of uniform metal houses and few public buildings it was more of a military camp than a city, though the inhabitants had done their best to brighten it up with terrestrial flowers. Some of these had grown to impressive sizes under the low gravity, and Oxford Circus was now ablaze with sunflowers thrice the height of a man. Though they were getting rather a nuisance no one had the heart to suggest their removal; if they continued at their present rate of growth it would soon take a skilled lumberjack to fell them without endangering the port hospital.

Gibson continued thoughtfully up Broadway until he

came to Marble Arch, at the meeting point of Domes One and Two. It was also, as he had quickly found, a meeting point in many other ways. Here, strategically placed near the multiple airlocks, was "George's," the only bar on Mars.

"Morning, Mr. Gibson," said George. "Hope the Chief was in a good temper."

As he had left the administration building less than ten minutes ago, Gibson thought this was pretty quick work. He was soon to find that news travelled very rapidly in Port Lowell, and most of it seemed to be routed through George.

George was an interesting character. Since tavern keepers were regarded as only relatively, and not absolutely, essential for the well-being of the Port, he had two official professions. On Earth he had been a well-known stage entertainer, but the unreasonable demands of the three or four wives he had acquired in a rush of youthful enthusiasm had made him decide to emigrate. He was now in charge of the Port's little theatre and seemed to be perfectly contented with life. Being in the middle forties, he was one of the oldest men on Mars.

"We've got a show on next week," he remarked, when he had served Gibson. "One or two quite good turns. Hope you'll be coming along."

"Certainly," said Gibson. "I'll look forward to it. How often do you have this sort of thing?"

"About once a month. We have film shows three times a week, so we don't really do too badly."

"I'm glad Port Lowell has some night-life."

"You'd be surprised. Still, I'd better not tell you about that or you'll be writing it all up in the papers."

"I don't write for *that* sort of newspaper," retorted Gibson, sipping thoughtfully at the local brew. It wasn't at all bad when you got used to it, though of course it was completely synthetic—the joint offspring of hydroponic farm and chemical laboratory.

The bar was quite deserted, for at this time of day everyone in Port Lowell would be hard at work. Gibson pulled out his notebook and began to make careful entries, whistling a little tune as he did so. It was an annoying habit, of which he was quite unconscious, and George counterattacked by turning up the bar radio.

For once it was a live programme, beamed to Mars from somewhere on the night side of Earth, punched across space by heaven-knows-how-many megawatts, then picked up and rebroadcast by the station on the low hills to the south of the city. Reception was good, apart from a trace of solar noise—static from that infinitely greater transmitter against whose background Earth was broadcasting. Gibson wondered if it was really worth all this trouble to send the voice of a somewhat mediocre soprano and a light orchestra from world to world. But half Mars was probably listening with varying degrees of sentimentality and homesickness—both of which would be indignantly denied.

Gibson finished the list of several score questions he had to ask someone. He still felt rather like a new boy at his first school; everything was so strange, nothing could be taken for granted. It was hard to believe that twenty metres on the other side of that transparent bubble lay a sudden death by suffocation. Somehow this feeling had never worried him on the *Ares;* after all, space was like that. But it seemed all wrong here, where one could look out across that brilliant green plain, now a battlefield on which the hardy Martian plants fought their annual struggle for existence—a struggle which would end in death for victors and vanquished alike with the coming of winter.

Suddenly Gibson felt an almost overwhelming desire to leave the narrow streets and go out beneath the open sky. For almost the first time, he found himself really missing Earth, the planet he had thought had so little more to offer him. Like Falstaff, he felt like babbling of green fields—with the added irony that green fields were all around him, tantalisingly visible yet barred from him by the laws of nature.

"George," said Gibson abruptly, "I've been here awhile and I haven't been outside yet. I'm not supposed to without someone to look after me. You won't have any customers for an hour or so. Be a sport and take me out through the airlock—just for ten minutes."

No doubt, thought Gibson a little sheepishly, George considered this a pretty crazy request. He was quite wrong; it had happened so often before that George took it very much for granted. After all, his job was attending to the whims of his customers, and most of the new boys seemed to feel this way after their first few days under the dome. George shrugged his shoulders philosophically, wondering if he should apply for additional credits as Port psychotherapist, and disappeared into his inner sanctum. He came back a moment later, carrying a couple of breathing masks and their auxiliary equipment.

"We won't want the whole works on a nice day like this," he said, while Gibson clumsily adjusted his gear. "Make sure that sponge rubber fits snugly around your neck. All right—let's go. But only ten minutes, mind!"

Gibson followed eagerly, like a sheepdog behind its master, until they came to the dome exit. There were two locks here, a large one, wide open, leading into Dome Two, and a smaller one which led out on to the open landscape. It was simply a metal tube, about three metres in diameter, leading through the glass-brick wall which anchored the flexible plastic envelope of the dome to the ground.

There were four separate doors, none of which could be opened unless the remaining three were closed. Gibson fully approved of these precautions, but it seemed a long time before the last of the doors swung inwards from its seals and that vivid green plain lay open before him. His exposed skin was tingling under the reduced pressure, but the thin air was reasonably warm and he soon felt quite comfortable. Completely ignoring George, he ploughed his way briskly through the low, closely packed vegetation, wondering as he did why it clustered so thickly round the dome. Perhaps it was attracted by the warmth of the slow seepage of oxygen from the city.

He stopped after a few hundred metres, feeling at last clear of that oppressive canopy and once more under the open sky of heaven. The fact that his head, at least, was still totally enclosed somehow didn't seem to matter. He bent down and examined the plants among which he was standing knee-deep.

He had, of course, seen photographs of Martian plants many times before. They were not really very exciting, and he was not enough of a botanist to appreciate their peculiarities. Indeed if he had met such plants in some out-of-the-way part of Earth he would hardly have looked at them twice. None were higher than his waist, and those around him now seemed to be made of sheets of brilliant green parchment, very thin but very tough, designed to catch as much sunlight as possible without losing precious water. These ragged sheets were spread like little sails in the sun, whose progress across the sky they would follow until they dipped westwards at dusk. Gibson wished there were some flowers to add a touch of contrasting colour to the vivid emerald, but there were no flowers on Mars. Perhaps there had been, once, when the air was thick enough to support insects, but now most of the Martian plant-life was self-fertilised.

George caught up with him and stood regarding the natives with a morose indifference. Gibson wondered if he was annoyed at being so summarily dragged out of doors, but his qualms of conscience were unjustified. George was simply brooding over his next production, wondering whether to risk a Noel Coward play after the disaster that had resulted the last time his company had tried its hand with period pieces. Suddenly he snapped out of his reverie and said to Gibson, his voice thin but clearly audible over this short distance: "This is rather amusing. Just stand still for a minute and watch that plant in your shadow."

Gibson obeyed this peculiar instruction. For a moment nothing happened. Then he saw that, very slowly, the parchment sheets were folding in on one another. The whole process was over in about three minutes; at the end of that time the plant had become a little ball of green paper, tightly crumpled together and only a fraction of its previous size.

George chuckled.

"It thinks night's fallen," he said, "and doesn't want to be caught napping when the sun's gone. If you move away, it will think things over for half an hour before it risks opening shop again. You could probably give it a nervous breakdown if you kept this up all day."

"Are these plants any use?" said Gibson. "I mean, can they be eaten, or do they contain any valuable chemicals?"

"They certainly can't be eaten—they're not poisonous but they'd make you feel mighty unhappy. You see they're not really like plants on Earth at all. That green is just a coincidence. It isn't—what do you call the stuff——"

"Chlorophyll?"

"Yes. They don't depend on the air as our plants do; everything they need they get from the ground. In fact they can grow in a complete vacuum, like the plants on the Moon, if they've got suitable soil and enough sunlight."

Quite a triumph of evolution, thought Gibson. But to what purpose? he wondered. Why had life clung so tenaciously to this little world, despite the worst that nature could do? Perhaps the Chief Executive had obtained some of his own optimism from these tough and resolute plants.

"Hey!" said George. "It's time to go back."

Gibson followed meekly enough. He no longer felt weighed down by that claustrophobic oppression which was, he knew, partly due to the inevitable reaction at finding Mars something of an anticlimax. Those who had come here for a definite job, and hadn't been given time to brood, would probably by-pass this stage altogether. But he had been turned loose to collect his impressions, and so far his chief one was a feeling of helplessness as he compared what man had so far achieved on Mars with the problems still to be faced. Why, even now three-quarters of the planet was still unexplored! That was some measure of what remained to be done.

The first days at Port Lowell had been busy and exciting enough. It had been a Sunday when he had arrived and Mayor Whittaker had been sufficiently free from the cares of office to show him round the city personally, once he had been installed in one of the four suites of the Grand Martian Hotel. (The other three had not yet been finished.) They had started at Dome One, the first to be built, and the Mayor had proudly traced the growth of his city from a group of pressurised huts only ten years ago. It was amusing—and rather touching—to see how the colonists had used wherever possible the names of familiar streets and squares from their own far-away cities. There was also a scientific system of numbering the streets in Port Lowell, but nobody ever used it.

Most of the living houses were uniform metal structures, two stories high, with rounded corners and rather small windows. They held two families and were none too large, since the birth-rate of Port Lowell was the highest in the known universe. This, of course, was hardly surprising since almost the entire population lay between the ages of twenty and thirty, with a few of the senior administrative staff creeping up into the forties. Every house had a curious porch which puzzled Gibson until he realised that it was designed to act as an airlock in an emergency.

Whittaker had taken him first to the administrative centre, the tallest building in the city. If one stood on its roof, one could almost reach up and touch the dome floating above. There was nothing very exciting about Admin. It might have been any office building on Earth, with its rows of desks and typewriters and filing cabinets.

Main Air was much more interesting. This, truly, was

the heart of Port Lowell; if it ever ceased to function, the city and all those it held would soon be dead. Gibson had been somewhat vague about the manner in which the settlement obtained its oxygen. At one time he had been under the impression that it was extracted from the surrounding air, having forgotten that even such scanty atmosphere as Mars possessed contained less than one per cent of the gas.

Mayor Whittaker had pointed to the great heap of red sand that had been bulldozed in from outside the dome. Everyone called it "sand," but it had little resemblance to the familiar sand of Earth. A complex mixture of metallic oxides, it was nothing less than the debris of a world that had rusted to death.

"All the oxygen we need's in these ores," said Whittaker, kicking at the caked powder. "And just about every metal you can think of. We've had one or two strokes of luck on Mars: this is the biggest."

He bent down and picked up a lump more solid than the rest.

"I'm not much of a geologist," he said, "but look at this. Pretty, isn't it? Mostly iron oxide, they tell me. Iron isn't much use, of course, but the other metals are. About the only one we can't get easily direct from the sand is magnesium. The best source of that's the old sea bed; there are some salt flats a hundred metres thick out in Xanthe and we just go and collect when we need it."

They walked into the low, brightly lit building, towards which a continual flow of sand was moving on a conveyor belt. There was not really a great deal to see, and though the engineer in charge was only too anxious to explain just what was happening, Gibson was content merely to learn that the ores were cracked in electric furnaces, the oxygen drawn off, purified and compressed, and the various metallic messes sent on for more complicated operations. A good deal of water was also produced here—almost enough for the settlement's needs, though other sources were available as well.

"Of course," said Mayor Whittaker, "in addition to storing the oxygen we've got to keep the air pressure at the correct value and to get rid of the CO_2. You realise, don't you, that the dome's kept up purely by the internal pressure and hasn't any other support at all?"

"Yes," said Gibson. "I suppose if that fell off the whole thing would collapse like a deflated balloon."

"Exactly. We keep 150 millimetres pressure in summer, a little more in winter. That gives almost the same oxygen pressure as in Earth's atmosphere. And we remove the CO_2 simply by letting plants do the trick. We imported enough for this job, since the Martian plants don't go in for photosynthesis."

"Hence the hypertrophied sunflowers in Oxford Circus, I suppose."

"Well, those are intended to be more ornamental than functional. I'm afraid they're getting a bit of a nuisance; I'll have to stop them from spraying seeds all over the city, or whatever it is that sunflowers do. Now let's walk over and look at the farm."

The name was a singularly misleading one for the big food-production plant filling Dome Three. The air was quite humid here, and the sunlight was augmented by batteries of fluorescent tubes so that growth could continue day and night. Gibson knew very little about hydroponic farming and so was not really impressed by the figures which Mayor Whittaker proudly poured into his ear. He could, however, appreciate that one of the greatest problems was meat production, and admired the ingenuity which had partly overcome this by extensive tissue-culture in great vats of nutrient fluid.

"It's better than nothing," said the Mayor a little wistfully. "But what I wouldn't give for a genuine lamb-chop! The trouble with natural meat production is that it takes up so much space and we simply can't afford it. However, when the new dome's up we're going to start a little farm with a few sheep and cows. The kids will love it—they've never seen any animals, of course."

This was not quite true, as Gibson was soon to discover: Mayor Whittaker had momentarily overlooked two of Port Lowell's best-known residents.

By the end of the tour Gibson began to suffer from slight mental indigestion. The mechanics of life in the city were so complicated, and Mayor Whittaker tried to show him *everything*. He was quite thankful when the trip was over and they returned to the Mayor's home for dinner.

"I think that's enough for one day," said Whittaker, "but I wanted to show you round because we'll all be busy tomorrow and I won't be able to spare much time. The Chief's away, you know, and won't be back until Thursday, so I've got to look after everything."

"Where's he gone?" asked Gibson, out of politeness rather than real interest.

"Oh, up to Phobos," Whittaker replied, with the briefest possible hesitation. "As soon as he gets back he'll be glad to see you."

The conversation had then been interrupted by the arrival of Mrs. Whittaker and family, and for the rest of the evening Gibson was compelled to talk about Earth. It was his first, but not by any means his last, experience of the insatiable interest which the colonists had in the home planet. They seldom admitted it openly, pretending to a stubborn indifference about the "old world" and its affairs. But their questions, and above all their rapid reactions to terrestrial criticisms and comments, belied this completely.

It was strange to talk to children who had never known Earth, who had been born and had spent all their short lives under the shelter of the great domes. What, Gibson wondered, did Earth mean to them? Was it any more real than the fabulous lands of fairy tales? All they knew of the world from which their parents had emigrated was at second hand, derived from books and pictures. As far as their own senses were concerned, Earth was just another star.

They had never known the coming of the seasons. Outside the dome, it was true, they could watch the long winter spread death over the land as the Sun descended in the northern sky, could see the strange plants wither and perish, to make way for the next generation when spring returned. But no hint of this came through the protecting barriers of the city. The engineers at the power plant simply threw in more heater circuits and laughed at the worst that Mars could do.

Yet these children, despite their completely artificial environment, seemed happy and well, and quite unconscious of all the things which they had missed. Gibson wondered just what their reactions would be if they ever came to Earth. It would be a very interesting experiment, but so far none of the children born on Mars were old enough to leave their parents.

The lights of the city were going down when Gibson left the Mayor's home after his first day on Mars. He said very little as Whittaker walked back with him to the hotel, for his mind was too full of jumbled impressions. In the morning he would start to sort them out, but at the moment his chief feeling was that the greatest city on Mars was nothing more than an over-mechanised village.

Gibson had not yet mastered the intricacies of the Martian calendar, but he knew that the week-days were the same as on Earth and that Monday followed Sunday in the usual way. (The months also had the same names, but were fifty to sixty days in length.) When he left the hotel at what he thought was a reasonable hour, the city appeared quite deserted. There were none of the gossiping groups of people who had watched his progress with such interest on the previous day. Everyone was at work in office, factory, or lab, and Gibson felt rather like a drone who had strayed into a particularly busy hive.

He found Mayor Whittaker beleaguered by secretaries and talking into two telephones at once. Not having the heart to intrude, Gibson tiptoed away and started a tour of exploration himself. There was not, after all, any great danger of becoming lost. The maximum distance he would travel in a straight line was less than half a kilometre. It was not the kind of exploration of Mars he had ever imagined in any of his books. . . .

So he had passed his first few days in Port Lowell wandering round and asking questions during working hours, spending the evenings with the families of Mayor Whittaker or other members of the senior staff. Already he felt as if he had lived here for years. There was nothing new to be seen; he had met everyone of importance, up to and including the Chief Executive himself.

But he knew he was still a stranger: he had really seen less than a thousand millionth of the whole surface of Mars. Beyond the shelter of the dome, beyond the crimson hills, over the edge of the emerald plain—all the rest of this world was mystery.

9

"Well, it's certainly nice to see you all again," said Gibson carrying the drinks carefully across from the bar. "Now I suppose you're going to paint Port Lowell red. I presume the first move will be to contact the local girl friends?"

"That's never very easy," said Norden. "They *will* get married between trips, and you've got to be tactful. By the way, George, what's happened to Miss Margaret Mackinnon?"

"You mean Mrs. Henry Lewis," said George. "Such a fine baby boy, too."

"Has she called it John?" asked Bradley, not particularly *sotto voce.*

"Oh, well," sighed Norden, "I hope she's saved me some of the wedding cake. Here's to you, Martin."

"And to the *Ares,*" said Gibson clinking glasses. "I hope you've put her together again. She looked in a pretty bad way the last time I saw her."

Norden chuckled.

"Oh, that! No, we'll leave all the plating off until we reload. The rain isn't likely to get in!"

"What do you think of Mars, Jimmy?" asked Gibson. "You're the only other new boy here besides myself."

"I haven't seen much of it yet," Jimmy replied cautiously. "Everything seems rather small, though."

Gibson spluttered violently and had to be patted on the back.

"I remember your saying just the oppsosite when we were on Deimos. But I guess you've forgotten it. You were slightly drunk at the time."

"I've never been drunk," said Jimmy indignantly.

"Then I compliment you on a first-rate imitation: it deceived me completely. But I'm interested in what you say, because that's exactly how I felt after the first couple of days, as soon as I'd seen all there was to look at inside the dome. There's only one cure—you have to go outside and stretch your legs. I've had a couple of short walk around, but now I've managed to grab a Sand Flea fron Transport. I'm going to gallop up into the hills tomorrow Like to come?"

Jimmy's eyes glistened.

"Thanks very much—I'd love to."

"Hey, what about us?" protested Norden.

"You've done it before," said Gibson. "But there'll b one spare seat, so you can toss for it. We've got to tak an official driver; they won't let us go out by ourselve with one of their precious vehicles, and I suppose you ca hardly blame them."

Mackay won the toss, whereupon the others immediate ly explained that they didn't really want to go anyway.

"Well, that settles that," said Gibson. "Meet me a Transport Section, Dome Four, at 10 tomorrow. Now must be off. I've got three articles to write—or at an rate one article with three different titles."

The explorers met promptly on time, carrying the fu protective equipment which they had been issued on ar rival but so far had found no occasion to use. This com prised the headpiece, oxygen cylinders, and air purifier— all that was necessary out of doors on Mars on a warn day—and the heat-insulating suit with its compact powe cells. This could keep one warm and comfortable eve when the temperature outside was more than a hundre below. It would not be needed on this trip, unless a accident to the Flea left them stranded a long way awa from home.

The driver was a tough young geologist who claime to have spent as much time outside Port Lowell as in i He looked extremely competent and resourceful, and Gib son felt no qualms at handing his valuable person int his keeping.

"Do these machines ever break down outside?" he aske as they climbed into the Flea.

"Not very often. They've got a terrific safety facto and there's really very little to go wrong. Of cours sometimes a careless driver gets stuck, but you can usua ly haul yourself out of anything with the winch. Ther have only been a couple of cases of people having t walk home in the last month."

"I trust we won't make a third," said Mackay, as th vehicle rolled into the lock.

"I shouldn't worry about that," laughed the driver, waiting for the outer door to open. "We won't be going far from base, so we can always get back even if the worst comes to the worst."

With a surge of power they shot through the lock and out of the city. A narrow road had been cut through the low, vivid vegetation—a road which circled the port and from which other highways radiated to the nearby mines, to the radio station and observatory on the hills, and to the landing ground on which even now the *Ares*' freight was being unloaded as the rockets ferried it down from Deimos.

"Well," said the driver, halting at the first junction. "It's all yours. Which way do we go?"

Gibson was struggling with a map three sizes too big for the cabin. Their guide looked at it with scorn.

"I don't know where you got hold of *that,*" he said. "I suppose Admin gave it to you. It's completely out of date, anyway. If you'll tell me where you want to go I can take you there without bothering about that thing."

"Very well," Gibson replied meekly. "I suggest we climb up into the hills and get a good look round. Let's go to the Observatory."

The Flea leapt forward along the narrow road and the brilliant green around them merged into a featureless blur.

"How fast can these things go?" asked Gibson, when he had climbed out of Mackay's lap.

"Oh, at least a hundred on a good road. But as there aren't any good roads on Mars, we have to take it easy. I'm doing sixty now. On rough ground you'll be lucky to average half that."

"And what about range?" said Gibson, obviously still a little nervous.

"A good thousand kilometres on one charge, even allowing pretty generously for heating, cooking, and the rest. For really long trips we tow a trailer with spare power cells. The record's about five thousand kilometres; I've done three before now, prospecting out in Argyre. When you're doing that sort of thing, you arrange to get supplies dropped from the air."

Though they had now been travelling for no more than a couple of minutes, Port Lowell was already falling below the horizon. The steep curvature of Mars made it very difficult to judge distances, and the fact that the domes were now half concealed by the curve of the planet made one imagine that they were much larger objects at a far greater distance than they really were.

Soon afterwards, they began to reappear as the Flea started climbing towards higher ground. The hills above Port Lowell were less than a kilometre high, but they formed a useful break for the cold winter winds from the south, and gave vantage points for radio station and observatory.

They reached the radio station half an hour after leaving the city. Feeling it was time to do some walking, they adjusted their masks and dismounted from the Flea, taking turns to go through the tiny collapsible airlock.

The view was not really very impressive. To the north, the domes of Port Lowell floated like bubbles on an emerald sea. Over to the west Gibson could just catch a glimpse of crimson from the desert which encircled the entire planet. As the crest of the hills still lay a little above him, he could not see southwards, but he knew that the green band of vegetation stretched for several hundred kilometres until it petered out into the Mare Erythraeum. There were hardly any plants here on the hilltop, and he presumed that this was due to the absence of moisture.

He walked over to the radio station. It was quite automatic, so there was no one he could buttonhole in the usual way, but he knew enough about the subject to guess what was going on. The giant parabolic reflector lay almost on its back, pointing a little east of the zenith—pointing to Earth, sixty million kilometres Sunwards. Along its invisible beam were coming and going the messages that linked these two worlds together. Perhaps at this very moment one of his own articles was flying Earthwards—or one of Ruth Goldstein's directives was winging its way towards him.

Mackay's voice, distorted and feeble in this thin air, made him turn round.

"Someone's coming in to land down there—over on the right."

With some difficulty, Gibson spotted the tiny arrowhead of the rocket moving swiftly across the sky, racing in on a free glide just as he had done a week before. It banked over the city and was lost behind the domes as it touched down on the landing strip. Gibson hoped it was bringing in the remainder of his luggage, which seemed to have taken a long time to catch up with him.

The Observatory was about five kilometres farther south, just over the brow of the hills, where the lights of Port Lowell would not interfere with its work. Gibson had half expected to see the gleaming domes which on Earth were the trademarks of the astronomers, but instead the only dome was the small plastic bubble of the living quarters. The instruments themselves were in the open, though there was provision for covering them up in the very rare event of bad weather.

Everything appeared to be completely deserted as the Flea approached. They halted beside the largest instrument—a reflector with a mirror which, Gibson guessed, was less than a metre across. It was an astonishingly small instrument for the chief observatory on Mars. There were two small refractors, and a complicated horizontal affair which Mackay said was a mirror-transit—whatever that might be. And this, apart from the pressurised dome, seemed to be about all.

There was obviously someone at home, for a small Sand Flea was parked outside the building.

"They're quite a sociable crowd," said the driver as he brought the vehicle to a halt. "It's a pretty dull life up here and they're always glad to see people. And there'll be room inside the dome for us to stretch our legs and have dinner in comfort."

"Surely we can't expect them to provide a meal for us," protested Gibson, who had a dislike of incurring obligations he couldn't readily discharge. The driver looked genuinely surprised; then he laughed heartily.

"This isn't Earth, you know. On Mars, everyone helps everyone else—we have to, or we'd never get anywhere. But I've brought our provisions along—all I want to use is their stove. If you'd ever tried to cook a meal inside a Sand Flea with four aboard you'd know why."

As predicted, the two astronmers on duty greeted them warmly, and the little plastic bubble's air-conditioning plant was soon dealing with the odours of cookery. While this was going on, Mackay had grabbed the senior member of the staff and started a technical discussion about the Observatory's work. Most of it was quite over Gibson's head, but he tried to gather what he could from the conversation.

Most of the work done here was, it seemed, positional astronomy—the dull but essential business of finding longitudes and latitudes, providing time signals and linking radio fixes with the main Martian grid. Very little observational work was done at all; the huge instruments on Earth's moon had taken *that* over long ago, and these small telescopes, with the additional handicap of an atmosphere above them, could not hope to compete. The parallaxes of a few nearer stars had been measured, but the very slight increase of accuracy provided by the wider orbit of Mars made it hardly worth while.

As he ate his dinner—finding to his surprise that his appetite was better than at any time since reaching Mars—Gibson felt a glow of satisfaction at having done a little to brighten the dull lives of these devoted men. Because he had never met enough of them to shatter the illusion, Gibson had an altogether disproportionate respect for astronomers, whom he regarded as leading lives of monkish dedication on their remote mountain eyries. Even his first encounter with the excellent cocktail bar on Mount Palomar had not destroyed this simple faith.

After the meal, at which everyone helped so conscientiously with the washing-up that it took twice as long as necessary, the visitors were invited to have a look through the large reflector. Since it was early afternoon, Gibson did not imagine that there would be a great deal to see; but this was an oversight on his part.

For a moment the picture was blurred, and he adjusted the focussing screw with clumsy fingers. It was not easy to observe with the special eyepiece needed when one was wearing a breathing mask, but after a while Gibson got the knack of it.

Hanging in the field of view, against the almost black sky near the zenith, was a beautiful pearly crescent like a three-day-old moon. Some markings were just visible on the illuminated portion, but though Gibson strained his eyes to the utmost he could not identify them. Too much of the planet was in darkness for him to see any of the major continents.

Not far away floated an identically shaped but much smaller and fainter crescent, and Gibson could distinctly see some of the familiar craters along its edge. They formed a beautiful couple, the twin planets Earth and Moon, but somehow they seemed too remote and ethereal to give him any feeling of homesickness or regret for all that he had left behind.

One of the astronomers was speaking, his helmet held close to Gibson's.

"When it's dark you can see the lights of the cities down there on the night side. New York and London are easy. The prettiest sight, though, is the reflections of the Sun off the sea. You get it near the edge of the disc when there's no cloud about—a sort of brilliant, shimmering star. It isn't visible now because it's mostly land on the crescent portion."

Before leaving the Observatory, they had a look at Deimos, which was rising in its leisurely fashion in the east. Under the highest power of the telescope the rugged little moon seemed only a few kilometres away, and to his surprise Gibson could see the *Ares* quite clearly as two gleaming dots close together. He also wanted to look at Phobos, but the inner moon had not yet risen.

When there was nothing more to be seen, they bade farewell to the two astronomers, who waved back rather glumly as the Flea drove off along the brow of the hill. The driver explained that he wanted to make a private detour to pick up some rock specimens, and as to Gibson one part of Mars was very much like another he raised no objection.

There was no real road over the hills, but ages ago all irregularities had been worn away so that the ground was perfectly smooth. Here and there a few stubborn boulders still jutted above the surface, displaying a fantastic riot of colour and shape, but these obstacles were easily avoided. Once or twice they passed small trees—if one could call them that—of a type which Gibson had never seen before. They looked rather like pieces of coral, completely stiff and petrified. According to their driver they were immensely old, for though they were certainly alive no one had yet been able to measure their rate of growth. The smallest value which could be derived for their age was fifty thousand years, and their method of reproduction was a complete mystery.

Towards mid-afternoon they came to a low but beautifully coloured cliff—"Rainbow Ridge," the geologist called it—which reminded Gibson irresistibly of the more flamboyant Arizona canyons, though on a much smaller scale. They got out of the Sand Flea and, while the driver chipped off his samples, Gibson happily shot off half a reel of the new Multichrome film he had brought with him for just such occasions. If it could bring out all those colours perfectly it must be as good as the makers claimed, but unfortunately he'd have to wait until he got back to Earth before it could be developed. No one on Mars knew anything about it.

"Well," said the driver, "I suppose it's time we started for home if we want to get back for tea. We can drive back the way we came, and keep to the high ground, or we can go round behind the hills. Any preferences?"

"Why not drive down into the plain? That would be the most direct route," said Mackay, who was now getting a little bored.

"And the slowest—you can't drive at any speed through those overgrown cabbages."

"I always hate retracing my steps," said Gibson. "Let's go round the hills and see what we can find there."

The driver grinned.

"Don't raise any false hopes. It's much the same on both sides. Here we go!"

The Flea bounced forward and Rainbow Ridge soon disappeared behind them. They were now winding their way through completely barren country, and even the petrified trees had vanished. Sometimes Gibson saw a patch of green which he thought was vegetation, but as they approached it invariably turned into another mineral outcrop. This region was fantastically beautiful, a geologist's paradise, and Gibson hoped that it would never be ravaged by mining operations. It was certainly one of the show places of Mars.

They had been driving for half an hour when the hills sloped down into a long, winding valley which was unmistakably an ancient watercourse. Perhaps fifty million years ago, the driver told them, a great river had flowed this way to lose its waters in the Mare Erythraeum—one of the few Martian "seas" to be correctly, if somewhat belatedly, named. They stopped the Flea and gazed down the empty river bed with mingled feelings. Gibson tried to picture this scene as it must have appeared in those remote days, when the great reptiles ruled the Earth and Man was still a dream of the distant future. The red cliffs would scarcely have changed in all that time, but between them the river would have made its unhurried way to the sea, flowing slowly under the weak gravity. It was a scene that might almost have belonged to Earth; and had it ever been witnessed by intelligent eyes? No one knew. Perhaps there had indeed been Martians in those days, but time had buried them completely.

The ancient river had left a legacy, for there was still moisture along the lower reaches of the valley. A narrow band of vegetation had come thrusting up from Erythraeum, its brilliant green contrasting vividly with the crimson of the cliffs. The plants were those which Gibson had already met on the other side of the hills, but here and there were strangers. They were tall enough to be called trees, but they had no leaves—only thin, whip-like branches which continually trembled despite the stillness of the air. Gibson thought they were some of the most sinister things he had ever seen—just the sort of ominous plant that would suddenly flick out its tentacles at an unsuspecting passer-by. In fact, as he was perfectly well aware, they were as harmless as everything else on Mars.

They had zigzagged down into the valley and were climbing the other slope when the driver suddenly brought the Flea to a halt.

"Hello!" he said. "This is odd. I didn't know there was any traffic in these parts."

For a moment Gibson, who was not really as observant as he liked to think, was at a loss. Then he noticed a faint track running along the valley at right angles to their present path.

"There have been some heavy vehicles here," said the driver. "I'm sure this track didn't exist the last time I came this way—let's see, about a year ago. And there haven't been any expeditions into Erythraeum in that time."

"Where does it lead?" asked Gibson.

"Well, if you go up the valley and over the top you'll be back in Port Lowell; that was what I intended to do. The other direction only leads out into the Mare."

"We've got time—let's go along it a little way."

Willingly enough, the driver swung the Flea around and headed down the valley. From time to time the track vanished as they went over smooth, open rock, but it always reappeared again. At last, however, they lost it completely.

The driver stopped the Flea.

"I know what's happened," he said. "There's only one way it could have gone. Did you notice that pass about a kilometre back? Ten to one it leads up there."

"And where would that take anyone?"

"That's the funny thing—it's a complete cul-de-sac. There's a nice little amphitheatre about two kilometres across, but you can't get out of it anywhere except the way you came in. I spent a couple of hours there once when we did the first survey of this region. It's quite a pretty little place, sheltered and with some water in the spring."

"A good hide-out for smugglers," laughed Gibson.

The driver grinned.

"That's an idea. Maybe there's a gang bringing in contraband beefsteaks from Earth. I'd settle for one a week to keep my mouth shut."

The narrow pass had obviously once contained a tributary of the main river, and the going was a good deal rougher than in the main valley. They had not driven very far before it became quite clear that they were on the right track.

"There's been some blasting here," said the driver. "This bit of road didn't exist when I came this way. I had to make a detour up that slope, and nearly had to abandon the Flea."

"What do you think's going on?" asked Gibson, now getting quite excited.

"Oh, there are several research projects that are so specialised that one doesn't hear a lot about them. Some things can't be done near the city, you know. They may be building a magnetic observatory here—there's been some talk of that. The generators at Port Lowell would be pretty well shielded by the hills. But I don't think that's the explanation, for I'd have heard—Good Lord!"

They had suddenly merged from the pass, and before them lay an almost perfect oval of green, flanked by the low, ochre hills. Once this might have been a lovely mountain lake; it was still a solace to the eye weary of lifeless, multicoloured rock. But for the moment Gibson scarcely noticed the brilliant carpet of vegetation; he was too astonished by the cluster of domes, like a miniature of Port Lowell itself, grouped at the edge of the little plain.

They drove in silence along the road that had been cut through the living green carpet. No one was moving outside the domes, but a large transporter vehicle, several times the size of the Sand Flea, showed that someone was certainly at home.

"This is quite a set-up," remarked the driver as he adjusted his mask. "There must be a pretty good reason for spending all this money. Just wait here while I go over and talk to them."

They watched him disappear into the airlock of the larger dome. It seemed to his impatient passengers that he was gone rather a long time. Then they saw the outer door open again and he walked slowly back towards them.

"Well?" asked Gibson eagerly as the driver climbed back into the cab. "What did they have to say?"

There was a slight pause; then the driver started the engine and the Sand Flea began to move off.

"I say—what about this famous Martian hospitality? Aren't we invited in?" cried Mackay.

The driver seemed embarrassed. He looked, Gibson thought, exactly like a man who had just discovered he's made a fool of himself. He cleared his throat nervously.

"It's a plant research station," he said, choosing his words with obvious care. "It's not been going for very long, which is why I hadn't heard of it before. We can't go inside because the whole place is sterile and they don't want spores brought in—we'd have to change all our clothes and have a bath of disinfectant."

"I see," said Gibson. Something told him it was no use asking any further questions. He knew, beyond all possibility of error, that his guide had told him only part of the truth—and the least important part at that. For the first time the little discrepancies and doubts that Gibson had hitherto ignored or forgotten began to crystallise in his mind. It had started even before he reached Mars, with the diversion of the *Ares* from Phobos. And now he had stumbled upon this hidden research station. It had been as big a surprise to their experienced guide as to them, but he was attempting to cover up his accidental indiscretion.

There was something going on. What it was, Gibson could not imagine. It must be big, for it concerned not only Mars but Phobos. It was something unknown to most of the colonists, yet something they would co-operate in keeping secret when they encountered it.

Mars was hiding something; and it could only be hiding it from Earth.

10

The Grand Martian Hotel now had no less than two residents, a state of affairs which imposed a severe strain on its temporary staff. The rest of his shipmates had made private arrangements for their accommodation in Port Lowell, but as he knew no one in the city Jimmy had decided to accept official hospitality. Gibson wondered if this was going to be a success; he did not wish to throw too great a strain on their still somewhat provisional friendship, and if Jimmy saw too much of him the results might be disastrous. He remembered an epigram which his best enemy had once concocted: "Martin's one of the nicest fellows you could meet, as long as you don't do it too often." There was enough truth in this to make it sting, and he had no wish to put it to the test again.

His life in the Port had now settled down to a fairly steady routine. In the morning he would work, putting on paper his impressions of Mars—rather a presumptuous thing to do when he considered just how much of the planet he had so far seen. The afternoon was reserved for tours of inspection and interviews with the city's inhabitants. Sometimes Jimmy went with him on these trips, and once the whole of the *Ares* crew came along to the hospital to see how Dr. Scott and his colleagues were progressing with their battle against Martian fever. It was still too early to draw any conclusions, but Scott seemed fairly optimistic. "What we'd like to have," he said rubbing his hands ghoulishly, "is a really good epidemic so that we could test the stuff properly. We haven't enough cases at the moment."

Jimmy had two reasons for accompanying Gibson on his tours of the city. In the first place, the older man could go almost anywhere he pleased and so could get into all the interesting places which might otherwise be out of bounds. The second reason was a purely personal one—

his increasing interest in the curious character of Martin Gibson.

Though they had now been thrown so closely together, they had never reopened their earlier conversation. Jimmy knew that Gibson was anxious to be friends and to make some recompense for whatever had happened in the past. He was quite capable of accepting this offer on a purely impersonal basis, for he realised well enough that Gibson could be extremely useful to him in his career. Like most ambitious young men, Jimmy had a streak of coldly calculating self-interest in his make-up, and Gibson would have been slightly dismayed at some of the appraisals which Jimmy had made of the advantages to be obtained from his patronage.

It would, however, be quite unfair to Jimmy to suggest that these material considerations were uppermost in his mind. There were times when he sensed Gibson's inner loneliness—the loneliness of the bachelor facing the approach of middle age. Perhaps Jimmy also realised—though not consciously as yet—that to Gibson he was beginning to represent the son he had never had. It was not a rôle that Jimmy was by any means sure he wanted, yet there were often times when he felt sorry for Gibson and would have been glad to please him. It is, after all, very difficult not to feel a certain affection towards someone who likes you.

The accident that introduced a new and quite unexpected element into Jimmy's life was really very trivial. He had been out alone one afternoon and, feeling thirsty, had dropped into the small café opposite the Administration building. Unfortunately he had not chosen his time well, for while he was quietly sipping a cup of tea which had never been within millions of kilometres of Ceylon, the place was suddenly invaded. It was the twenty-minute afternoon break when all work stopped on Mars—a rule which the Chief Executive had enforced in the interests of efficiency, though everyone would have much preferred to do without it and leave work twenty minutes earlier instead.

Jimmy was rapidly surrounded by an army of young women, who eyed him with alarming candour and a complete lack of diffidence. Although half a dozen men had been swept in on the flood, they crowded round one table for mutual protection, and judging by their intense expressions, continued to battle mentally with the files they had left on their desks. Jimmy decided to finish his drink as quickly as he could and get out.

A rather tough-looking woman in her late thirties—probably a senior secretary—was sitting opposite him, talking to a much younger girl on his side of the table. It was quite a squeeze to get past, and as Jimmy pushed into the crowd swirling through the narrow gangway, he tripped over an outstretched foot. He grabbed the table as he fell and managed to avoid complete disaster, but only at the cost of catching his elbow a sickening crack on the glass top. Forgetting in his agony that he was no longer back in the *Ares*, he relieved his feelings with a few well-chosen words. Then, blushing furiously, he recovered and bolted to freedom. He caught a glimpse of the elder woman trying hard not to laugh, and the younger one not even attempting such self-control.

And then, though it seemed inconceivable in retrospect, he forgot all about them both.

It was Gibson who quite accidentally provided the second stimulus. They were talking about the swift growth of the city during the last few years, and wondering if it would continue in the future. Gibson had remarked on the abnormal age distribution caused by the fact that no one under twenty-one had been allowed to emigrate to Mars, so that there was a complete gap between the ages of ten and twenty-one—a gap which, of course, the high birth-rate of the colony would soon fill. Jimmy had been listening half-heartedly when one of Gibson's remarks made him suddenly look up.

"That's funny," he said. "Yesterday I saw a girl who couldn't have been more than eighteen."

And then he stopped. For, like a delayed-action bomb, the memory of that girl's laughing face as he had stumbled from the café suddenly exploded in his mind.

He never heard Gibson tell him that he must have been mistaken. He only knew that, whoever she was and wherever she had come from, he had to see her again.

In a place the size of Port Lowell, it was only a matter of time before one met everybody: the laws of chance would see to that. Jimmy, however, had no intention of waiting until these doubtful allies arranged a second encounter. The following day, just before the afternoon break, he was drinking tea at the same table in the little café.

This not very subtle move had caused him some mental anguish. In the first case, it might seem altogether too obvious. Yet why shouldn't he have tea here when most of Admin did the same? A second and weightier objection was the memory of the previous day's debacle. But Jimmy remembered an apt quotation about faint hearts and fair ladies.

His qualms were unnecessary. Though he waited until the café had emptied again, there was no sign of the girl or her companion. They must have gone somewhere else.

It was an annoying but only temporary setback to so resourceful a young man as Jimmy. Almost certainly she worked in the Admin building, and there were innumerable excuses for visiting that. He could think up enquiries about his pay, though these would hardly get him into the depths of the filing system or the stenographer's office, where she probably worked.

It would be best simply to keep an eye on the building when the staff arrived and left, though how this could be done unobtrusively was a considerable problem. Before he had made any attempt to solve it, Fate stepped in again, heavily disguised as Martin Gibson, slightly short of breath.

"I've been looking everywhere for you, Jimmy. Better hurry up and get dressed. You know there's a show tonight? Well, we've all been invited to have dinner with the Chief before going. That's in two hours."

"What does one wear for formal dinners on Mars?" asked Jimmy.

"Black shorts and white tie, I think," said Gibson, a little doubtfully. "Or is it the other way round? Anyway, they'll tell us at the hotel. I hope they can find something that fits me."

They did, but only just. Evening dress on Mars, where in the heat and air-conditioned cities all clothes were kept to a minimum, consisted simply of a white silk shirt with two rows of pearl buttons, a black bow tie, and black satin shorts with a belt of wide aluminium links on an elastic backing. It was smarter than might have been expected, but when fitted out Gibson felt something midway between a Boy Scout and Little Lord Fauntleroy. Norden and Hilton, on the other hand, carried it off quite well,

Mackay and Scott were less successful, and Bradley obviously didn't give a damn.

The Chief's residence was the largest private house on Mars, though on Earth it would have been a very modest affair. They assembled in the lounge for a chat and sherry—real sherry—before the meal. Mayor Whittaker, being Hadfield's second-in-command, had also been invited, and as he listened to them talking to Norden, Gibson understood for the first time with what respect and admiration the colonists regarded the men who provided their sole link with Earth. Hadfield was holding forth at some length about the *Ares,* waxing quite lyrical over her speed and payload, and the effects these would have on the economy of Mars.

"Before we go in," said the Chief, when they had finished the sherry, "I'd like you to meet my daughter. She's just seeing to the arrangements—excuse me a moment while I fetch her."

He was gone only a few seconds.

"This is Irene," he said, in a voice that tried not to be proud but failed completely. One by one he introduced her to his guests, coming to Jimmy last.

Irene looked at him and smiled sweetly.

"I think we've met before," she said.

Jimmy's colour heightened, but he held his ground and smiled back.

"So we have," he replied.

It was really very foolish of him not to have guessed. If he had even started to think properly he would have known who she must have been. On Mars, the only man who could break the rules was the one who enforced them. Jimmy remembeerd hearing that the Chief had a daughter, but he had never connected the facts together. It all fell into place now: when Hadfield and his wife came to Mars they had brought their only child with them as part of the contract. No one else had ever been allowed to do so.

The meal was an excellent one, but it was largely wasted on Jimmy. He had not exactly lost his appetite—that would have been unthinkable—but he ate with a distracted air. As he was seated near the end of the table, he could see Irene only by dint of craning his neck in a most ungentlemanly fashion. He was very glad when the meal was over and they adjourned for coffee.

The other two members of the Chief Executive's household were waiting for the guests. Already occupying the best seats, a pair of beautiful Siamese cats regarded the visitors with fathomless eyes. They were introduced as Topaz and Turquoise, and Gibson, who loved cats, immediately started to try and make friends with them.

"Are you fond of cats?" Irene asked Jimmy.

"Rather," said Jimmy, who loathed them. "How long have they been here?"

"Oh, about a year. Just fancy—they're the only animals on Mars! I wonder if they appreciate it?"

"I'm sure Mars does. Don't they get spoiled?"

"They're too independent. I don't think they really care for anyone—not even Daddy, though he likes to pretend they do."

With great subtlety—though to any spectator it would have been fairly obvious that Irene was always one jump ahead of him—Jimmy brought the conversation round to more personal matters. He discovered that she worked in the accounting section, but knew a good deal of everything that went on in Administration, where she one day hoped to hold a responsible executive post. Jimmy guessed that her father's position had been, if anything, a slight handicap to her. Though it must have made life easier in some ways, in others it would be a definite disadvantage, as Port Lowell was fiercely democratic.

It was very hard to keep Irene on the subject of Mars. She was much more anxious to hear about Earth, the planet which she had left when a child and so must have, in her mind, a dream-like unreality. Jimmy did his best to answer her questions, quite content to talk about anything which held her interest. He spoke of Earth's great cities, its mountains and seas, its blue skies and scudding clouds, its rivers and rainbows—all the things which Mars had lost. And as he talked, he fell deeper and deeper beneath the spell of Irene's laughing eyes. That was the only word to describe them: she always seemed to be on the point of sharing some secret joke.

Was she still laughing at him? Jimmy wasn't sure—and he didn't mind. What rubbish it was, he thought, to imagine that one became tongue-tied on these occasions! He had never been more fluent in his life. . . .

He was suddenly aware that a great silence had fallen. Everyone was looking at him and Irene.

"Humph!" said the Chief Executive. "If you two have quite finished, we'd better get a move on. The show starts in ten minutes."

Most of Port Lowell seemed to have squeezed into the little theatre by the time they arrived. Mayor Whittaker, who had hurried ahead to check the arrangements, met them at the door and shepherded them into their seats, a reserved block occupying most of the front row. Gibson, Hadfield, and Irene were in the centre, flanked by Norden and Hilton—much to Jimmy's chagrin. He had no alternative but to look at the show.

Like all such amateur performances, it was good in parts. The musical items were excellent and there was one mezzosoprano who was up to the best professional standards of Earth. Gibson was not surprised when he saw against her name on the programme: "Late of the Royal Covent Garden Opera."

A dramatic interlude then followed, the distressed heroine and oldtime villain hamming it for all they were worth. The audience loved it, cheering and booing the appropriate characters and shouting gratuitous advice.

Next came one of the most astonishing ventriloquist acts that Gibson had ever seen. It was nearly over before he realised—only a minute before the performer revealed it deliberately—that there was a radio receiver inside the doll and an accomplice off-stage.

The next item appeared to be a skit on life in the city, and was so full of local allusions that Gibson understood only part of it. However, the antics of the main character—a harassed official obviously modelled on Mayor Whittaker—drew roars of laughter. These increased still further when he began to be pestered by a fantastic person who was continually asking ridiculous questions, noting the answers in a little book (which he was always losing), and photographing everything in sight.

It was several minutes before Gibson realised just what was going on. For a moment he turned a deep red; then he realised that there was only one thing he could do. He would have to laugh louder than anyone else.

The proceedings ended with community singing, a form of entertainment which Gibson did not normally go out of his way to seek—rather the reverse, in fact. But he found it more enjoyable than he had expected, and as he joined in the last choruses a sudden wave of emotion swept over him, causing his voice to peter out into nothingness. For a moment he sat, the only silent man in all that crowd, wondering what had happened to him.

The faces around provided the answer. Here were men and women united in a single task, driving towards a common goal, each knowing that their work was vital to the community. They had a sense of fulfilment which very few could know on Earth, where all the frontiers had long ago been reached. It was a sense heightened and made more personal by the fact that Port Lowell was still so small that everyone knew everybody else.

Of course, it was too good to last. As the colony grew, the spirit of these pioneering days would fade. Everything would become too big and too well organised; the development of the planet would be just another job of work. But for the present it was a wonderful sensation, which a man would be lucky indeed to experience even once in his lifetime. Gibson knew it was felt by all those around him, yet he could not share it. He was an outsider: that was the rôle he had always preferred to play—and now he had played it long enough. It if was not too late, he wanted to join in the game.

That was the moment, if indeed there was such a single point in time, when Martin Gibson changed his allegiance from Earth to Mars. No one ever knew. Even those beside him, if they noticed anything at all, were aware only that for a few seconds he had stopped singing, but had now joined in the chorus again with redoubled vigour.

In twos and threes, laughing, talking and singing, the audience slowly dissolved into the night. Gibson and his friends started back towards the hotel, having said goodbye to the Chief and Mayor Whittaker. The two men who virtually ran Mars watched them disappear down the narrow streets; then Hadfield turned to his daughter and remarked quietly: "Run along home now, dear—Mr. Whittaker and I are going for a little walk. I'll be back in half an hour."

They waited, answering good-nights from time to time, until the tiny square was deserted. Mayor Whittaker, who guessed what was coming, fidgeted slightly.

"Remind me to congratulate George on tonight's show," said Hadfield.

"Yes," Whittaker replied. "I loved the skit on our mutual headache, Gibson. I suppose you want to conduct a post-mortem on his latest exploit?"

The Chief was slightly taken aback by this direct approach.

"It's rather too late now—and there's no real evidence that any real harm was done. I'm just wondering how to prevent future accidents."

"It was hardly the driver's fault. He didn't know about the Project and it was pure bad luck that he stumbled on it."

"Do you think Gibson suspects anything?"

"Frankly, I don't know. He's pretty shrewd."

"Of all the times to send a reporter here! I did everything I could to keep him away, heaven knows!"

"He's bound to find out that something's happening before he's here much longer. I think there's only one solution."

"What's that?"

"We'll just have to tell him. Perhaps not everything, but enough."

They walked in silence for a few yards. Then Hadfield remarked:

"That's pretty drastic. You're assuming he can be trusted completely."

"I've seen a good deal of him these last weeks. Fundamentally, he's on our side. You see, we're doing the sort of things he's been writing about all his life, though he can't quite believe it yet. What would be fatal would be to let him go back to Earth, suspecting something but not knowing what."

There was another long silence. They reached the limit of the dome and stared across the glimmering Martian landscape, dimly lit by the radiance spilling out from the city.

"I'll have to think it over," said Hadfield, turning to retrace his footsteps. "Of course, a lot depends on how quickly things move."

"Any hints yet?"

"No, confound them. You never can pin scientists down to a date."

A young couple, arms twined together, strolled past them obliviously. Whittaker chuckled.

"That reminds me. Irene seems to have taken quite a fancy to that youngster—what's his name—Spencer."

"Oh, I don't know. It's a change to see a fresh face

around. And space travel is so much more romantic than the work we do here."

"All the nice girls love a sailor, eh? Well, don't say I didn't warn you!"

That something had happened to Jimmy was soon perfectly obvious to Gibson, and it took him no more than two guesses to arrive at the correct answer. He quite approved of the lad's choice: Irene seemed a very nice child, from what little he had seen of her. She was rather unsophisticated, but this was not necessarily a handicap. Much more important was the fact that she had a gay and cheerful disposition, though once or twice Gibson had caught her in a mood of wistfulness that was very attractive. She was also extremely pretty; Gibson was now old enough to realise that this was not all-important, though Jimmy might have different views on the subject.

At first, he decided to say nothing about the matter until Jimmy raised it himself. In all probability, the boy was still under the impression that no one had noticed anything in the least unusual. Gibson's self-control gave way, however, when Jimmy announced his intention of taking a temporary job in Port Lowell. There was nothing odd about this; indeed, it was a common practice among visiting space-crews, who soon got bored if they had nothing to do between trips. The work they chose was invariably technical and related in some way to their professional activities; Mackay, for example, was running evening classes in mathematics, while poor Dr. Scott had had no holiday at all, but had gone straight to the hospital immediately on reaching Port Lowell.

But Jimmy, it seemed, wanted a change. They were short of staff in the accounting section, and he thought his knowledge of mathematics might help. He put up an astonishingly convincing argument, to which Gibson listened with genuine pleasure.

"My dear Jimmy," he said, when it was finished. "Why tell *me* all this? There's nothing to stop your going right ahead if you want to."

"I know," said Jimmy, "but you see a lot of Mayor Whittaker and it might save trouble if you had a word with him."

"I'll speak to the Chief if you like."

"Oh no, I shouldn't——" Jimmy began. Then he tried

to retrieve his blunder. "It isn't worth bothering him about such details."

"Look here, Jimmy," said Gibson with great firmness. "Why not come clean? Is this your idea, or did Irene put you up to it?"

It was worth travelling all the way to Mars to see Jimmy's expression. He looked rather like a fish that had been breathing air for some time and had only just realised it.

"Oh," he said at last, "I didn't know you knew. You won't tell anyone, will you?"

Gibson was just about to remark that this would be quite unnecessary, but there was something in Jimmy's eyes that made him abandon all attempts at humour. The wheel had come full circle; he was back again in that twenty-year-old-buried spring. He knew exactly what Jimmy was feeling now, and knew also that nothing which the future could bring to him would ever match the emotions he was discovering, still as new and fresh as on the first morning of the world. He might fall in love again in later days, but the memory of Irene would shape and colour all his life—just as Irene herself must be the memory of some ideal he had brought with him into this universe.

"I'll do what I can," said Gibson gently, and meant it with all his heart. Though history might repeat itself, it never did so exactly, and one generation could learn from the errors of the last. Some things were beyond planning or foresight, but he would do all he could to help; and this time, perhaps, the outcome might be different.

11

The amber light was on. Gibson took a last sip of water, cleared his throat gently, and checked that the papers of his script were in the right order. No matter how many times he broadcast, his throat always felt this initial tightness. In the control room, the programme engineer held up her thumb; the amber changed abruptly to red.

"Hello, Earth. This is Martin Gibson speaking to you from Port Lowell, Mars. It's a great day for us here. This morning the new dome was inflated and now the city's increased its size by almost a half. I don't know if I can convey any impression of what a triumph this means, what a feeling of victory it gives to us here in the battle against Mars. But I'll try.

"You all know that it's impossible to breathe the Martian atmosphere—it's far too thin and contains practically no oxygen. Port Lowell, our biggest city, is built under six domes of transparent plastic held up by the pressure of the air inside—air which we can breathe comfortably though it's still much less dense than yours.

"For the last year a seventh dome has been under construction, a dome twice as big as any of the others. I'll describe it as it was yesterday, when I went inside before the inflation started.

"Imagine a great circular space half a kilometre across, surrounded by a thick wall of glass bricks twice as high as a man. Through this wall lead the passages to the other domes, and the exits direct on to the brilliant green Martian landscape all around us. These passages are simply metal tubes with great doors which close automatically if air escapes from any of the domes. On Mars, we don't believe in putting all our eggs in one basket!

"When I entered Dome Seven yesterday, all this great circular space was covered with a thin transparent sheet fastened to the surrounding wall, and lying limp on the ground in huge folds beneath which we had to force our way. If you can imagine being inside a deflated balloon you'll know exactly how I felt. The envelope of the dome is a very strong plastic, almost perfectly transparent and quite flexible—a kind of thick cellophane.

"Of course, I had to wear my breathing mask, for though we were sealed off from the outside there was still practically no air in the dome. It was being pumped in as rapidly as possible, and you could see the great sheets of plastic straining sluggishly as the pressure mounted.

"This went on all through the night. The first thing this morning I went into the dome again, and found that the envelope had now blown itself into a big bubble at the centre, though round the edges it was still lying flat. That huge bubble—it was about a hundred metres across—kept trying to move around like a living creature, and all the time it grew.

"About the middle of the morning it had grown so much that we could see the complete dome taking shape; the envelope had lifted away from the ground everywhere. Pumping was stopped for a while to test for leaks, then resumed again around midday. By now the sun was helping too, warming up the air and making it expand.

"Three hours ago the first stage of the inflation was finished. We took off our masks and let out a great cheer. The air still wasn't really thick enough for comfort, but it was breathable and the engineers could work inside without bothering about masks any more. They'll spend the next few days checking the great envelope for stresses, and looking for leaks. There are bound to be some, of course, but as long as the air loss doesn't exceed a certain value it won't matter.

"So now we feel we've pushed our frontier on Mars back a little further. Soon the new buildings will be going up under Dome Seven, and we're making plans for a small park and even a lake—the only one on Mars, that will be, for free water can't exist here in the open for any length of time.

"Of course, this is only a beginning, and one day it will seem a very small achievement; but it's a great step forward in our battle—it represents the conquest of another slice of Mars. And it means living space for another thousand people. Are you listening, Earth? Good night."

The red light faded. For a moment Gibson sat staring

at the microphone, musing on the fact that his first words, though travelling at the speed of light, would only now be reaching Earth. Then he gathered up his papers and walked through the padded doors into the control room.

The engineer held up a telephone for him. "A call's just come through for you, Mr. Gibson," she said. "Someone's been pretty quick off the mark!"

"They certainly have," he replied with a grin. "Hello, Gibson here."

"This is Hadfield. Congratulations. I've just been listening—it went out over our local station, you know."

"I'm glad you liked it."

Hadfield chuckled.

"You've probably guessed that I've read most of your earlier scripts. It's been quite interesting to watch the change of attitude."

"What change?"

"When you started, we were 'they.' Now we're 'we.' Not very well put, perhaps, but I think my point's clear."

He gave Gibson no time to answer this, but continued without a break.

"I really rang up about this. I've been able to fix your trip to Skia at last. We've got a passenger jet going over there on Wednesday, with room for three aboard. Whittaker will give you the details. Good-bye."

The phone clicked into silence. Very thoughtfully, but not a little pleased, Gibson replaced it on the stand. What the Chief had said was true enough. He had been here for almost a month, and in that time his outlook towards Mars had changed completely. The first schoolboy excitement had lasted no more than a few days; the subsequent disillusionment only a little longer. Now he knew enough to regard the colony with a tempered enthusiasm not wholly based on logic. He was afraid to analyse it, lest it disappear completely. Some part of it, he knew, came from his growing respect for the people around him—his admiration for the keen-eyed competence, the readiness to take well-calculated risks, which had enabled them not merely to survive on this heartbreakingly hostile world, but to lay the foundations of the first extra-terrestrial culture. More than ever before, he felt a longing to identify himself with their work, wherever it might lead.

Meanwhile, his first real chance of seeing Mars on the large scale had arrived. On Wednesday he would be taking off for Port Schiaparelli, the planet's second city, ten thousand kilometres to the east in Trivium Charontis. The trip had been planned a fortnight ago, but every time something had turned up to postpone it. He would have to tell Jimmy and Hilton to get ready—they had been the lucky ones in the draw. Perhaps Jimmy might not be quite so eager to go now as he had been once. No doubt he was now anxiously counting the days left to him on Mars, and would resent anything that took him away from Irene. But if he turned down *this* chance, Gibson would have no sympathy for him at all.

"Neat job, isn't she?" said the pilot proudly. "There are only six like her on Mars. It's quite a trick designing a jet that can fly in this atmosphere, even with the low gravity to help you."

Gibson did not know enough about aerodynamics to appreciate the finer points of the aircraft, though he could see that the wing area was abnormally large. The four jet units were neatly buried just outboard of the fuselage, only the slightest of bulges betraying their position. If he had met such a machine on a terrestrial airfield Gibson would not have given it a second thought, though the sturdy tractor undercarriage might have surprised him. This machine was built to fly fast and far—and to land on any surface which was approximately flat.

He climbed in after Jimmy and Hilton and settled himself as comfortably as he could in the rather restricted space. Most of the cabin was taken up by large packing cases securely strapped in position—urgent freight for Skia, he supposed. It hadn't left a great deal of space for the passengers.

The motors accelerated swiftly until their thin whines hovered at the edge of hearing. There was the familiar pause while the pilot checked his instruments and controls; then the jets opened full out and the runway began to slide beneath them. A few seconds later there came the sudden reassuring surge of power as the take-off rockets fired and lifted them effortlessly up into the sky. The aircraft climbed steadily into the south, then swung round to starboard in a great curve that took it over the city.

The aircraft levelled out on an easterly course and the great island of Aurorae Sinus sank over the edge of the planet. Apart from a few oases, the open desert now lay ahead for thousands of kilometres.

The pilot switched his controls to automatic and came amidships to talk to his passengers.

"We'll be at Charontis in about four hours," he said. "I'm afraid there isn't much to look at on the way, though you'll see some fine colour effects when we go over Euphrates. After that it's more or less uniform desert until we hit the Syrtis Major."

Gibson did some rapid mental arithmetic.

"Let's see—we're flying east and we started rather late—it'll be dark when we get there."

"Don't worry about that—we'll pick up the Charontis beacon when we're a couple of hundred kilometres away. Mars is so small that you don't often do a long-distance trip in daylight all the way."

"How long have you been on Mars?" asked Gibson, who had now ceased taking photos through the observation ports.

"Oh, five years."

"Flying all the time?"

"Most of it."

"Wouldn't you prefer being in spaceships?"

"Not likely. No excitement in it—just floating around in nothing for months." He grinned at Hilton, who smiled amiably but showed no inclination to argue.

"Just what do you mean by 'excitement'?" said Gibson anxiously.

"Well, you've got some scenery to look at, you're not away from home for very long, and there's always the chance you may find something new. I've done half a dozen trips over the poles, you know—most of them in summer, but I went across the Mare Boreum last winter. A hundred and fifty degrees below outside! That's the record so far for Mars."

"I can beat that pretty easily," said Hilton. "At night it reaches two hundred below on Titan." It was the first time Gibson had ever heard him refer to the Saturnia expedition.

"By the way, Fred," he asked, "is this rumour true?"

"What rumour?"

"*You* know—that you're going to have another shot at Saturn."

Hilton shrugged his shoulders.

"It isn't decided—there are a lot of difficulties. But I think it will come off; it would be a pity to miss the chance. You see, if we can leave next year we can go past Jupiter on the way, and have our first really good look at him. Mac's worked out a very interesting orbit for us. We go rather close to Jupiter—right inside *all* the satellites—and let his gravitational field swing us round so that we head out in the right direction for Saturn. It'll need rather accurate navigation to give us just the orbit we want, but it can be done."

"Then what's holding it up?"

"Money, as usual. The trip will last two and a half years and will cost about fifty million. Mars can't afford it—it would mean doubling the usual deficit! At the moment we're trying to get Earth to foot the bill."

"It would come to that anyway in the long run," said Gibson. "But give me all the facts when we get home and I'll write a blistering exposé about cheeseparing terrestrial politicians. You mustn't underestimate the power of the press."

The talk then drifted from planet to planet, until Gibson suddenly remembered that he was wasting a magnificent chance of seeing Mars at first hand. Obtaining permission to occupy the pilot's seat—after promising not to touch anything—he went forward and settled himself comfortably behind the controls.

Five kilometres below, the coloured desert was streaking past him to the west. They were flying at what, on Earth, would have been a very low altitude, for the thinness of the Martian air made it essential to keep as near the surface as safety allowed. Gibson had never before received such an impression of sheer speed, for though he had flown in much faster machines on Earth, that had always been at heights where the ground was invisible. The nearness of the horizon added to the effect, for an object which appeared over the edge of the planet would be passing beneath a few minutes later.

From time to time the pilot came forward to check the course, though it was a pure formality, as there was nothing he need do until the voyage was nearly over. At mid-point some coffee and light refreshments were produced, and Gibson rejoined his companions in the cabin. Hilton and the pilot were now arguing briskly about Venus—quite a sore point with the Martian colonists, who regarded that peculiar planet as a complete waste of time.

The sun was now very low in the west and even the stunted Martian hills threw long shadows across the desert. Down there the temperature was already below freezing point, and falling fast. The few hardy plants that had survived in this almost barren waste would have folded their leaves tightly together, conserving warmth and energy against the rigours of the night.

Gibson yawned and stretched himself. The swiftly unfolding landscape had an almost hypnotic effect and it was difficult to keep awake. He decided to catch some sleep in the ninety or so minutes that were left of the voyage.

Some change in the failing light must have woken him. For a moment it was impossible to believe that he was not still dreaming; he could only sit and stare, paralysed with sheer astonishment. No longer was he looking out across a flat, almost featureless landscape meeting the deep blue of the sky at the far horizon. Desert and horizon had both vanished; in their place towered a range of crimson mountains, reaching north and south as far as the eye could follow. The last rays of the setting sun caught their peaks and bequeathed to them its dying glory; already the foothills were lost in the night that was sweeping onwards to the west.

For long seconds the splendour of the scene robbed it of all reality and hence all menace. Then Gibson awoke from his trance, realising in one dreadful instant that they were flying far too low to clear those Himalayan peaks.

The sense of utter panic lasted only a moment—to be followed at once by a far deeper terror. Gibson had remembered now what the first shock had banished from his mind—the simple fact he should have thought of from the beginning.

There were no mountains on Mars.

Hadfield was dictating an urgent memorandum to the Interplanetary Development Board when the news came through. Port Schiaparelli had waited the regulation fifteen minutes after the aircraft's expected time of arrival, and Port Lowell Control had stood by for another ten before sending out the "Overdue" signal. One precious aircraft from the tiny Martian fleet was already standing by to search the line of flight as soon as dawn came. The high speed and low altitude essential for flight would make such a search very difficult, but when Phobos rose the telescopes up there could join in with far greater prospects of success.

The news reached Earth an hour later, at a time when there was nothing much else to occupy press or radio. Gibson would have been well satisfied by the resultant publicity: everywhere people began reading his last articles with a morbid interest. Ruth Goldstein knew nothing about it until an editor she was dealing with arrived waving the evening paper. She immediately sold the second reprint rights of Gibson's latest series for half as much again as her victim had intended to pay, then retired to her private room and wept copiously for a full minute. Both these events would have pleased Gibson enormously.

In a score of newspaper offices, the copy culled from the morgue began to be set up in type so that no time would be wasted. And in London a publisher who had paid Gibson a rather large advance began to feel very unhappy indeed.

Gibson's shout was still echoing through the cabin when the pilot reached the controls. Then he was flung to the floor as the machine turned over in an almost vertical bank in a desperate attempt to swing round to the north. When Gibson could climb to his feet again, he caught a glimpse of a strangely blurred orange cliff sweeping down upon them from only kilometres away. Even in that moment of panic, he could see that there was something very curious about that swiftly approaching barrier, and suddenly the truth dawned upon him at last. This was no mountain range, but something that might be no less deadly. They were running into a wind-borne wall of sand reaching from the desert almost to the edge of the stratosphere.

The hurricane hit them a second later. Something slapped the machine violently from side to side, and through the insulation of the hull came an angry whistling roar that was the most terrifying sound Gibson had ever heard in his life. Night had come instantly upon them and they were flying helplessly through a howling darkness.

It was all over in five minutes, but it seemed a lifetime. Their sheer speed had saved them, for the ship had cut through the heart of the hurricane like a projectile. There was a sudden burst of deep ruby twilight, the ship ceased to be pounded by a million sledge-hammers, and a ringing silence seemed to fill the little cabin. Through the rear observation port Gibson caught a last glimpse of the storm as it moved westwards, tearing up the desert in its wake.

His legs feeling like jellies, Gibson tottered thankfully into his seat and breathed an enormous sigh of relief. For a moment he wondered if they had been thrown badly off course, then realised that this scarcely mattered considering the navigational aids they carried.

It was only then, when his ears had ceased to be deafened by the storm, that Gibson had his second shock. The motors had stopped.

The little cabin was very tense and still. Then the pilot called out over his shoulder: "Get your masks on! The hull may crack when we come down." His fingers feeling very clumsy, Gibson dragged his breathing equipment from under the seat and adjusted it over his head. When he had finished, the ground already seemed very close, though it was hard to judge distances in the failing twilight.

A low hill swept by and was gone into the darkness. The ship banked violently to avoid another, then gave a sudden spasmodic jerk as it touched ground and bounced. A moment later it made contact again and Gibson tensed himself for the inevitable crash.

It was an age before he dared relax, still unable to believe that they were, safely down. Then Hilton stretched himself in his seat, removed his mask, and called out to the pilot: "That was a very nice landing, Skipper. Now how far have we got to walk?"

For a moment there was no reply. Then the pilot called, in a rather strained voice: "Can anyone light me a cigarette? I've got the twitch."

"Here you are," said Hilton, going forward. "Let's have the cabin lights on now, shall we?"

The warm, comfortable glow did much to raise their spirits by banishing the Martian night, which now lay all around. Everyone began to feel ridiculously cheerful and there was much laughing at quite feeble jokes. The reaction had set in: they were so delighted at still being alive that the thousand kilometres separating them from the nearest base scarcely seemed to matter.

"That was quite a storm," said Gibson. "Does this sort of thing happen very often on Mars? And why didn't we get any warning?"

The pilot, now that he had got over his initial shock, was doing some quick thinking, the inevitable court of enquiry obviously looming large in his mind. Even on autopilot, he *should* have gone forward more often. . . .

"I've never seen one like it before," he said, "though I've done at least fifty trips between Lowell and Skia. The trouble is that we don't know anything about Martian meteorology, even now. And there are only half a dozen met stations on the planet—not enough to give us an accurate picture."

"What about Phobos? Couldn't they have seen what was happening and warned us?"

The pilot grabbed his almanac and ruffled rapidly through the pages.

"Phobos hasn't risen yet," he said after a brief calculation. "I guess the storm blew up suddenly out of Hades—appropriate name, isn't it?—and has probably collapsed again now. I don't suppose it went anywhere near Charontis, so *they* couldn't have warned us either. It was just one of those accidents that's nobody's fault."

This thought seemed to cheer him considerably, but Gibson found it hard to be so philosophical.

"Meanwhile," he retorted, "we're stuck in the middle of nowhere. How long will it take them to find us? Or is there any chance of repairing the ship?"

"Not a hope of that; the jets are ruined. They were made to work on air, not sand, you know!"

"Well, can we radio Skia?"

"Not now we're on the ground. But when Phobos rises in—let's see—an hour's time, we'll be able to call the observatory and they can relay us on. That's the way we've got to do all our long-distance stuff here, you know. The ionosphere's too feeble to bounce signals round the way you do on Earth. Anyway, I'll go and check that the radio is O.K."

He went forward and started tinkering with the ship's transmitter, while Hilton busied himself checking the heaters and cabin air pressure, leaving the two remaining passengers looking at each other a little thoughtfully.

"This is a fine kettle of fish!" exploded Gibson, half in anger and half in amusement. "I've come safely from Earth to Mars—more than fifty million kilometres—and as soon as I set foot inside a miserable aeroplane *this* is what happens! I'll stick to spaceships in future."

Jimmy grinned. "It'll give us something to tell the others when we get back, won't it? Maybe we'll be able to do some real exploring at last." He peered through the windows, cupping his hands over his eyes to keep out the cabin light. The surrounding landscape was now in complete darkness, apart from the illumination from the ship.

"There seem to be hills all round us; we were lucky to get down in one piece. Good Lord—there's a cliff here on this side—another few metres and we'd have gone smack into it!"

"Any idea where we are?" Gibson called to the pilot. This tactless remark earned him a very stony stare.

"About 120 east, 20 north. The storm can't have thrown us very far off course."

"Then we're somewhere in the Aetheria," said Gibson, bending over the maps. "Yes—there's a hilly region marked here. Not much information about it."

"It's the first time anyone's ever landed here—that's why. This part of Mars is almost unexplored; it's been thoroughly mapped from the air, but that's all."

Gibson was amused to see how Jimmy brightened at this news. There was certainly something exciting about being in a region where no human foot had ever trodden before.

"I hate to cast a gloom over the proceedings," remarked Hilton, in a tone of voice hinting that this was exactly what he was going to do, "but I'm not at all sure you'll be able to radio Phobos even when it does rise."

"What!" yelped the pilot. "The set's O.K.—I've just tested it."

"Yes—but have you noticed where we are? We can't even *see* Phobos. That cliff's due south of us and blocks the view completely. That means that they won't be able to pick up our microwave signals. What's even worse, they won't be able to locate us in their telescopes."

There was a shocked silence.

"*Now* what do we do?" asked Gibson. He had a horrible vision of a thousand-kilometre trek across the desert to Charontis, but dismissed it from his mind at once.

They couldn't possibly carry the oxygen for the trip, still less the food and equipment necessary. And no one could spend the night unprotected on the surface of Mars, even here near the Equator.

"We'll just have to signal in some other way," said Hilton calmly. "In the morning we'll climb those hills and have a look round. Meanwhile I suggest we take it easy." He yawned and stretched himself, filling the cabin from ceiling to floor. "We've got no immediate worries; there's air for several days, and power in the batteries to keep us warm almost indefinitely. We may get a bit hungry if we're here more than a week, but I don't think that's at all likely to happen."

By a kind of unspoken mutual consent, Hilton had taken control. Perhaps he was not even consciously aware of the fact, but he was now the leader of the little party. The pilot had delegated his own authority without a second thought.

"Phobos rises in an hour, you said?" asked Hilton.

"Yes."

"When does it transit? I can never remember what this crazy little moon of yours gets up to."

"Well, it rises in the west and sets in the east about four hours later."

"So it'll be due south around midnight?"

"That's right. Oh Lord—that means we won't be able to see it anyway. It'll be eclipsed for at least an hour!"

"*What* a moon!" snorted Gibson. "When you want it most badly, you can't even see the blasted thing!"

"That doesn't matter," said Hilton calmly. "We'll know just where it is, and it won't do any harm to try the radio then. That's all we can do tonight. Has anyone got a pack of cards? No? Then what about entertaining us, Martin, with some of your stories?"

It was a rash remark, and Gibson seized his chance immediately.

"I wouldn't dream of doing that," he said. "*You're* the one who has the stories to tell."

Hilton stiffened, and for a moment Gibson wondered if he had offended him. He knew that Hilton seldom talked about the Saturnian expedition, but this was too good an opportunity to miss. The chance would never come again, and, as is true of all great adventures, its telling would do their morale good. Perhaps Hilton realised this too, for presently he relaxed and smiled.

"You've got me nicely cornered, haven't you, Martin? Well, I'll talk—but on one condition."

"What's that?"

"No direct quotes, please!"

"As if I would!"

"And when you *do* write it up, let me see the manuscript first."

"Of course."

This was better than Gibson had dared to hope. He had no immediate intention of writing about Hilton's adventures, but it was nice to know that he could do so if he wished. The possibility that he might never have the chance simply did not cross his mind.

Outside the walls of the ship, the fierce Martian night reigned supreme—a night studded with needle-sharp, unwinking stars. The pale light of Deimos made the surrounding landscape dimly visible, as if lit with a cold phosphorescence. Out of the east Jupiter, the brightest object in the sky, was rising in his glory. But the thoughts of the four men in the crashed aircraft were six hundred million kilometres still farther from the sun.

It still puzzled many people—the curious fact that man had visited Saturn but not Jupiter, so much closer at hand. But in space-travel, sheer distance is of no importance, and Saturn had been reached because of a single astonishing stroke of luck that still seemed too good to be true. Orbiting Saturn was Titan, the largest satellite in the Solar System—about twice the size of Earth's moon. As far back as 1944 it had been discovered that Titan possessed an atmosphere. It was not an atmosphere one could breathe: it was immensely more valuable than that. For it was an atmosphere of methane, one of the ideal propellants for atomic rockets.

This had given rise to a situation unique in the history of spaceflight. For the first time, an expedition could be sent to a strange world with the virtual certainty that refuelling would be possible on arrival.

The *Arcturus* and her crew of six had been launched in space from the orbit of Mars. She had reached the Saturnian systems only nine months later, with just enough fuel to land safely on Titan. Then the pumps had been started, and the great tanks replenished from the countless trillions of tons of methane that were there for the taking. Refuelling on Titan whenever necessary, the *Arcturus* had visited every one of Saturn's fifteen known moons, and had even skirted the great ring system itself. In a few months, more was learned about Saturn than in all the previous centuries of telescopic examination.

There had been a price to pay. Two of the crew had died of radiation sickness after emergency repairs to one of the atomic motors. They had been buried on Dione, the fourth moon. And the leader of the expedition, Captain Envers, had been killed by an avalanche of frozen air on Titan; his body had never been found. Hilton had assumed command, and had brought the *Arcturus* safely back to Mars a year later, with only two men to help him.

All these bare facts Gibson knew well enough. He could still remember listening to those radio messages that had come trickling back through space, relayed from world to world. But it was a different thing altogether to hear Hilton telling the story in his quiet, curiously impersonal manner, as if he had been a spectator rather than a participant.

He spoke of Titan and its smaller brethren, the little moons which, circling Saturn, made the planet almost a scale model of the Solar System. He described how at last they had landed on the innermost moon of all, Mimas, only half as far from Saturn as the Moon is from the Earth.

"We came down in a wide valley between a couple of mountains, where we were sure the ground would be pretty solid. We weren't going to make the mistake we did on Rhea! It was a good landing, and we climbed into our suits to go outside. It's funny how impatient you always are to do that, no matter how many times you've set down on a new world.

"Of course, Mimas hasn't much gravity—only a hundredth of Earth's. That was enough to keep us from jumping off into space. I liked it that way; you knew you'd always come down safely again if you waited long enough.

"It was early in the morning when we landed. Mimas has a day a bit shorter than Earth's—it goes round Saturn in twenty-two hours, and as it keeps the same face towards the planet its day and month are the same length—just as they are on the Moon. We'd come down in the northern hemisphere, not for from the Equator, and most of Saturn was above the horizon. It looked quite weird—a huge crescent horn sticking up into the sky, like some impossibly bent mountain thousands of miles high.

"Of course you've all seen the films we made—especially the speeded-up colour one showing a complete cycle of Saturn's phases. But I don't think they can give you much idea of what it was like to live with that enormous thing always there in the sky. It was so big, you see, that one couldn't take it in in a single view. If you stood facing it and held your arms wide open, you could just imagine your finger tips touching the opposite ends of the rings. We couldn't see the rings themselves very well, because they were almost edge-on, but you could always tell they were there by the wide, dusky band of shadow they cast on the planet.

"None of us ever got tired of watching it. It's spinning so fast, you know—the pattern was always changing. The cloud formations, if that's what they were, used to whip round from one side of the disc to the other in a few hours, changing continually as they moved. And there were the most wonderful colours—greens and browns and yellows chiefly. Now and then there'd be great, slow eruptions, and something as big as Earth would rise up out of the depths and spread itself sluggishly in a huge stain half-way round the planet.

"You could never take your eyes off it for long. Even when it was new and so completely invisible, you could still tell it was there because of the great hole in the stars. And here's a funny thing which I haven't reported because I was never quite sure of it. Once or twice, when we were in the planet's shadow and its disc should have been completely dark, I thought I saw a faint phosphorescent glow coming from the night side. It didn't last long—if it really happened at all. Perhaps it was some kind of chemical reaction going on down there in that spinning cauldron.

"Are you surprised that I want to go to Saturn again? What I'd like to do is to get *really* close this time—and by that I mean within a thousand kilometres. It should be quite safe and wouldn't take much power. All you need do is to go into a parabolic orbit and let yourself fall in like a comet going round the Sun. Of course, you'd only spend a few minutes actually close to Saturn, but you could get a lot of records in that time.

"And I want to land on Mimas again, and see that great shining crescent reaching half-way up the sky. It'll be worth the journey, just to watch Saturn waxing and waning, and to see the storms chasing themselves round his Equator. Yes—it would be worth it, even if *I* didn't get back this time."

There were no mock heroics in this closing remark. It was merely a simple statement of fact, and Hilton's listeners believed him completely. While the spell lasted, every one of them would be willing to strike the same bargain.

Gibson ended the long silence by going to the cabin window and peering out into the night.

"Can we have the lights off?" he called. Complete darkness fell as the pilot obeyed his request. The others joined him at the window.

"Look," said Gibson. "Up there—you can just see it if you crane your neck."

The cliff against which they were lying was no longer a wall of absolute and unrelieved darkness. On its very topmost peaks a new light was playing, spilling over the broken crags and filtering down into the valley. Phobos had leapt out of the west and was climbing on its meteoric rise towards the south, racing backwards across the sky.

Minute by minute the light grew stronger, and presently the pilot began to send out his signals. He had barely begun when the pale moonlight was snuffed out so suddenly that Gibson gave a cry of astonishment. Phobos had gone hurtling into the shadow of Mars, and though it was still rising it would cease to shine for almost an hour. There was no way of telling whether or not it would peep over the edge of the great cliff and so be in the right position to receive their signals.

They did not give up hope for almost two hours. Suddenly the light reappeared on the peaks, but shining now from the east. Phobos had emerged from its eclipse, and was now dropping down towards the horizon which it would reach in little more than an hour. The pilot switched off his transmitter in disgust.

"It's no good," he said. "We'll have to try something else."

"I know!" Gibson exclaimed excitedly. "Can't we carry the transmitter up the top of the hill?"

"I'd thought of that, but it would be the devil's own job to get it out without proper tools. The whole thing—aerials and all—is built into the hull."

"There's nothing more we can do tonight, anyway," said Hilton. "I suggest we all get some sleep before dawn. Good night, everybody."

It was excellent advice, but not easy to follow. Gibson's mind was still racing ahead, making plans for the morrow. Not until Phobos had at last plunged down into the east, and its light had ceased to play mockingly on the cliff above them, did he finally pass into a fitful slumber.

Even then he dreamed that he was trying to fix a belt-drive from the motors to the tractor undercarriage so that they could taxi the last thousand kilometres to Port Schiaparelli. . . .

12

When Gibson woke it was long after dawn. The sun was invisible behind the cliffs, but its rays reflected from the scarlet crags above them flooded the cabin with an unearthly, even a sinister light. He stretched himself stiffly; these seats had not been designed to sleep in, and he had spent an uncomfortable night.

He looked round for his companions—and realised that Hilton and the pilot had gone. Jimmy was still fast asleep; the others must have awakened first and gone out to explore. Gibson felt a vague annoyance at being left behind, but knew that he would have been still more annoyed if they had interrupted his slumbers.

There was a short message from Hilton pinned prominently on the wall. It said simply: "Went outside at 6.30. Will be gone about an hour. We'll be hungry when we get back. Fred."

The hint could hardly be ignored. Besides, Gibson felt hungry himself. He rummaged through the emergency food pack which the aircraft carried for such accidents, wondering as he did so just how long it would have to last them. His attempts to brew a hot drink in the tiny pressure-boiler aroused Jimmy, who looked somewhat sheepish when he realised he was the last to wake.

"Had a good sleep?" asked Gibson, as he searched round for the cups.

"Awful," said Jimmy, running his hands through his hair. "I feel I haven't slept for a week. Where are the others?"

His question was promptly answered by the sounds of someone entering the airlock. A moment later Hilton appeared, followed by the pilot. They divested themselves of masks and heating equipment—it was still around freezing point outside—and advanced eagerly on the pieces of chocolate and compressed meat which Gibson had portioned out with impeccable fairness.

"Well," said Gibson anxiously, "what's the verdict?"

"I can tell you one thing right away," said Hilton between mouthfuls. "We're damn lucky to be alive."

"I know that."

"You don't know the half of it—you haven't seen just where we landed. We came down parallel to this cliff for almost a kilometre before we stopped. If we'd swerved a couple of degrees to starboard—bang! When we touched down we did swing inwards a bit, but not enough to do any damage.

"We're in a long valley, running east and west. It looks like a geological fault rather than an old river bed, though that was my first guess. The cliff opposite us is a good hundred metres high, and practically vertical—in fact, it's got a bit of overhang near the top. Maybe it can be climbed farther along, but we didn't try. There's no need to, anyway—if we want Phobos to see us we've only got to walk a little way to the north, until the cliff doesn't block the view. In fact, I think that may be the answer—if we can push this ship out into the open. It'll mean we can use the radio, and will give the telescopes and air search a better chance of spotting us."

"How much does this thing weigh?" said Gibson doubtfully.

"About thirty tones with full load. There's a lot of stuff we can take out, of course."

"No there isn't!" said the pilot. "That would mean letting down our pressure, and we can't afford to waste air."

"Oh Lord, I'd forgotten that. Still, the ground's fairly smooth and the undercart's perfectly O.K."

Gibson made noises indicating extreme doubt. Even under a third of Earth's gravity, moving the aircraft was not going to be an easy proposition.

For the next few minutes his attention was diverted to the coffee, which he had tried to pour out before it had cooled sufficiently.

Releasing the pressure on the boiler immediately filled the room with steam, so that for a moment it looked as if everyone was going to inhale their liquid refreshment. Making hot drinks on Mars was always a nuisance, since water under normal pressure boiled at around sixty degrees Centigrade, and cooks who forgot this elementary fact usually met with disaster.

The dull but nourishing meal was finished in silence, as the castaways pondered their pet plans for rescue. They were not really worried; they knew that an intensive search would now be in progress, and it could only be a matter of time before they were located. But that time could be reduced to a few hours if they could get some kind of signal to Phobos.

After breakfast they tried to move the ship. By dint of much pushing and pulling they managed to shift it a good five metres. Then the caterpillar tracks sank into soft ground, and as far as their combined efforts were concerned the machine might have been completely bogged. They retired, panting, into the cabin to discuss the next move.

"Have we anything white which we could spread out over a large area?" asked Gibson.

This excellent idea came to nothing when an intensive search of the cabin revealed six handkerchiefs and a few pieces of grimy rag. It was agreed that, even under the most favourable conditions, these would not be visible from Phobos.

"There's only one thing for it," said Hilton. "We'll have to rip out the landing lights, run them out on a cable until they're clear of the cliff, and aim them at Phobos. I didn't want to do this if it could be avoided; it might make a mess of the wing and it's a pity to break up a good aeroplane."

By his glum expression, it was obvious that the pilot agreed with these sentiments.

Jimmy was suddenly struck with an idea.

"Why not fix up a heliograph?" he asked. "If we flashed a mirror on Phobos they ought to be able to see that."

"Across six thousand kilometres?" said Gibson doubtfully.

"Why not? They've got telescopes that magnify more than a thousand up there. Couldn't you see a mirror flashing in the sun if it was only six kilometres away?"

"I'm sure there's something wrong with that calculation, though I don't know what," said Gibson. "Things never work out as simply as that. But I agree with the general idea. Now who's got a mirror?"

After a quarter hour's search, Jimmy's scheme had to be abandoned. There simply was no such thing as a mirror on the ship.

"We could cut out a piece of the wing and polish that

up," said Hilton thoughtfully. "That would be almost as good."

"This magnesium alloy won't take much of a polish," said the pilot, still determined to defend his machine to the last.

Gibson suddenly shot to his feet.

"Will someone kick me three times round the cabin?" he announced to the assembly.

"With pleasure," grinned Hilton, "but tell us why."

Without answering, Gibson went to the rear of the ship and began rummaging among his luggage, keeping his back to the interested spectators. It took him only a moment to find what he wanted; then he swung quickly round.

"Here's the answer," he said triumphantly.

A flash of intolerable light suddenly filled the cabin, flooding every corner with a harsh brilliance and throwing distorted shadows on the wall. It was as if lightning had struck the ship, and for several minutes everyone was half-blinded, still carrying on their retinas a frozen picture of the cabin as seen in that moment of searing incandescence.

"I'm sorry," said Gibson contritely. "I've never used it at full power indoors before—that was intended for night work in the open."

"Phew!" said Hilton, rubbing his eyes. "I thought you'd let off an atomic bomb. Must you scare everyone to death when you photograph them?"

"It's only like *this* for normal indoor use," said Gibson, demonstrating. Everyone flinched again, but this time the flash seemed scarcely noticeable. "It's a special job I had made for me before I left Earth. I wanted to be quite sure I could do colour photography at night if I wanted to. So far I haven't had a real chance of using it."

"Let's have a look at the thing," said Hilton.

Gibson handed over the flash-gun and explained its operation.

"It's built round a super-capacity condenser. There's enough for about a hundred flashes on one charge, and it's practically full."

"A hundred of the high-powered flashes?"

"Yes; it'll do a couple of thousand of the normal ones."

"Then there's enough electrical energy to make a good bomb in that condenser. I hope it doesn't spring a leak."

Hilton was examining the little gas-discharge tube, only the size of a marble, at the centre of the small reflector.

"Can we focus this thing to get a good beam?" he asked.

"There's a catch behind the reflector—that's the idea. It's rather a broad beam, but it'll help."

Hilton looked very pleased.

"They ought to see this thing on Phobos, even in broad daylight, if they're watching this part with a good telescope. We mustn't waste flashes, though."

"Phobos is well up now, isn't it?" asked Gibson. "I'm going out to have a shot right away."

He got to his feet and began to adjust his breathing equipment.

"Don't use more than ten flashes," warned Hilton. "We want to save them for night. And stand in any shadow you can find."

"Can I go out too?" asked Jimmy.

"All right," said Hilton. "But keep together and don't go wandering off to explore. I'm going to stay here and see if there's anything we can do with the landing lights."

The fact that they now had a definite plan of action had raised their spirits considerably. Clutching his camera and the precious flash-gun close to his chest, Gibson bounded across the valley like a young gazelle. It was a curious fact that on Mars one quickly adjusted one's muscular efforts to the lower gravity, and so normally used strides no greater than on Earth. But the reserve of power was available, when necessity or high spirits demanded it.

They soon left the shadow of the cliff, and had a clear view of the open sky. Phobos was already high in the west, a little half-moon which would rapidly narrow to a thin crescent as it raced towards the south. Gibson regarded it thoughtfully, wondering if at this very moment someone might be watching this part of Mars. It seemed highly probable, for the approximate position of their crash would be known. He felt an irrational impulse to dance around and wave his arms—even to shout: "Here we are—can't you see us?"

What would this region look like in the telescopes which were, he hoped, now sweeping Aetheria? They would show the mottled green of the vegetation through which he was trudging, and the great cliff would be clearly visible as a red band casting a broad shadow over the valley when the sun was low. There would be scarcely any shadow now, for it was only a few hours from noon. The best thing to do, Gibson decided, was to get in the middle of the darkest area of vegetation he could find.

About a kilometre from the crashed ship the ground sloped down slightly, and here, in the lowest part of the valley, was a wide brownish belt which seemed to be covered with tall weeds. Gibson headed for this, Jimmy following close behind.

They found themselves among slender, leathery plants of a type they had never seen before. The leaves rose vertically out of the ground in long, thin streamers, and were covered with numberless pods which looked as if they might contain seeds. The flat sides were all turned towards the Sun, and Gibson was interested to note that while the sunlit sides of the leaves were black, the shadowed parts were a greyish white. It was a simple but effective trick to reduce loss of heat.

Without wasting time to botanise, Gibson pushed his way into the centre of the little forest. The plants were not crowded too closely together, and it was fairly easy to force a passage through them. When he had gone far enough he raised his flash-gun and squinted along it at Phobos.

The satellite was now a thin crescent not far from the Sun, and Gibson felt extremely foolish aiming his flash into the full glare of the summer sky. But the time was really well chosen, for it would be dark on the side of Phobos towards them and the telescopes there would be observing under favourable conditions.

He let off his ten shots in five pairs, spaced well apart. This seemed the most economical way of doing it while still making sure that the signals would look obviously artificial.

"That'll do for today," said Gibson. "We'll save the rest of our ammunition until after dark. Now let's have a look at these plants. Do you know what they remind me of?"

"Overgrown seaweed," replied Jimmy promptly.

"Right first time. I wonder what's in those pods? Have you got a knife on you—thanks."

Gibson began carving at the nearest frond until he had punctured one of the little black balloons. It apparently held gas, and under considerable pressure, for a faint hiss could be heard as the knife penetrated.

"What queer stuff!" said Gibson. "Let's take some back with us."

Not without difficulty, he hacked off one of the long black fronds near the roots. A dark brown fluid began to ooze out of the severed end, releasing tiny bubbles of gas as it did so. With this souvenir hanging over his shoulder, Gibson began to make his way back to the ship.

He did not know that he was carrying with him the future of a world.

They had gone only a few paces when they encountered a denser patch and had to make a detour. With the sun as a guide there was no danger of becoming lost, especially in such a small region, and they had made no attempt to retrace their footsteps exactly. Gibson was leading the way, and finding it somewhat heavy going. He was just wondering whether to swallow his pride and change places with Jimmy when he was relieved to come across a narrow, winding track leading more or less in the right direction.

To any observer, it would have been an interesting demonstration of the slowness of some mental processes. For both Gibson and Jimmy had walked a good six paces before they remembered the simple but shattering truth that footpaths do not, usually, make themselves.

"It's about time our two explorers came back, isn't it?" said the pilot as he helped Hilton detach the floodlights from the underside of the aircraft's wing This had proved, after all, to be a fairly straight-forward job, and Hilton hoped to find enough wiring inside the machine to run the lights far enough away from the cliff to be visible from Phobos when it rose again. They would not have the brilliance of Gibson's flash, but their steady beams would give them a better chance of being detected.

"How long have they been gone now?" said Hilton.

"About forty minutes. I hope they've had the sense not to get lost."

"Gibson's too careful to go wandering off. I wouldn't trust young Jimmy by himself, though—he'd want to start looking for Martians!"

"Oh, here they are. They seem to be in a bit of a hurry."

Two tiny figures had emerged from the middle distance and were bounding across the valley. Their haste was so obvious that the watchers downed tools and observed their approach with rising curiosity.

The fact that Gibson and Jimmy had returned so promptly represented a triumph of caution and self-control. For a long moment of incredulous astonishment they had stood staring at that pathway through the thin brown plants. On Earth, nothing could have been more commonplace; it was just the sort of track that cattle make across a hill, or wild animals through a forest. Its very familiarity had at first prevented them from noticing it, and even when they had forced their minds to accept its presence, they still kept trying to explain it away.

Gibson had spoken first, in a very subdued voice—almost as if he was afraid of being overheard.

"It's a path all right, Jimmy. But what could have made it, for heaven's sake? No one's ever been here before."

"It must have been some kind of animal."

"A fairly large one, too."

"Perhaps as big as a horse."

"Or a tiger."

The last remark produced an uneasy silence. Then Jimmy said: "Well, if it comes to a fight, that flash of yours should scare anything."

"Only if it had eyes," said Gibson. "Suppose it had some other sense?"

It was obvious that Jimmy was trying to think of good reasons for pressing ahead.

"I'm sure we could run faster, and jump higher, than anything else on Mars."

Gibson liked to believe that his decision was based on prudence rather than cowardice.

"We're not taking any risks," he said firmly. "We're going straight back to tell the others. *Then* we'll think about having a look round."

Jimmy had sense enough not to grumble, but he kept looking back wistfully as they returned to the ship. Whatever faults he might have, lack of courage was not among them.

It took some time to convince the others that they were not attempting a rather poor practical joke. After all, everyone knew why there couldn't be animal life on Mars. It was a question of metabolism: animals burned fuel so much faster than plants, and therefore could not exist in this thin, practically inert atmosphere. The biologists had been quick to point this out as soon as conditions on the surface of Mars had been accurately determined, and for the last ten years the question of animal life on the planet had been regarded as settled—except by incurable romantics.

"Even if you saw what you think," said Hilton, "there must be some natural explanation."

"Come and see for yourself," retorted Gibson. "I tell you it was a well-worn track."

"Oh, I'm coming," said Hilton.

"So am I," said the pilot.

"Wait a minute! We can't all go. At least one of us has got to stay behind."

For a moment Gibson felt like volunteering. Then he realised that he would never forgive himself if he did.

"*I* found the track," he said firmly.

"Looks as if I've got a mutiny on my hands," remarked Hilton. "Anyone got some money? Odd man out of you three stays behind."

"It's a wild goose chase, anyway," said the pilot, when he produced the only head. "I'll expect you home in an hour. If you take any longer I'll want you to bring back a genuine Martian princess, *à la* Edgar Rice Burroughs."

Hilton, despite his scepticism, was taking the matter more seriously.

"There'll be three of us," he said, "so it should be all right even if we do meet anything unfriendly. But just in case *none* of us come back, you've to sit right here and not go looking for us. Understand?"

"Very well. I'll sit tight."

The trio set off across the valley towards the little forest, Gibson leading the way. After reaching the tall thin fronds of "seaweed," they had no difficulty in finding the track again. Hilton stared at it in silence for a good minute, while Gibson and Jimmy regarded him with "I told you so" expressions. Then he remarked: "Let's have your flash-gun, Martin. I'm going first."

It would have been silly to argue. Hilton was taller, stronger, and more alert. Gibson handed over his weapon without a word.

There can be no weirder sensation than that of walking along a narrow track between high leafy walls, knowing that at any moment you may come face to face with a totally unknown and perhaps unfriendly creature. Gibson tried to remind himself that animals which had never before encountered man were seldom hostile—though there were enough exceptions to this rule to make life interesting.

They had gone about half-way through the forest when the track branched into two. Hilton took the turn to the right, but soon discovered that this was a *cul-de-sac*. It led to a clearing about twenty metres across, in which all the plants had been cut—or eaten—to within a short distance of the ground, leaving only the stumps showing. These were already beginning to sprout again, and it was obvious that this patch had been deserted for some time by whatever creatures had come here.

"Herbivores," whispered Gibson.

"And fairly intelligent," said Hilton. "See the way they've left the roots to come up again? Let's go back along the other branch."

They came across the second clearing five minutes later. It was a good deal larger than the first, and it was not empty.

Hilton tightened his grip on the flash-gun, and in a single smooth, well-practised movement Gibson swung his camera into position and began to take the most famous photographs ever made on Mars. Then they all relaxed, and stood waiting for the Martians to notice them.

In that moment centuries of fantasy and legend were swept away. All Man's dreams of neighbours not unlike himself vanished into limbo. With them, unlamented, went Wells' tentacled monstrosities and the other legions of crawling, nightmare horrors. And there vanished also the myth of coldly inhuman intelligences which might look down dispassionately on Man from their fabulous heights of wisdom—and might brush him aside with no more malice than he himself might destroy a creeping insect.

There were ten of the creatures in the glade, and they were all too busy eating to take any notice of the intruders. In appearance they resembled very plump kangaroos, their almost spherical bodies balanced on two large, slender hindlimbs. They were hairless, and their skin had a curious waxy sheen like polished leather. Two thin forearms, which seemed to be completely flexible, sprouted from the upper part of the body and ended in tiny hands like the claws of a bird—too small and feeble, one would have thought, to have been of much practical use. Their heads were set directly on the trunk with no suspicion of a neck, and bore two large pale eyes with wide pupils. There were no nostrils—only a very odd triangular mouth with three stubby bills which were making short work of the foliage. A pair of large, almost transparent ears hung limply from the head, twitching occasionally and sometimes folding themselves into trumpets which looked as if they might be extremely efficient sound detectors, even in this thin atmosphere.

The largest of the beasts was about as tall as Hilton, but all the others were considerably smaller. One baby, less than a metre high, could only be described by the overworked adjective "cute." It was hopping excitedly about in an effort to reach the more succulent leaves, and from time to time emitted thin, piping cries which were irresistibly pathetic.

"How intelligent would you say they are?" whispered Gibson at last.

"It's hard to say. Notice how they're careful not to destroy the plants they eat? Of course, that may be pure instinct—like bees knowing how to build their hives."

"They move very slowly, don't they? I wonder if they're warm-blooded."

"I don't see why they should have blood at all. Their metabolism must be pretty weird for them to survive in this climate."

"It's about time they took some notice of us."

"The big fellow knows we're here. I've caught him looking at us out of the corner of his eye. Do you notice the way his ears keep pointing towards us?"

"Let's go out into the open."

Hilton thought this over.

"I don't see how they can do us much harm, even if they want to. Those little hands look rather feeble—but I suppose those three-sided beaks could do some damage. We'll go forward, very slowly, for six paces. If they come at us, I'll give them a flash with the gun while you make a bolt for it. I'm sure we can outrun them easily. They certainly don't look built for speed."

Moving with a slowness which they hoped would appear reassuring rather than stealthy, they walked forward into the glade. There was now no doubt that the Martians saw them; half a dozen pairs of great, calm eyes stared at them, then looked away as their owners got on with the more important business of eating.

"They don't even seem to be inquisitive," said Gibson, somewhat disappointed. "Are we as uninteresting as all this?"

"Hello—Junior's spotted us! What's he up to?"

The smallest Martian had stopped eating and was staring at the intruders with an expression that might have meant anything from rank disbelief to hopeful anticipation of another meal. It gave a couple of shrill squeaks which were answered by a noncommittal "honk" from one of the adults. Then it began to hop towards the interested spectators.

It halted a couple of paces away, showing not the slightest signs of fear or caution.

"How do you do?" said Hilton solemnly. "Let me introduce us. On my right, James Spencer; on my left, Martin Gibson. But I'm afraid I didn't quite catch your name."

"Squeak," said the small Martian.

"Well, Squeak, what can we do for you?"

The little creature put out an exploring hand and tugged at Hilton's clothing. Then it hopped towards Gibson, who had been busily photographing this exchange of courtesies. Once again it put forward an enquiring paw, and Gibson moved the camera round out of harm's way. He held out his hand, and the little fingers closed round it with surprising strength.

"Friendly little chap, isn't he?" said Gibson, having disentangled himself with difficulty. "At least he's not as stuck-up as his relatives."

The adults had so far taken not the slightest notice of the proceedings. They were still munching placidly at the other side of the glade.

"I wish we had something to give him, but I don't suppose he could eat any of our food. Lend me your knife, Jimmy. I'll cut down a bit of seaweed for him, just to prove that we're friends."

This gift was gratefully received and promptly eaten, and the small hands reached out for more.

"You seem to have made a hit, Martin," said Hilton.

"I'm afraid it's cupboard love," sighed Gibson. "Hey, leave my camera alone—you can't eat that!"

"I say," said Hilton suddenly. "There's something odd here. What colour would you say this little chap is?"

"Why, brown in the front and—oh, a dirty grey at the back."

"Well, just walk to the other side of him and offer another bit of food."

Gibson obliged, Squeak rotating on his haunches so that he could grab the new morsel. And as he did so, an extraordinary thing happened.

The brown covering on the front of his body slowly faded, and in less than a minute had become a dingy grey. At the same time, exactly the reverse happened on the creature's back, until the interchange was complete.

"Good Lord!" said Gibson. "It's just like a chameleon. What do you think the idea is? Protective coloration?"

"No, it's cleverer than that. Look at those others over there. You see, they're always brown—or nearly black—on the side towards the sun. It's simply a scheme to catch as much heat as possible, and avoid re-radiating it. The plants do just the same—I wonder who thought of it first? It wouldn't be any use on an animal that had to move quickly, but some of those big chaps haven't changed position in the last five minutes."

Gibson promptly set to work photographing this peculiar phenomenon—not a very difficult feat to do, as wherever he moved Squeak always turned hopefully towards him and sat waiting patiently. When he had finished, Hilton remarked:

"I hate to break up this touching scene, but we said we'd be back in an hour."

"We needn't all go. Be a good chap, Jimmy—run back and say that we're all right."

But Jimmy was staring at the sky—the first to realise that for the last five minutes an aircraft had been circling high over the valley.

Their united cheer disturbed even the placidly browsing Martians, who looked round disapprovingly. It scared Squeak so much that he shot backwards in one tremendous hop, but soon got over his fright and came forward again.

"See you later!" called Gibson over his shoulder as they hurried out of the glade. The natives took not the slightest notice.

They were half-way out of the little forest when Gibson suddenly became aware of the fact that he was being followed. He stopped and looked back. Making heavy weather, but still hopping along gamely behind him, was Squeak.

"Shoo!" said Gibson, flapping his arms around like a distraught scarecrow. "Go back to Mother! I haven't got anything for you."

It was not the slightest use, and his pause had merely enabled Squeak to catch up with him. The others were already out of sight, unaware that Gibson had dropped back. They therefore missed a very interesting cameo as Gibson tried, without hurting Squeak's feelings, to disengage himself from his new-found friend.

He gave up the direct approach after five minutes, and tried guile. Fortunately he had failed to return Jimmy's knife, and after much panting and hacking managed to collect a small pile of "seaweed" which he laid in front of Squeak. This, he hoped, would keep him busy for quite a while.

He had just finished this when Hilton and Jimmy came hurrying back to find what had happened to him.

"O.K.—I'm coming along now," he said. "I had to get rid of Squeak somehow. *That'll* stop him following."

The pilot in the crashed aircraft had been getting anxious, for the hour was nearly up and there was still no sign of his companions. By climbing on to the top of the fuselage he could see half-way across the valley, and to the dark area of vegetation into which they had disappeared. He was examining this when the rescue aircraft came driving out of the east and began to circle the valley.

When he was sure it had spotted him he turned his attention to the ground again. He was just in time to see a group of figures emerging into the open plain—and a moment later he rubbed his eyes in rank disbelief.

Three people had gone into the forest; but four were coming out. And the fourth looked a very odd sort of person indeed.

13

After what was later to be christened the most successful crash in the history of Martian exploration, the visit to Trivium Charontis and Port Schiaparelli was, inevitably, something of an anticlimax. Indeed Gibson had wished to postpone it altogether and to return to Port Lowell immediately with his prize. He had soon abandoned all attempts to jettison Squeak, and as everyone in the colony would be on tenterhooks to see a real, live Martian it had been decided to fly the little creature back with them.

But Port Lowell would not let them return; indeed, it was ten days before they saw the capital again. Under the great domes, one of the decisive battles for the possession of the planet was now being fought. It was a battle which Gibson knew of only through the radio reports—a silent but deadly battle which he was thankful to have missed.

The epidemic which Dr. Scott had asked for had arrived. At its peak, a tenth of the city's population was sick with Martian fever. But the serum from Earth broke the attack, and the battle was won with only three fatal casualties. It was the last time that the fever ever threatened the colony.

Taking Squeak to Port Schiaparelli involved considerable difficulties, for it meant flying large quantities of his staple diet ahead of him. At first it was doubted if he could live in the oxygenated atmosphere of the domes, but it was soon discovered that this did not worry him in the least—though it reduced his appetite considerably. The explanation of this fortunate accident was not discovered until a good deal later. What never was discovered at all was the reason for Squeak's attachment to Gibson. Someone suggested, rather unkindly, that it was because they were approximately the same shape.

Before they continued their journey, Gibson and his colleagues, with the pilot of the rescue plane and the repair crew who arrived later, made several visits to the little family of Martians. They discovered only the one group, and Gibson wondered if these were the last specimens left on the planet. This, as it later turned out, was not the case.

The rescue plane had been searching along the track of their flight when it had received a radio message from Phobos reporting brilliant flashes in Aetheria. (Just how those flashes had been made had puzzled everyone considerably until Gibson, with justifiable pride, gave the explanation.) When they discovered it would take only a few hours to replace the jet units on their plane, they had decided to wait while the repairs were carried out and to use the time studying the Martians in their natural haunts. It was then that Gibson first suspected the secret of their existence.

In the remote past they had probably been oxygen breathers, and their life processes still depended on the element. They could not obtain it direct from the soil, where it lay in such countless trillions of tons; but the plants they ate could do so. Gibson quickly found that the numerous "pods" in the seaweed-like fronds contained oxygen under quite high pressure. By slowing down their metabolism, the Martians had managed to evolve a balance—almost a symbiosis—with the plants which provided them, literally, with food and air. It was a precarious balance which, one would have thought, might have been upset at any time by some natural catastrophe. But conditions on Mars had long ago reached stability, and the balance would be maintained for ages yet—unless Man disturbed it.

The repairs took a little longer than expected, and they did not reach Port Schiaparelli until three days after leaving Port Lowell. The second city of Mars held less than a thousand people, living under two domes on a long, narrow plateau. This had been the site of the orginal landing on Mars, and so the position of the city was really an historical accident. Not until some years later, when the planet's resources began to be better known, was it decided to move the colony's centre of gravity to Lowell and not to expand Schiaparelli any further.

The little city was in many respects an exact replica of its larger and more modern rival. Its specialty was light engineering, geological—or rather aerological—research, and the exploration of the surrounding regions. The fact that Gibson and his colleagues had accidentally stumbled on the greatest discovery so far made on Mars, less than an hour's flight from the city, was thus the cause of some heartburning.

The visit must have had a demoralising effect on all normal activity in Port Schiaparelli, for wherever Gibson went everything stopped while crowds gathered around Squeak. A favourite occupation was to lure him into a field of uniform illumination and to watch him turn black all over, as he blissfully tried to extract the maximum advantage from this state of affairs. It was in Schiaparelli that someone hit on the deplorable scheme of projecting simple pictures onto Squeak, and photographing the result before it faded. One day Gibson was very annoyed to come across a photo of his pet bearing a crude but recognisable caricature of a well-known television star.

On the whole, their stay in Port Schiaparelli was not a very happy one. After the first three days they had seen everything worth seeing, and the few trips they were able to make into the surrounding countryside did not provide much of interest. Jimmy was continually worrying about Irene, and putting through expensive calls to Port Lowell. Gibson was impatient to get back to the big city which, not so long ago, he had called an overgrown village. Only Hilton, who seemed to possess unlimited reserves of patience, took life easily and relaxed while the others fussed around him.

There was one excitement during their stay in the city. Gibson had often wondered, a little apprehensively, what would happen if the pressurising dome ever failed. He received the answer—or as much of it as he had any desire for—one quiet afternoon when he was interviewing the city's chief engineer in his office. Squeak had been with them, propped up on his large, flexible lower limbs like some improbable nursery doll.

As the interview progressed, Gibson became aware that his victim was showing more than the usual signs of restiveness. His mind was obviously very far away, and he seemed to be waiting for something to happen. Suddenly, without warning, the whole building trembled slightly as if hit by an earthquake. Two more shocks, equally spaced, came in quick succession. From a loudspeaker on the wall a voice called urgently: "Blowout! Practice only! You have ten seconds to reach shelter! Blowout! Practice only!"

Gibson had jumped out of his chair, but immediat realised there was nothing he need do. From far aw there came a sound of slamming doors—then silence. T engineer got to his feet and walked over to the windc overlooking the city's only main street.

"Everyone seems to have got to cover," he said. " course, it isn't possible to make these tests a compl surprise. There's one a month, and we have to tell peo what day it will be because they might think it was t real thing."

"Just what are we all supposed to do?" asked Gibs who had been told at least twice but had become a lit rusty on the subject.

"As soon as you hear the signal—that's the three grou explosions—you've got to get under cover. If you're doors you have to grab your breathing mask to resc anyone who can't make it. You see, if pressure goes eve house becomes a self-contained unit with enough air f several hours."

"And anyone out in the open?"

"It would take a few seconds for the pressure to go rig down, and as every building has its own airlock it shou always be possible to reach shelter in time. Even if y collapsed in the open, you'd probably be all right if y were rescued inside two minutes—unless you'd got a b heart. And no one comes to Mars if he's got a b heart."

"Well, I hope you never have to put this theory in practice."

"So do we! But on Mars one has to be prepared f anything. Ah, there goes the All Clear."

The speaker had burst into life again.

"Exercise over. Will all those who failed to reach shelt in the regulation time please inform Admin in the us way? End of message."

"Will they?" asked Gibson. "I should have thoug they'd keep quiet."

The engineer laughed.

"That depends. They probably will if it was their o fault. But it's the best way of showing up weak points our defences. Someone will come and say: 'Look here- was cleaning one of the ore furnaces when the alarm we it took me two minutes to get out of the blinking thi

What am *I* supposed to do if there's a real blow-out?' Then we've got to think of an answer, if we can."

Gibson looked enviously at Squeak, who seemed to be asleep, though an occasional twitch of the great translucent ears showed that he was taking some interest in the conversation.

"It would be nice if we could be like him and didn't have to bother about air-pressure. Then we could really do something with Mars."

"I wonder!" said the engineer thoughtfully. "What have *they* done except survive? It's always fatal to adapt oneself to one's surroundings. The thing to do is to alter your surroundings to suit you."

The words were almost an echo of the remark that Hadfield had made at their first meeting. Gibson was to remember them often in the years to come.

Their return to Port Lowell was almost a victory parade. The capital was in a mood of elation over the defeat of the epidemic, and it was now anxiously waiting to see Gibson and his prize. The scientists had prepared quite a reception for Squeak, the zoologists in particular being busily at work explaining away their early explanations for the absence of animal life on Mars.

Gibson had handed his pet over to the experts only when they had solemnly assured him that no thought of dissection had ever for a moment entered their minds. Then, full of ideas, he had hurried to see the Chief.

Hadfield had greeted him warmly. There was, Gibson was interested to note, a distinct change in the Chief's attitude towards him. At first it had been—well, not unfriendly, but at least somewhat reserved. He had not attempted to conceal the fact that he considered Gibson's presence on Mars something of a nuisance—another burden to add to those he already carried. This attitude had slowly changed until it was now obvious that the Chief Executive no longer regarded him as an unmitigated calamity.

"You've added some interesting citizens to my little empire," Hadfield said with a smile. "I've just had a look at your engaging pet. He's already bitten the Chief Medical Officer."

"I hope they're treating him properly," said Gibson anxiously.

"Who—the C.M.O.?"

"No—Squeak, of course. What I'm wondering is whether there are any other forms of animal life we haven't discovered yet—perhaps more intelligent."

"In other words, are these the only genuine Martians?"

"Yes."

"It'll be years before we know for certain, but I rather expect they are. The conditions which make it possible for them to survive don't occur in many places on the planet."

"That was one thing I wanted to talk to you about." Gibson reached into his pocket and brought out a frond of the brown "seaweed." He punctured one of the fronds, and there was the faint hiss of escaping gas.

"If this stuff is cultivated properly, it may solve the oxygen problem in the cities and do away with all our present complicated machinery. With enough sand for it to feed on, it would give you all the oxygen you need."

"Go on," said Hadfield noncommittally.

"Of course, you'd have to do some selective breeding to get the variety that gave most oxygen," continued Gibson, warming to his subject.

"Naturally," replied Hadfield.

Gibson looked at his listener with a sudden suspicion, aware that there was something odd about his attitude. A faint smile was playing about Hadfield's lips.

"I don't think you're taking me seriously!" Gibson protested bitterly.

Hadfield sat up with a start.

"On the contrary!" he retorted. "I'm taking you much more seriously than you imagine." He toyed with his paperweight, then apparently came to a decision. Abruptly he leaned towards his desk microphone and pressed a switch.

"Get me a Sand Flea and a driver," he said. "I want them at Lock One West in thirty minutes."

He turned to Gibson.

"Can you be ready by then?"

"What—yes, I suppose so. I've only got to get my breathing gear from the hotel."

"Good—see you in half an hour."

Gibson was there ten minutes early, his brain in a whirl. Transport had managed to produce a vehicle in time, and the Chief was punctual as ever. He gave the driver instructions which Gibson was unable to catch, and the Flea jerked out of the dome on to the road circling the city.

"I'm doing something rather rash, Gibson," said Hadfield as the brilliant green landscape flowed past them. "Will you give me your word that you'll say nothing of this until I authorise you?"

"Why, certainly," said Gibson, startled.

"I'm trusting you because I believe you're on our side, and haven't been as big a nuisance as I expected."

"Thank you," said Gibson dryly.

"And because of what you've just taught us about our own planet. I think we owe you something in return."

The Flea had swung round to the south, following the track that led up into the hills. And, quite suddenly, Gibson realised where they were going.

"Were you very upset when you heard that we'd crashed?" asked Jimmy anxiously.

"Of course I was," said Irene. "Terribly upset. I couldn't sleep for worrying about you."

"Now it's all over, though, don't you think it was worth it?"

"I suppose so, but somehow it keeps reminding me that in a month you'll be gone again. Oh, Jimmy, what shall we do then?"

Deep despair settled upon the two lovers. All Jimmy's present satisfaction vanished into gloom. There was no escaping from this inevitable fact. The *Ares* would be leaving Deimos in less than four weeks, and it might be years before he could return to Mars. It was a prospect too terrible for words.

"I can't possibly stay on Mars, even if they'd let me," said Jimmy. "I can't earn a living until I'm qualified, and I've still got two years' post-graduate work *and* a trip to Venus to do! There's only one thing for it!"

Irene's eyes brightened; then she relapsed into gloom.

"Oh, we've been through that before. I'm sure Daddy wouldn't agree."

"Well, it won't do any harm to try. I'll get Martin to tackle him."

"Mr. Gibson? Do you think he would?"

"I know he will, if I ask him. And he'll make it sound convincing."

"I don't see why he should bother."

"Oh, he likes me," said Jimmy with easy self-assurance. "I'm sure he'll agree with us. It's not right that you should stick here on Mars and never see anything of Earth. Paris—New York—London—why, you haven't lived until you've visited them. Do you know what I think?"

"What?"

"Your father's being selfish in keeping you here."

Irene pouted a little. She was very fond of her father and her first impulse was to defend him vigorously. But she was now torn between two loyalties, though in the long run there was no doubt which would win.

"Of course," said Jimmy, realising that he might have gone too far, "I'm sure he really means to do the best for you, but he's got so many things to worry about. He's probably forgotten what Earth is like and doesn't realise what you're losing! No, you must get away before it's too late."

Irene still looked uncertain. Then her sense of humour, so much more acute than Jimmy's, came to the rescue.

"I'm quite sure that if we were on Earth, and you had to go back to Mars, you'd be able to prove just as easily that I ought to follow you there!"

Jimmy looked a little hurt, then realised that Irene wasn't really laughing at him.

"All right," he said. "That's settled. I'll talk to Martin as soon as I see him—and ask him to tackle your Dad. So let's forget all about it until then, shall we?"

They did, very nearly.

The little amphitheatre in the hills above Port Lowell was just as Gibson had remembered it, except that the green of its lush vegetation had darkened a little, as if it had already received the first warning of the still far-distant autumn. The Sand Flea drove up to the largest of the four small domes, and they walked over to the airlock.

"When I was here before," said Gibson dryly, "I was told we'd have to be disinfected before we could enter."

"A slight exaggeration to discourage unwanted visitors," said Hadfield, unabashed. The outer door had opened at his signal, and they quickly stripped off their breathing apparatus. "We used to take such precautions, but they're no longer necessary."

The inner door slid aside and they stepped through into the dome. A man wearing the white smock of the scientific worker—the *clean* white smock of the very senior scientific worker—was waiting for them.

"Hello, Baines," said Hadfield. "Gibson—this is Professor Baines. I expect you've heard of each other."

They shook hands. Baines, Gibson knew, was one of the world's greatest experts on plant genetics. He had read a year or two ago that he had gone to Mars to study its flora.

"So you're the chap who's just discovered *Oxyfera,*" said Baines dreamily. He was a large, rugged man with an absentminded air which contrasted strangely with his massive frame and determined features.

"Is that what you call it?" asked Gibson. "Well, I *thought* I'd discovered it. But I'm beginning to have doubts."

"You certainly discovered something quite as important," Hadfield reassured him. "But Baines isn't interested in animals, so it's no good talking to him about your Martian friends."

They were walking between low temporary walls which, Gibson saw, partitioned the dome into numerous rooms and corridors. The whole place looked as if it had been built in a great hurry; they came across beautiful scientific apparatus supported on rough packing cases, and everywhere there was an atmosphere of hectic improvisation. Yet, curiously enough, very few people were at work. Gibson obtained the impression that whatever task had been going on here was now completed and that only a skeleton staff was left.

Baines led them to an airlock connecting with one of the other domes, and as they waited for the last door to open he remarked quietly: "This may hurt your eyes a bit." With this warning, Gibson put up his hand as a shield.

His first impression was one of light and heat. It was almost as if he had moved from Pole to Tropics in a single step. Overhead, batteries of powerful lamps were blasting the hemispherical chamber with light. There was something heavy and oppressive about the air that was not only due to the heat, and he wondered what sort of atmosphere he was breathing.

This dome was not divided up by partitions; it was simply a large, circular space laid out into neat plots on which grew all the Martian plants which Gibson had ever seen, and many more besides. About a quarter of the area was covered by tall brown fronds which Gibson recognised at once.

"So you've known about them all the time?" he said, neither surprised nor particularly disappointed. (Hadfield was quite right: the Martians were *much* more important.)

"Yes," said Hadfield. "They were discovered about two years ago and aren't very rare along the equatorial belt. They only grow where there's plenty of sunlight, and your little crop was the farthest north they've ever been found."

"It takes a great deal of energy to split the oxygen out of the sand," explained Baines. "We've been helping them here with these lights, and trying some experiments of our own. Come and look at the result."

Gibson walked over to the plot, keeping carefully to the narrow path. These plants weren't, after all, exactly the same as those he had discovered, though they had obviously descended from the same stock. The most surprising difference was the complete absence of gas-pods, their place having been taken by myriads of minute pores.

"This is the important point," said Hadfield. "We've bred a variety which releases its oxygen directly into the air, because it doesn't need to store it any more. As long as it's got plenty of light and heat, it can extract all it needs from the sand and will throw off the surplus. *All the oxygen you're breathing now comes from these plants*—there's no other source in this dome."

"I see," said Gibson slowly. "So you'd already thought of my idea—and gone a good deal further. But I still don't understand the need for all this secrecy."

"What secrecy?" said Hadfield with an air of injured innocence.

"Really!" protested Gibson. "You've just asked me not to say anything about this place."

"Oh, that's because there will be an official announcement in a few days, and we haven't wanted to raise false hopes. But there hasn't been any real secrecy."

Gibson brooded over this remark all the way back to Port Lowell. Hadfield had told him a good deal, but had he told him everything? Where—if at all—did Phobos come into the picture? Gibson wondered if his suspicions about the inner moon were completely unfounded; it could obviously have no connection with this particular project. He felt like trying to force Hadfield's hand by a direct question, but thought better of it. He might only make himself look a fool if he did.

The domes of Port Lowell were climbing up over the steeply convex horizon when Gibson broached the subject that had been worrying him for the past fortnight.

"The *Ares* is going back to Earth in three weeks, isn't she?" he remarked to Hadfield. The other merely nodded; the question was obviously a purely rhetorical one for Gibson knew the answer as well as anybody.

"I've been thinking," said Gibson slowly, "that I'd like to stay on Mars a bit longer. Maybe until next year."

"Oh," said Hadfield. The exclamation revealed neither congratulation nor disapproval, and Gibson felt a little piqued that his shattering announcement had fallen flat. "What about your work?" continued the Chief.

"All that can be done just as easily here as on Earth."

"I suppose you realise," said Hadfield, "that if you stay here you'll have to take up some useful profession." He smiled a little wryly. "That wasn't very tactful, was it? What I mean is that you'll have to do something to help run the colony. Have you any particular ideas in this line?"

This was a little more encouraging; at least it meant that Hadfield had not dismissed the suggestion at once. But it was a point that Gibson had overlooked in his first rush of enthusiasm.

"I wasn't thinking of making a permanent home here," he said a little lamely. "But I want to spend some time studying the Martians, and I'd like to see if I can find any more of them. Besides, I don't want to leave Mars just when things are getting interesting."

"What do you mean?" said Hadfield swiftly.

"Why—these oxygen plants, and getting Dome Seven into operation. I want to see what comes of all this in the next few months."

Hadfield looked thoughtfully at his passenger. He was less surprised than Gibson might have imagined, for he had seen this sort of thing happen before. He had even wondered if it was going to happen to Gibson, and was by no means displeased at the turn of events.

The explanation was really very simple. Gibson was happier now than he had ever been on Earth; he had done something worth while, and felt that he was becoming part of the Martian community. The identification was now nearly complete, and the fact that Mars had already made one attempt on his life had merely strengthened his determination to stay. If he returned to Earth, he would not be going home—he would be sailing into exile.

"Enthusiasm isn't enough, you know," said Hadfield.

"I quite understand that."

"This little world of ours is founded on two things—skill and hard work. Without both of them, we might just as well go back to Earth."

"I'm not afraid of work, and I'm sure I could learn some of the administrative jobs you've got here—and a lot of the routine technical ones."

This, Hadfield thought, was probably true. Ability to do these things was a function of intelligence, and Gibson had plenty of that. But more than intelligence was needed; there were personal factors as well. It would be best not to raise Gibson's hopes until he had made further enquiries and discussed the matter with Whittaker.

"I'll tell you what to do," said Hadfield. "Put in a provisional application to stay, and I'll have it signalled to Earth. We'll get their answer in about a week. Of course, if they turn you down there's nothing we can do."

Gibson doubted this, for he knew just how much notice Hadfield took of terrestrial regulations when they interfered with his plans. But he merely said: "And if Earth agrees, then I suppose it's up to you?"

"Yes. I'll start thinking about my answer then."

That, thought Gibson, was satisfactory as far as it went. Now that he had taken the plunge, he felt a great sense of relief, as if everything was now outside his control. He had merely to drift with the current, awaiting the progress of events.

The door of the airlock opened before them and the Flea crunched into the city. Even if he had made a mistake, no great harm would be done. He could always go back to Earth by the next ship—or the one after.

But there was no doubt that Mars had changed him. He knew what some of his friends would say when they read the news. "Have you heard about Martin? Looks as if Mars has made a man out of him! Who'd have thought it?"

Gibson wriggled uncomfortably. He had no intention of becoming an elevating object lesson for anyone, if he could help it. Even in his most maudlin moments he had never had the slightest use for those smug Victorian parables about lazy, self-centred men becoming useful members of the community. But he had a horrible fear that something uncommonly like this was beginning to happen to him.

14

"Out with it, Jimmy. What's on your mind? You don't seem to have much appetite this morning."

Jimmy toyed fretfully with the synthetic omelette on his plate, which he had already carved into microscopic fragments.

"I was thinking about Irene, and what a shame it is she's never had a chance of seeing Earth."

"Are you sure she wants to? I've never heard anyone here say a single good word for the place."

"Oh, she wants to all right. I've asked her."

"Stop beating about the bush. What are you two planning now? Do you want to elope in the *Ares?*"

Jimmy gave a rather sickly grin.

"That's an idea, but it would take a bit of doing! Honestly though—don't you think Irene ought to go back to Earth to finish her education? If she stays here she'll grow up into a—a——"

"A simple unsophisticated country girl—a raw colonial? Is that what you were thinking?"

"Well, something like that, but I wish you wouldn't put it so crudely."

"Sorry—I didn't mean to. As a matter of fact, I rather agree with you; it's a point that's occurred to me. I think someone ought to mention it to Hadfield."

"That's exactly what——" began Jimmy excitedly.

"—what you and Irene want me to do?"

Jimmy threw up his hands in mock despair.

"It's no good trying to kid you. Yes."

"If you'd said that at the beginning, think of the time we'd have saved. But tell me frankly, Jimmy—just how serious are you about Irene?"

Jimmy looked back at him with a level, steadfast gaze that was in itself a sufficient answer.

"I'm dead serious; you ought to know that. I want to marry her as soon as she's old enough—and I can earn my living."

There was a dead silence, then Gibson replied:

"You could do a lot worse; she's a very nice girl. And I think it would do her a lot of good to have a year or so on Earth. Still, I'd rather not tackle Hadfield at the moment. He's very busy and—well, he's already got one request from me."

"Oh?" said Jimmy, looking up with interest.

Gibson cleared his throat.

"It's got to come out some time, but don't say anything to the others yet. I've applied to stay on Mars."

"Good Lord!" exclaimed Jimmy. "That's—well, quite a thing to do."

Gibson suppressed a smile.

"Do you think it's a good thing?"

"Why, yes. I'd like to do it myself."

"Even if Irene was going back to Earth?" asked Gibson dryly.

"That isn't fair! But how long do you expect to stay?"

"Frankly, I don't know; it depends on too many factors. For one thing, I'll have to learn a job!"

"What sort of job?"

"Something that's congenial—and productive. Any ideas?"

Jimmy sat in silence for a moment, his forehead wrinkled with concentration. Gibson wondered just what he was thinking. Was he sorry that they might soon have to separate? In the last few weeks the strain and animosities which had once both repelled and united them had dissolved away. They had reached a state of emotional equilibrium which was pleasant, yet not as satisfactory as Gibson would have hoped. Perhaps it was his own fault; perhaps he had been afraid to show his deeper feelings and had hidden them behind banter and even occasional sarcasm. If so, he was afraid he might have succeeded only too well. Once he had hoped to earn Jimmy's trust and confidence; now, it seemed, Jimmy only came to him when he wanted something. No—that wasn't fair. Jimmy certainly liked him, perhaps as much as many sons liked their fathers. That was a positive achievement of which he could be proud. He could take some credit, too, for the great improvement in Jimmy's disposition since they had left Earth. He was no longer awkward and shy; though he was still rather serious, he was never sullen. This, thought Gibson, was something in which he could take a good deal of satisfaction. But now there was little more he could do. Jimmy was slipping out of his world—Irene was the only thing that mattered to him now.

"I'm afraid I don't seem to have any ideas," said Jimmy. "Of course, you could have my job here! Oh, that reminds me of something I picked up in Admin the other day." His voice dropped to a conspiratorial whisper and he leaned across the table. "Have you ever heard of 'Project Dawn'?"

"No; what is it?"

"That's what I'm trying to find out. It's something very secret, and I think it must be pretty big."

"Oh!" said Gibson, suddenly alert. "Perhaps I have heard about it after all. Tell me what you know."

"Well, I was working late one evening in the filing section, and was sitting on the floor between some of the cabinets, sorting out papers, when the Chief and Mayor Whittaker came in. They didn't know I was there, and were talking together. I wasn't trying to eavesdrop, but you know how it is. All of a sudden Mayor Whittaker said something that made me sit up with a bang. I think these were his exact words: 'Whatever happens, there's going to be hell to pay as soon as Earth knows about Project Dawn—even if it's successful.' Then the Chief gave a queer little laugh, and said something about success excusing everything. That's all I could hear; they went out soon afterwards. What do you think about it?"

"Project Dawn!" There was a magic about the name that made Gibson's pulse quicken. Almost certainly it must have some connection with the research going on up in the hills above the city—but that could hardly justify Whittaker's remark. Or could it?

Gibson knew a little about the interplay of political forces between Earth and Mars. He appreciated, from occasional remarks of Hadfield's and comments in the local press, that the colony was now passing through a critical period. On Earth, powerful voices were raised in protest against its enormous expense, which, it seemed, would extend indefinitely into the future with no sign of any ultimate reduction. More than once Hadfield had spoken bitterly of schemes which he had been compelled to abandon on grounds of economy, and of other projects for which permission could not be obtained at all.

"I'll see what I can find out from my—er—various

sources of information," said Gibson. "Have you mentioned it to anyone else?"

"No."

"I shouldn't, if I were you. After all, it may not be anything important. I'll let you know what I find out."

"You won't forget to ask about Irene?"

"As soon as I get the chance. But it may take some time—I'll have to catch Hadfield in the right mood!"

As a private detective agency, Gibson was not a success. He made two rather clumsy direct attempts before he decided that the frontal approach was useless. George the barman had been his first target, for he seemed to know everything that was happening on Mars and was one of Gibson's most valuable contacts. This time, however, he proved of no use at all.

"Project Dawn?" he said, with a puzzled expression. "I've never heard of it."

"Are you quite sure?" asked Gibson, watching him narrowly.

George seemed to lose himself in deep thought.

"Quite sure," he said at last. And that was that. George was such an excellent actor that it was quite impossible to guess whether he was lying or speaking the truth.

Gibson did a trifle better with the editor of the "Martian Times." Westerman was a man he normally avoided, as he was always trying to coax articles out of him and Gibson was invariably behind with his terrestrial commitments. The staff of two therefore looked up with some surprise as their visitor entered the tiny office of Mars' only newspaper.

Having handed over some carbon copies as a peace offering, Gibson sprang his trap.

"I'm trying to collect all the information I can on 'Project Dawn,' " he said casually. "I know it's still under cover, but I want to have everything ready when it can be published."

There was dead silence for several seconds. Then Westerman remarked: "I think you'd better see the Chief about that."

"I didn't want to bother him—he's so busy," said Gibson innocently.

"Well, I can't tell you anything."

"You mean you don't know anything about it?"

"If you like. There are only a few dozen people on Mars who could even tell you what it is."

That, at least, was a valuable piece of information.

"Do you happen to be one of them?" asked Gibson.

Westerman shrugged his shoulders.

"I keep my eyes open, and I've done a bit of guessing."

That was all that Gibson could extract from him. He strongly suspected that Westerman knew little more about the matter than he did himself, but was anxious to conceal his ignorance. The interview had, however, confirmed two main facts. "Project Dawn" certainly did exist, and it was extremely well hidden. Gibson could only follow Westerman's example, keeping his eyes open and guessing what he could.

He decided to abandon the quest for the time being and to go round to the Biophysics Lab, where Squeak was the guest of honour. The little Martian was sitting on his haunches taking life easily while the scientists stood conversing in a corner, trying to decide what to do next. As soon as he saw Gibson, he gave a chirp of delight and bounded across the room, bringing down a chair as he did so but luckily missing any valuable apparatus. The bevy of biologists regarded this demonstration with some annoyance; presumably it could not be reconciled with their views on Martian psychology.

"Well," said Gibson to the leader of the team, when he had disentangled himself from Squeak's clutches. "Have you decided how intelligent he is yet?"

The scientist scratched his head.

"He's a queer little beast. Sometimes I get the feeling he's just laughing at us. The odd thing is that he's quite different from the rest of his tribe. We've got a unit studying them in the field, you know."

"In what way is he different?"

"The others don't show any emotions at all, as far as we can discover. They're completely lacking in curiosity. You can stand beside them and if you wait long enough they'll eat right round you. As long as you don't actively interfere with them they'll take no notice of you."

"And what happens if you do?"

"They'll try and push you out of the way, like some obstacle. If they can't do that, they'll just go somewhere else. Whatever you do, you can't make them annoyed."

"Are they good-natured, or just plain stupid?"

"I'd be inclined to say it's neither one nor the other. They've had no natural enemies for so long that they can't imagine that anyone would try to hurt them. By now they must be largely creatures of habit; life's so tough for them that they can't afford expensive luxuries like curiosity and the other emotions."

"Then how do you explain this little fellow's behaviour?" asked Gibson, pointing to Squeak, who was now investigating his pockets. "He's not really hungry—I've just offered him some food—so it must be pure inquisitiveness."

"It's probably a phase they pass through when they're young. Think how a kitten differs from a full-grown cat—or a human baby from an adult, for that matter."

"So when Squeak grows up he'll be like the others?"

"Probably, but it isn't certain. We don't know what capacity he has for learning new habits. For instance, he's very good at finding his way out of mazes—once you can persuade him to make the effort."

"Poor Squeak!" said Gibson. "Sometimes I feel quite guilty about taking you away from home. Still, it was your own idea. Let's go for a walk."

Squeak immediately hopped towards the door.

"Did you see that?" exclaimed Gibson. "He understands what I'm saying."

"Well, so can a dog when it hears a command. It may simply be a question of habit again—you've been taking him out this time every day and he's got used to it. Can you bring him back inside half an hour? We're fixing up the encephalograph to get some EEG records of his brain."

These afternoon walks were a way of reconciling Squeak to his fate and at the same time salving Gibson's conscience. He sometimes felt rather like a baby-snatcher who had abandoned his victim immediately after stealing it. But it was all in the cause of science, and the biologists had sworn they wouldn't hurt Squeak in any way.

The inhabitants of Port Lowell were now used to seeing this strangely assorted pair taking their daily stroll along the streets, and crowds no longer gathered to watch them pass. When it was outside school hours Squeak usually collected a retinue of young admirers who wanted to play with him, but it was now early afternoon and the juvenile population was still in durance vile. There was no one in sight when Gibson and his companion swung into Broadway, but presently a familiar figure appeared in the distance. Hadfield was carrying out his daily tour of inspection, and as usual he was accompanied by his pets.

It was the first time that Topaz and Turquoise had met Squeak, and their aristocratic calm was seriously disturbed, though they did their best to conceal the fact. They tugged on their leads and tried to shelter unobtrusively behind Hadfield, while Squeak took not the slightest notice of them at all.

"Quite a menagerie!" laughed Hadfield. "I don't think Topaz and Turquoise appreciate having a rival—they've had the place to themselves so long that they think they own it."

"Any news from Earth yet?" asked Gibson, anxiously.

"Oh, about your application?" Good heavens, I only sent it off two days ago! You know just how quickly things move down there. It will be at least a week before we get an answer."

The Earth was always "down," the outer planets "up," so Gibson had discovered. The terms gave him a curious mental picture of a great slope leading down to the Sun, with the planets lying on it at varying heights.

"I don't really see what it's got to do with Earth," Gibson continued. "After all, it's not as if there's any question of allocating shipping space. I'm here already—in fact it'll save trouble if I *don't* go back!"

"You surely don't imagine that such commonsense arguments carry much weight with the policy-makers back on Earth!" retorted Hadfield. "Oh, dear no! Everything has to go through the Proper Channels."

Gibson was fairly sure that Hadfield did not usually talk about his superiors in this light-hearted fashion, and he felt that peculiar glow of satisfaction that comes when one is permitted to share a deliberate indiscretion. It was another sign that the C.E. trusted him and considered that he was on his side. Dare he mention the two other matters that were occupying his mind—Project Dawn and Irene? As far as Irene was concerned, he had made his promise and would have to keep it sooner or later. But first he really ought to have a talk with Irene herself—yes, that was a perfectly good excuse for putting it off.

He put it off so long that the matter was taken right out of his hands. Irene herself made the plunge, no doubt egged on by Jimmy, from whom Gibson had a full report the next day. It was easy to tell from Jimmy's face what the result had been.

Irene's suggestion must have been a considerable shock to Hadfield, who no doubt believed that he had given his daughter everything she needed, and thus shared a delusion common among parents. Yet he had taken it calmly and there had been no scenes. Hadfield was too intelligent a man to adopt the attitude of the deeply wounded father. He had merely given lucid and compelling reasons why Irene couldn't possibly go to Earth until she was twenty-one, when he planned to return for a long holiday during which they could see the world together. And that was only three years away.

"Three years!" lamented Jimmy. "It might just as well be three lifetimes!"

Gibson deeply sympathised, but tried to look on the bright side of things.

"It's not so long, really. You'll be fully qualified then and earning a lot more money than most young men at that age. And it's surprising how quickly the time goes."

This Job's comforting produced no alleviation of Jimmy's gloom. Gibson felt like adding the comment that it was just as well that ages on Mars were still reckoned by Earth time, and not according to the Martian year of 687 days. However, he thought better of it and remarked instead: "What does Hadfield think about all this, anyway? Has he discussed you with Irene?"

"I don't think he knows anything about it."

"You can bet your life he does! You know, I really think it would be a good idea to go and have it out with him."

"I've thought of that, once or twice," said Jimmy. "But I guess I'm scared."

"You'll have to get over that some time if he's going to be your father-in-law!" retorted Gibson. "Besides, what harm could it do?"

"He might stop Irene seeing me in the time we've still got."

"Hadfield isn't that sort of man, and if he was he'd have done it long ago."

Jimmy thought this over and was unable to refute it. To some extent Gibson could understand his feelings, for he remembered his own nervousness at his first meeting with Hadfield. In this he had had much less excuse than

Jimmy, for experience had long ago taught him that few great men remain great when one gets up close to them. But to Jimmy, Hadfield was still the aloof and unapproachable master of Mars.

"If I *do* go and see him," said Jimmy at last, "what do you think I ought to say?"

"What's wrong with the plain, unvarnished truth? It's been known to work wonders on such occasions."

Jimmy shot him a slightly hurt look; he was never quite sure whether Gibson was laughing with him or at him. It was Gibson's own fault, and was the chief obstacle to their complete understanding.

"Look," said Gibson. "Come along with me to the Chief's house tonight, and have it out with him. After all, look at it from his point of view. For all he can tell, it may be just an ordinary flirtation with neither side taking it very seriously. But if you go and tell him you want to get engaged—then it's a different matter."

He was much relieved when Jimmy agreed with no more argument. After all, if the boy had anything in him he should make these decisions himself, without any prompting. Gibson was sensible enough to realise that, in his anxiety to be helpful, he must not run the risk of destroying Jimmy's self-reliance.

It was one of Hadfield's virtues that one always knew where to find him at any given time—though woe betide anyone who bothered him with routine official matters during the few hours when he considered himself off duty. This matter was neither routine nor official; and it was not, as Gibson had guessed, entirely unexpected either, for Hadfield had shown no surprise at all when he saw whom Gibson had brought with him. There was no sign of Irene, she had thoughtfully effaced herself. As soon as possible, Gibson did the same.

He was waiting in the library, running through Hadfield's books and wondering how many of them the Chief had actually had time to read, when Jimmy came in.

"Mr. Hadfield would like to see you," he said.

"How did you get on?"

"I don't know yet, but it wasn't so bad as I'd expected."

"It never is. And don't worry. I'll give you the best reference I can without actual perjury."

When Gibson entered the study, he found Hadfield sunk

in one of the armchairs, staring at the carpet as though he had never seen it before in his life. He motioned his visitor to take the other chair.

"How long have you known Spencer?" he asked.

"Only since leaving Earth. I'd never met him before boarding the *Ares*."

"And do you think that's long enough to form a clear opinion of his character?"

"Is a lifetime long enough to do that?" countered Gibson.

Hadfield smiled, and looked up for the first time.

"Don't evade the issue," he said, though without irritation. "What do you really think about him? Would *you* be willing to accept him as a son-in-law?"

"Yes," said Gibson, without hesitation. "I'd be glad to."

It was just as well that Jimmy could not overhear their conversation in the next ten minutes—though in other ways, perhaps, it was rather a pity, for it would have given him much more insight into Gibson's feelings. In his carefully probing cross-examination, Hadfield was trying to learn all he could about Jimmy, but he was testing Gibson as well. This was something that Gibson should have anticipated; the fact that he had overlooked it in serving Jimmy's interests was no small matter to his credit. When Hadfield's interrogation suddenly switched its point of attack, he was totally unprepared for it.

"Tell me, Gibson," said Hadfield abruptly. "Why are you taking all this trouble for young Spencer? You say you only met him five months ago."

"That's perfectly true. But when we were a few weeks out I discovered that I'd known both his parents very well—we were all at college together."

It had slipped out before he could stop it. Hadfield's eyebrows went up slightly; no doubt he was wondering why Gibson had never taken his degree. But he was far too tactful to pursue this subject, and merely asked a few casual questions about Jimmy's parents, and when he had known them.

At least, they seemed casual questions—just the kind Hadfield might have been expected to ask, and Gibson answered them innocently enough. He had forgotten that he was dealing with one of the keenest minds in the Solar System, one at least as good as his own at analysing the springs and motives of human conduct. When he realised what had happened, it was already too late.

"I'm sorry," said Hadfield, with deceptive smoothness, "but this whole story of yours simply lacks conviction. I don't say that what you've told me isn't the truth. It's perfectly possible that you might take such an interest in Spencer because you knew his parents very well twenty years ago. But you've tried to explain away too much, and it's quite obvious that the whole affair touches you at an altogether deeper level." He leaned forward suddenly and stabbed at Gibson with his finger.

"I'm not a fool, Gibson, and men's minds are my business. You've no need to answer this if you don't want to, but I think you owe it to me now. *Jimmy Spencer is your son, isn't he?*"

The bomb had dropped—the explosion was over. And in the silence that followed Gibson's only emotion was one of overwhelming relief.

"Yes," he said. "He is my son. How did you guess?"

Hadfield smiled; he looked somewhat pleased with himself, as if he had just settled a question that had been bothering him for some time.

"It's extraordinary how blind men can be to the effects of their own actions—and how easily they assume that no one else has any powers of observation. There's a slight but distinct likeness between you and Spencer; when I first met you together I wondered if you were related and was quite surprised when I heard you weren't."

"It's very curious," interjected Gibson, "that we were together in the *Ares* for three months, and no one noticed it there."

"Is it so curious? Spencer's crewmates thought they knew his background, and it never occurred to them to associate it with you. That probably blinded them to the resemblance which I—who hadn't any preconceived ideas—spotted at once. But I'd have dismissed it as pure coincidence if you hadn't told me your story. That provided the missing clues. Tell me—does Spencer know this?"

"I'm sure he doesn't even suspect it."

"Why are you so sure? And why haven't you told him?"

The cross-examination was ruthless, but Gibson did not resent it. No one had a better right than Hadfield to ask these questions. And Gibson needed someone in whom to confide—just as Jimmy had needed him, back in the

Ares when this uncovering of the past had first begun. To think that he had started it all himself! He had certainly never dreamed where it would lead. . . .

"I think I'd better go back to the beginning," said Gibson, shifting uneasily in his chair. "When I left college I had a complete breakdown and was in hospital for over a year. After I came out I'd lost all contact with my Cambridge friends; though a few tried to keep in touch with me, I didn't want to be reminded of the past. Eventually, of course, I ran into some of them again, but it wasn't until several years later that I heard what had happened to Kathleen—to Jimmy's mother. By then, she was already dead."

He paused, still remembering, across all these years, the puzzled wonder he had felt because the news had brought him so little emotion.

"I heard there was a son, and thought little of it. We'd always been—well, careful, or so we believed—and I just assumed that the boy was Gerald's. You see, I didn't know when they were married, or when Jimmy was born. I just wanted to forget the whole business, and pushed it out of my mind. I can't even remember now if it even occurred to me that the boy might have been mine. You may find it hard to believe this, but it's the truth.

"And then I met Jimmy, and that brought it all back again. I felt sorry for him at first, and then began to get fond of him. But I never guessed who he was. I even found myself trying to trace his resemblance to Gerald—though I can hardly remember him now."

Poor Gerald! He, of course, had known the truth well enough, but he had loved Kathleen and had been glad to marry her on any terms he could. Perhaps he was to be pitied as much as she, but that was something that now would never be known.

"And when," persisted Hadfield, "did you discover the truth?"

"Only a few weeks ago, when Jimmy asked me to witness some official document he had to fill in—it was his application to start work here, in fact. That was when I first learned his date of birth."

"I see," said Hadfield thoughtfully. "But even that doesn't give absolute proof, does it?"

"I'm perfectly sure," Gibson replied with such obvious pique that Hadfield could not help smiling, "that there was no one else. Even if I'd had any doubts left, you've dispelled them yourself."

"And Spencer?" asked Hadfield, going back to his original question. "You've not told me why you're so confident he knows nothing. Why shouldn't he have checked a few dates? His parents' wedding day, for example? Surely what you've told him must have roused his suspicions?"

"I don't think so," said Gibson slowly, choosing his words with the delicate precision of a cat walking over a wet roadway. "You see, he rather idealises his mother, and though he may guess I haven't told him everything, I don't believe he's jumped to the right conclusion. He's not the sort who could have kept quiet about it if he had. And besides, he'd still have no proof even if he knows when his parents were married—which is more than most people do. No, I'm sure Jimmy doesn't know, and I'm afraid it will be rather a shock to him when he finds out."

Hadfield was silent; Gibson could not even guess what he was thinking. It was not a very creditable story, but at least he had shown the virtue of frankness.

Then Hadfield shrugged his shoulders in a gesture that seemed to hold a lifetime's study of human nature.

"He likes you," he said. "He'll get over it all right."

Gibson relaxed with a sigh of relief. He knew that the worst was past.

"Gosh, you've been a long time," said Jimmy. "I thought you were never going to finish; what happened?"

Gibson took him by the arm.

"Don't worry," he said. "It's quite all right. Everything's going to be all right now."

He hoped and believed he was telling the truth. Hadfield had been sensible, which was more than some fathers would have been even in this day and age.

"I'm not particularly concerned," he had said, "who Spencer's parents were or were not. This isn't the Victorian era. I'm only interested in the fellow himself, and I must say I'm favourably impressed. I've also had quite a chat about him with Captain Norden, by the way, so I'm not relying merely on tonight's interview. Oh yes, I saw all this coming a long time ago! There was even a certain inevitability about it, since there are very few youngsters of Spencer's age on Mars."

He had spread his hands in front of him—in a habit which Gibson had noticed before—and stared intently at his fingers as if seeing them for the first time in his life.

"The engagement can be announced tomorrow," he'd said softly. "And now—what about *your* side of the affair?" He'd stared keenly at Gibson, who returned his gaze without flinching.

"I want to do whatever is best for Jimmy," he had said. "Just as soon as I can decide what that is."

"And you still want to stay on Mars?" asked Hadfield.

"I'd thought of that aspect of it too," Gibson had said. "But if I went back to Earth, what good would that do? Jimmy'll never be there more than a few months at a time —in fact, from now on I'll see a lot more of him if I stay on Mars!"

"Yes, I suppose that's true enough," Hadfield had said, smiling. "How Irene's going to enjoy having a husband who spends half his life in space remains to be seen—but then, sailors' wives have managed to put up with this sort of thing for quite a long time." He paused abruptly.

"Do you know what I think you ought to do?" he said.

"I'd be very glad of your views," Gibson had replied with feeling.

"Do nothing until the engagement's over and the whole thing's settled. If you revealed your identity now I don't see what good it would do, and it might conceivably cause harm. Later, though, you must tell Jimmy who you are —or who he is, whichever way you like to look at it. But I don't think the right moment will come for quite a while."

It was the first time that Hadfield had referred to Spencer by his Christian name. He was probably not even conscious of it, but to Gibson it was a clear and unmistakable sign that he was already thinking of Jimmy as his son-in-law. The knowledge brought him a sudden sense of kinship and sympathy towards Hadfield. They were united in selfless dedication towards the same purpose—the happiness of the two children in whom they saw their own youth reborn.

Looking back upon it later, Gibson was to identify this moment with the beginning of his friendship with

Hadfield—the first man to whom he was ever able to give his unreserved admiration and respect. It was a friendship that was to play a greater part in the future of Mars than either could have guessed.

15

It had opened just like any other day in Port Lowell. Jimmy and Gibson had breakfasted quietly together—very quietly, for they were both deeply engrossed with their personal problems. Jimmy was still in what could best be described as an ecstatic condition, though he had occasional fits of depression at the thought of leaving Irene, while Gibson was wondering if Earth had yet made any move regarding his application. Sometimes he was sure the whole thing was a great mistake, and even hoped that the papers had been lost. But he knew he'd have to go through with it, and decided to stir things up at Admin.

He could tell that something was wrong the moment he entered the office. Mrs. Smyth, Hadfield's secretary, met him as she always did when he came to see the Chief. Usually she showed him in at once; sometimes she explained that Hadfield was extremely busy, or putting a call through to Earth, and could he come back later? This time she simply said: "I'm sorry, Mr. Hadfield isn't there. He won't be back until tomorrow."

"Won't be back?" queried Gibson. "Has he gone to Skia?

"Oh no," said Mrs. Smyth, wavering slightly but obviously on the defensive. "I'm afraid I can't say. But he'll be back in twenty-four hours."

Gibson decided to puzzle over this later. He presumed that Mrs. Smyth knew all about his affairs, so she could probably answer his question.

"Do you know if there's been any reply yet to my application?" he asked.

Mrs. Smyth looked even unhappier.

"I think there has," she said. "But it was a personal signal to Mr. Hadfield and I can't discuss it. I expect he'll want to see you about it as soon as he gets back."

This was most exasperating. It was bad enough not to have a reply, but it was even worse to have one you weren't allowed to see. Gibson felt his patience evaporating.

"Surely there's no reason why you shouldn't tell me about it!" he exclaimed. "Especially if I'll know tomorrow, anyway."

"I'm really awfully sorry, Mr. Gibson. But I know Mr. Hadfield will be most annoyed if I say anything now."

"Oh, very well," said Gibson, and went off in a huff.

He decided to relieve his feelings by tackling Mayor Whittaker—always assuming that he was still in the city. He was, and he did not look particularly happy to see Gibson, who settled himself firmly down in the visitor's chair in a way that obviously meant business.

"Look here, Whittaker," he began. "I'm a patient man and I think you'll agree I don't often make unreasonable requests." As the other showed no signs of making the right reply. Gibson continued hastily:

"There's something very peculiar going on round here and I'm anxious to get to the bottom of it."

Whittaker sighed. He had been expecting this to happen sooner or later. A pity Gibson couldn't have waited until tomorrow: it wouldn't have mattered then. . . .

"What's made you suddenly jump to this conclusion?" he asked.

"Oh, lots of things—and it isn't at all sudden. I've just tried to see Hadfield, and Mrs. Smyth told me he's not in the city and then closed up like a clam when I tried to ask a few innocent questions."

"I can just imagine her doing that!" grinned Whittaker cheerfully.

"If you try the same thing I'll start throwing the furniture around. At least if you can't tell me what's going on, for goodness' sake tell me *why* you can't tell me. It's Project Dawn, isn't it?"

That made Whittaker sit up with a start.

"How did you know?" he asked.

"Never mind; I can be stubborn too."

"I'm not trying to be stubborn," said Whittaker plaintively. "Don't think we like secrecy for the sake of it; it's a confounded nuisance. But suppose you start telling me what you know."

"Very well, if it'll soften you up. Project Dawn is something to do with that plant genetics place up in the hills where you've been cultivating—what do you call it?—*Oxyfera*. As there seems no point in keeping that quiet, I can only assume it's part of a much bigger plan. I suspect Phobos is mixed up with it, though I can't imagine how. You've managed to keep it so secret that the few people on Mars who know anything about it just won't talk. But you haven't been trying to conceal it from Mars so much as from Earth. Now what have you got to say?"

Whittaker appeared to be not in the least abashed.

"I must compliment you on your—er—perspicacity," he said. "You may also be interested to know that, a couple of weeks ago, I suggested to the Chief that we ought to take you fully into our confidence. But he couldn't make up his mind, and since then things have happened rather more rapidly than anyone expected."

He doodled absentmindedly on his writing pad, then came to a decision.

"I won't jump the gun," he said, "and I can't tell you what's happening now. But here's a little story that may amuse you. Any resemblance to—ah—real persons and places is quite coincidental."

"I understand," grinned Gibson. "Go on."

"Let's suppose that in the first rush of interplanetary enthusiasm world A has set up a colony on world B. After some years it finds that this is costing a lot more than it expected, and has given no tangible returns for the money spent. Two factions then arise on the mother world. One, the conservative group, wants to close the project down—to cut its losses and get out. The other group, the progressives, wants to continue the experiment because they believe that in the long run Man has got to explore and master the material universe, or else he'll simply stagnate on his own world. But this sort of argument is no use with the taxpayers, and the conservatives are beginning to get the upper hand.

"All this, of course, is rather unsettling to the colonists, who are getting more and more independently minded and don't like the idea of being regarded as poor relations living on charity. Still, they don't see any way out—until one day a revolutionary scientific discovery is made. (I should have explained at the beginning that planet B has been attracting the finest brains of A, which is another reason why A is getting annoyed.) This discovery opens up almost unlimited prospects for the future of B, but to apply it involves certain risks, as well as the diversion of a good deal of B's limited resources. Still, the plan is put forward—and is promptly turned down by A. There is a protracted tug-of-war behind the scenes, but the home planet is adamant.

"The colonists are then faced with two alternatives. They can force the issue out into the open, and appeal to the public on world A. Obviously they'll be at a great disadvantage, as the men on the spot can shout them down. The other choice is to carry on with the plan without informing Earth—I mean, planet A—and this is what they finally decided to do.

"Of course, there were a lot of other factors involved —political and personal, as well as scientific. It so happened that the leader of the colonists was a man of unusual determination who wasn't scared of anything or anyone, on either of the planets. He had a team of first-class scientists behind him, and they backed him up. So the plan went ahead; but no one knows yet if it will be successful. I'm sorry I can't tell you the end of the story; you know how these serials always break off at the most exciting place."

"I think you've told me just about everything," said Gibson. "Everything, that is, except one minor detail. I *still* don't know what Project Dawn is." He rose to go. "Tomorrow I'm coming back to hear the final instalment of your gripping serial."

"There won't be any need to do that," Whittaker replied. He glanced unconsciously at the clock. "You'll know long before then."

As he left the Administration Building, Gibson was intercepted by Jimmy.

"I'm supposed to be at work," he said breathlessly, "but I had to catch you. Something important's going on."

"I know," replied Gibson rather impatiently. "Project Dawn's coming to the boil, and Hadfield's left town."

"Oh," replied Jimmy, a little taken aback. "I didn't think you'd have heard. But you won't know this, anyway. Irene's very upset. She told me her father said good-bye last night as if—well, as if he mightn't see her again."

Gibson whistled. That put things in a different light. Project Dawn was not only big, it might be dangerous. This was a possibility he had not considered.

"Whatever's happening," he said, "we'll know all about it tomorrow—Whittaker's just told me that. But I think I can guess where Hadfield is right now."

"Where?"

"He's up on Phobos. For some reason, that's the key to Project Dawn, and that's where you'll find the Chief right now."

Gibson would have made a large bet on the accuracy of this guess. It was just as well that there was no one to take it, for he was quite wrong. Hadfield was now almost as far away from Phobos as he was from Mars. At the moment he was sitting in some discomfort in a small spaceship, which was packed with scientists and their hastily dismantled equipment. He was playing chess, and playing it very badly, against one of the greatest physicists in the Solar System. His opponent was playing equally badly, and it would soon have become quite obvious to any observer that they were simply trying to pass the time. Like everyone on Mars, they were waiting; but they were the only ones who knew exactly what they were waiting for.

The long day—one of the longest that Gibson had ever known—slowly ebbed away. It was a day of wild rumours and speculation: everyone in Port Lowell had some theory which they were anxious to air. But as those who knew the truth said nothing, and those who knew nothing said too much, when night came the city was in a state of extreme confusion. Gibson wondered if it was worth while staying up late, but around midnight he decided to go to bed. He was fast asleep when, invisibly, soundlessly, hidden from him by the thickness of the planet, Project Dawn came to its climax. Only the men in the watching spaceship saw it happen, and changed suddenly from grave scientists to shouting, laughing schoolboys as they turned to race for home.

In the very small hours of the morning Gibson was wakened by a thunderous banging on his door. It was Jimmy, shouting to him to get up and come outside. He dressed hastily, but when he reached the door Jimmy had already gone out into the street. He caught him up at the doorway. From all sides, people were beginning to appear, rubbing their eyes sleepily and wondering what had happened. There was a rising buzz of voices and distant shouts; Port Lowell sounded like a beehive that had been suddenly disturbed.

It was a full minute before Gibson understood what had awakened the city. Dawn was just breaking: the eastern sky was aglow with the first light of the rising Sun. The eastern sky? *My God, that dawn was breaking in the west.*

No one could have been less superstitious than Gibson, but for a moment the upper levels of his mind were submerged by a wave of irrational terror. It lasted only a moment; then reason reasserted itself. Brighter and brighter grew the light spilling over the horizon; now the first rays were touching the hills above the city. They were moving swiftly—far, far too swiftly for the Sun—and suddenly a blazing, golden meteor leapt up out of the desert, climbing almost vertically towards the zenith.

Its very speed betrayed its identity. This was Phobos—or what had been Phobos a few hours before. Now it was a yellow disc of fire, and Gibson could feel the heat of its burning upon his face. The city around him was now utterly silent, watching the miracle and slowly waking to a dim awareness of all that it might mean to Mars.

So this was Project Dawn—it had been well named. The pieces of the jig-saw puzzle were falling into place, but the main pattern was still not clear. To have turned Phobos into a second sun was an incredible feat of—presumably—nuclear engineering, yet Gibson did not see how it could solve the colony's problems. He was still worrying over this when the seldom used public-address system of Port Lowell burst into life and Whittaker's voice came drifting softly down the streets.

"Hello, everybody," he said. "I guess you're all awake by now and have seen what's happened. The Chief Executive's on his way back from space and would like to speak to you. Here he is."

There was a click; then someone said, *sotto voce:* "You're on to Port Lowell, sir." A moment later Hadfield's voice came out of the speakers. He sounded tired but triumphant, like a man who had fought a great battle and won through to victory.

"Hello, Mars," he said. "Hadfield speaking. I'm still in space on the way home—I'll be landing in about an hour.

"I hope you like your new sun. According to our calculations, it will take nearly a thousand years to burn itself out. We triggered Phobos off when it was well below your horizon, just in case the initial radiation peak was too high. The reaction's now stabilised at exactly the level we expected, though it may increase by a few per cent during the next week. It's mainly a meson resonance reaction, very efficient but not very violent, and there's no chance of a fully fledged atomic explosion with the material composing Phobos.

"Your new luminary will give you about a tenth of the Sun's heat, which will bring up the temperature of much of Mars to nearly the same value as Earth's. But that isn't the reason why we blew up Phobos—at least, it isn't the main reason.

"Mars wants oxygen more badly than heat—and all the oxygen needed to give it an atmosphere almost as good as Earth's is lying beneath your feet, locked up in the sand. Two years ago we discovered a plant that can break the sand down and release the oxygen. It's a tropical plant—it can exist only on the equator and doesn't really flourish even there. If there was enough sunlight available, it could spread over Mars—with some assistance from us—and in fifty years there'd be an atmosphere here that men could breathe. *That's* the goal we're aiming at: when we've reached it, we can go where we please on Mars and forget about our domed cities and breathing masks. It's a dream that many of you will live to see realised, and it'll mean that we've given a new world to mankind.

"Even now, there are some benefits we'll derive right away. It will be very much warmer, at least when Phobos and the Sun are shining together, and the winters will be much milder. Even though Phobos isn't visible above latitude seventy degrees, the new convection winds will warm the polar regions too, and will prevent our precious moisture from being locked up in the ice caps for half of every year.

"There'll be some disadvantages—the seasons and nights are going to get complicated now!—but they'll be far outweighed by the benefits. And every day, as you see the beacon we have now lit climbing across the sky, it will remind you of the new world we're bringing to birth. We're making history, remember, for this is the first time that Man has tried his hand at changing the face of a planet. If we succeed here, others will do the same elsewhere. In the ages to come, whole civilisations on worlds of which we've never heard will owe their existence to what we've done tonight.

"That's all I've got to say now. Perhaps you may regret the sacrifice we've had to make to bring life to this world again. But remember this—though Mars has lost a Moon, it's gained a Sun—and who can doubt which is the more valuable?

"And now—good night to you all."

But no one in Port Lowell went back to sleep. As far as the city was concerned, the night was over and the new day had dawned. It was hard to take one's eyes off that tiny golden disc as it climbed steadily up the sky, its warmth growing greater minute by minute. What would the Martian plants be making of it? Gibson wondered. He walked along the street until he came to the nearest section of the dome, and looked out through the transparent wall. It was as he had expected: they had all awakened and turned their faces to the new Sun. He wondered just what they would do when both Suns were in the sky together. . . .

The Chief's rocket landed half an hour later, but Hadfield and the scientists of Project Dawn avoided the crowds by coming into the city on foot through Dome Seven, and sending the transport on to the main entrance as a decoy. This ruse worked so well that they were all safely indoors before anyone realised what had happened, or could start celebrations which they were too tired to appreciate. However, this did not prevent numerous private parties forming all over the city—parties at which everyone tried to claim that they had known what Project Dawn was all the time.

Phobos was approaching the zenith, much nearer and therefore much warmer than it had been on rising, when Gibson and Jimmy met their crewmates in the crowd that had good-naturedly but firmly insisted to George that he had better open up the bar. Each party claimed it had only homed on this spot because it was sure it would find the other there.

Hilton, who as Chief Engineer might be expected to know more about nucleonics than anyone else in the assembly, was soon pushed to the fore and asked to explain just what had happened. He modestly denied his competence to do anything of the sort.

"What they've done up on Phobos," he protested, "is years ahead of anything I ever learned at college. Why, even meson reactions hadn't been discovered then—let alone how to harness them. In fact, I don't think anyone on Earth knows how to do that, even now. It must be something that Mars has learned for itself."

"Do you mean to tell me," said Bradley, "that Mars is ahead of Earth in nuclear physics—or anything else for that matter?"

This remark nearly caused a riot and Bradley's colleagues had to rescue him from the indignant colonists—which they did in a somewhat leisurely fashion. When peace had been restored, Hilton nearly put *his* foot in it by remarking: "Of course, you know that a lot of Earth's best scientists have been coming here in the last few years, so it's not as surprising as you might think."

The statement was perfectly true, and Gibson remembered the remark that Whittaker had made to him that very morning. Mars had been a lure to many others besides himself, and now he could understand why. What prodigies of persuasion, what intricate negotiations and downright deceptions Hadfield must have performed in these last few years! It had, perhaps, been not too difficult to attract the really first-rate minds; they could appreciate the challenge and respond to it. The second-raters, the equally essential rank-and-file of science, would have been harder to find. One day, perhaps, he would learn the secrets behind the secret, and discover just how Project Dawn had been launched and guided to success.

What was left of the night seemed to pass very swiftly. Phobos was dropping down into the eastern sky when the Sun rose up to greet its rival. It was a duel that all the city watched in silent fascination—a one-sided conflict that could have only a predetermined outcome. When it shone alone in the night sky, it was easy to pretend that Phobos was almost as brilliant as the Sun, but the first light of the true dawn banished the illusion. Minute by minute Phobos faded, though it was still well above the horizon, as the Sun came up out of the desert. Now one could tell how pale and yellow it was by comparison. There was little danger that the slowly turning plants would be confused in their quest for light; when the Sun was shining, one scarcely noticed Phobos at all.

But it was bright enough to perform its task, and for a thousand years it would be the lord of the Martian night. And thereafter? When its fires were extinguished, by the exhaustion of whatever elements it was burning now, would Phobos become again an ordinary moon, shining only by the Sun's reflected glory?

Gibson knew that it would not matter. Even in a century it would have done its work, and Mars would have an atmosphere which it would not lose again for geological ages. When at last Phobos guttered and died, the science of that distant day would have some other answer—perhaps an answer as inconceivable to this age as the detonation of a world would have been only a century ago.

For a little while, as the first day of the new age grew to maturity, Gibson watched his double shadow lying upon the ground. Both shadows pointed to the west, but though one scarcely moved, the fainter lengthened even as he watched, becoming more and more difficult to see, until at last it was snuffed out as Phobos dropped down below the edge of Mars.

Its sudden disappearance reminded Gibson abruptly of something that he—and most of Port Lowell—had forgotten in the last few hours' excitement. By now the news would have reached Earth; perhaps—though he wasn't sure of this—Mars must now be spectacularly brighter in terrestrial skies.

In a very short time, Earth would be asking some extremely pointed questions.

16

It was one of those little ceremonies so beloved by the TV newsreels. Hadfield and all his staff were gathered in a tight group at the edge of the clearing, with the domes of Port Lowell rising behind them. It was, thought the cameraman, a nicely composed picture, though the constantly changing double illumination made things a little difficult.

He got the cue from the control room and started to pan from left to right to give the viewers a bit of movement before the real business began. Not that there was really much to see: the landscape was so flat and they'd miss all its interest in this monochrome transmission. (One couldn't afford the band-width for colour on a live transmission all the way to Earth; even on black-and-white it was none too easy.) He had just finished exploring the scene when he got the order to swing back to Hadfield, who was now making a little speech. That was going out on the other sound channel and he couldn't hear it, though in the control room it would be mated to the picture he was sending. Anyway, he knew just what the Chief would be saying—he'd heard it all before.

Mayor Whittaker handed over the shovel on which he had been gracefully leaning for the last five minutes, and Hadfield began to tip in the sand until he had covered the roots of the tall, drab Martian plant standing there, held upright in its wooden frame. The "airweed," as it was now universally called, was not a very impressive object: it scarcely looked strong enough to stand upright, even under this low gravity. It certainly didn't look as if it could control the future of a planet. . . .

Hadfield had finished his token gardening; someone else could complete the job and fill in the hole. (The planting team was already hovering in the background, waiting for the bigwigs to clear out of the way so that they could get on with their work.) There was a lot of hand-shaking and back-slapping; Hadfield was hidden by the crowd that had gathered round him. The only person who wasn't taking the slightest notice of all this was Gibson's pet Martian, who was rocking on his haunches like one of those weighted dolls that always come the same way up however you put them down. The cameraman swung towards him and zoomed to a close-up; it would be the first time anyone on Earth would have seen a real Martian—at least in a live programme like this.

Hello—what was he up to? Something had caught his interest—the twitching of those huge, membranous ears gave him away. He was beginning to move in short, cautious hops. The camerman chased him and widened the field at the same time to see where he was going. No one else had noticed that he'd begun to move; Gibson was still talking to Whittaker and seemed to have completely forgotten his pet.

So *that* was the game! This was going to be good; the folk back on Earth would love it. Would he get there before he was spotted? Yes—he'd made it! With one final bound he hopped down into the little pit, and the small triangular beak began to nibble at the slim Martian plant that had just been placed there with such care. No doubt he thought it so kind of his friends to go to all this trouble for him. . . . Or did he really know he was being naughty? That devious approach had been so skilful that it was hard to believe it was done in complete innocence. Anyway, the cameraman wasn't going to spoil his fun; it would make too good a picture. He cut for a moment back to Hadfield and Company, still congratulating themselves on the work which Squeak was rapidly undoing.

It was too good to last. Gibson spotted what was happening and gave a great yell which made everyone jump. Then he raced towards Squeak, who did a quick look round, decided that there was nowhere to hide, and just sat still with an air of injured innocence. He let himself be led away quietly, not aggravating his offence by resisting the forces of the law when Gibson grabbed one of his ears and tugged him away from the scene of the crime. A group of experts then gathered anxiously around the airweed, and to everyone's relief it was soon decided that the damage was not fatal.

It was a trivial incident, which no one would have imagined to have any consequences beyond the immediate moment. Yet, though he never realised the fact, it was to inspire one of Gibson's most brilliant and fruitful ideas.

Life for Martin Gibson had suddenly become very complicated—and intensely interesting. He had been one of the first to see Hadfield after the inception of Project Dawn. The C.E. had called for him, but had been able to give him only a few minutes of his time. That, however, had been enough to change the pattern of Gibson's future.

"I'm sorry I had to keep you waiting," Hadfield said, "but I got the reply from Earth only just before I left. The answer is that you can stay here if you can be absorbed into our administrative structure—to use the official jargon. As the future of our 'administrative structure' depended somewhat largely on Project Dawn, I thought it best to leave the matter until I got back home."

The weight of uncertainty had lifted from Gibson's mind. It was all settled now; even if he had to make a mistake—and he did not believe he had—there was now no going back. He had thrown in his lot with Mars; he would be part of the colony in its fight to regenerate this world that was now stirring sluggishly in its sleep.

"And what job have you got for me?" Gibson asked a little anxiously.

"I've decided to regularise your unofficial status," said Hadfield, with a smile.

"What do you mean?"

"Do you remember what I said at our very first meeting? I asked you to help us by giving Earth not the mere facts of the situation, but also some idea of our goals and—I suppose you could call it—the spirit we've built up here on Mars. You've done well, despite the fact that you didn't know about the project on which we'd set our greatest hopes. I'm sorry I had to keep Dawn from you, but it would have made your job much harder if you'd known our secret and weren't able to say anything. Don't you agree?"

Gibson had not thought of it in that light, but it certainly made sense.

"I've been very interested," Hadfield continued, "to see what result your broadcasts and articles have had. You may not know that we've got a delicate method of testing this."

"How?" asked Gibson in surprise.

"Can't you guess? Every week about ten thousand people, scattered all over Earth, decide they want to come here, and something like three per cent pass the preliminary tests. Since your articles started appearing regularly, that figure's gone up to fifteen thousand a week, and it's still rising."

"Oh," said Gibson, very thoughtfully. He gave an abrupt little laugh. "I also seem to remember," he added, "that you didn't want me to come here in the first place."

"We all make mistakes, but I've learned to profit by mine," smiled Hadfield. "To sum it all up, what I'd like you to do is to lead a small section which, frankly, will be our propaganda department. Of course, we'll think of a nicer name for it! Your job will be to sell Mars. The opportunities are far greater now that we've really got something to put in out shop window. If we can get enough people clamouring to come here, then Earth will be forced to provide the shipping space. And the quicker that's done, the sooner we can promise Earth we'll be standing on our own feet. What do you say?"

Gibson felt a fleeting disappointment. Looked at from one point of view, this wasn't much of a change. But the C.E. was right: he could be of greater use to Mars in this way than in any other.

"I can do it," he said. "Give me a week to sort out my terrestrial affairs and clear up my outstanding commitments."

A week was somewhat optimistic, he thought, but that should break the back of the job. He wondered what Ruth was going to say. She'd probably think he was mad, and she'd probably be right.

"The news that you're going to stay here," said Hadfield with satisfaction, "will cause a lot of interest and will be quite a boost to our campaign. You've no objection to our announcing it right away?"

"I don't think so."

"Good. Whittaker would like to have a word with you now about the detailed arrangements. You realise, of course, that your salary will be that of a Class II Administrative Officer of your age?"

"Naturally I've looked into that," said Gibson. He did not add, because it was unncessary, that this was largely of theoretical interest. His salary on Mars, though less than a tenth of his total income, would be quite adequate for a comfortable standard of living on a planet where there were very few luxuries. He was not sure just how he could use his terrestrial credits, but no doubt they could be employed to squeeze something through the shipping bottleneck.

After a long session with Whittaker—who nearly succeeded in destroying his enthusiasm with laments about lack of staff and accommodation—Gibson spent the rest of the day writing dozens of radiograms. The longest was to Ruth, and was chiefly, but by no means wholly, concerned with business affairs. Ruth had often commented on the startling variety of things she did for her ten per cent, and Gibson wondered what she was going to say to this request that she keep an eye on one James Spencer, and generally look after him when he was in New York—which, since he was completing his studies at M.I.T., might be fairly often.

It would have made matters much simpler if he could have told her the facts; she would probably guess them, anyway. But that would be unfair to Jimmy; Gibson had made up his mind that he would be the first to know. There were times when the strain of not telling him was so great that he felt almost glad they would soon be parting. Yet Hadfield, as usual, had been right. He had waited a generation—he must wait a little longer yet. To reveal himself now might leave Jimmy confused and hurt—might even cause the breakdown of his engagement to Irene. The time to tell him would be when they had been married and, Gibson hoped, were still insulated from any shocks which the outside world might administer.

It was ironic that, having found his son so late, he must now lose him again. Perhaps that was part of the punishment for the selfishness and lack of courage—to put it no more strongly—he had shown twenty years ago. But the past must bury itself; he must think of the future now.

Jimmy would return to Mars as soon as he could—there was no doubt of that. And even if he had missed the pride and satisfaction of parenthood, there might be compensations later in watching his grandchildren come into the world he was helping to remake. For the first time in his life, Gibson had a future to which he could look forward with interest and excitement—a future which would not be merely a repetition of the past.

Earth hurled its thunderbolt four days later. The first Gibson knew about it was when he saw the headline across the front page of the "Martian Times." For a ment the two words staring back at him were so asto ing that he forgot to read on.

HADFIELD RECALLED

We have just received news that the Interplaneta Development Board has requested the Chief Exec tive to return to Earth on the *Ares,* which leav Deimos in four days. No reason is given.

That was all, but it would set Mars ablaze. No re was given—and none was necessary. Everyone knew actly why Earth wanted to see Warren Hadfield.

"What do you think of this?" Gibson asked Jimm he passed the paper across the breakfast table.

"Good Lord!" gasped Jimmy. "There'll be tro now! What do you think he'll do?"

"What can he do?"

"Well, he can refuse to go. Everyone here would tainly back him up."

"That would only make matters worse. He'll go right. Hadfield isn't the sort of man to run away fr fight."

Jimmy's eyes suddenly brightened.

"That means that Irene will be going too."

"Trust you to think of that!" laughed Gibson. "I pose you hope it will be an ill wind blowing the pa you some good. But don't count on it—Hadfield leave Irene behind."

He thought this very unlikely. When the Chief retu he would need all the moral support he could get.

Despite the amount of work he had awaiting him, son paid one brief call to Admin, where he found e one in a state of mingled indignation and suspense. nation because of Earth's cavalier treatment of the C suspense because no one yet knew what action he going to take. Hadfield had arrived early that morning so far had not seen anyone except Whittaker and hi vate secretary. Those who had caught a glimpse of stated that for a man who was, technically, about recalled in disgrace, he looked remarkably cheerful.

Gibson was thinking over this news as he made a d towards the Biology Lab. He had missed seeing his Martian friend for two days, and felt rather guilty abo

As he walked slowly along Regent Street, he wondered what sort of defence Hadfield would be able to put up. Now he understood that remark that Jimmy had overheard. *Would* success excuse everything? Success was still a long way off; as Hadfield had said, to bring Project Dawn to its conclusion would take half a century, even assuming the maximum assistance from Earth. It was essential to secure that support, and Hadfield would do his utmost not to antagonise the home planet. The best that Gibson could do to support him would be to provide long-range covering fire from his propaganda department.

Squeak, as usual, was delighted to see him, though Gibson returned his greeting somewhat absentmindedly. As he invariably did, he proffered Squeak a fragment of airweed from the supply kept in the Lab. That simple action must have triggered something in his subconscious mind, for he suddenly paused, then turned to the chief biologist.

"I've just had a wonderful idea," he said. "You know you were telling me about the tricks you've been able to teach Squeak?"

"Teach him! The problem now is to stop him learning them!"

"You also said you were fairly sure the Martians could communicate with each other, didn't you?"

"Well, our field party's proved that they can pass on simple thoughts, and even some abstract ideas like colour. That doesn't prove much, of course. Bees can do the same."

"Then tell me what you think of this. Why shouldn't we teach them to cultivate the airweed for us? You see what a colossal advantage they've got—they can go anywhere on Mars they please, while we'd have to do everything with machines. They needn't *know* what they're doing, of course. We'd simply provide them with the shoots—it does propagate that way, doesn't it?—teach them the necessary routine, and reward them afterwards."

"Just a moment! It's a pretty idea, but haven't you overlooked some practical points? I think we could train them in the way you suggest—we've certainly learned enough about their psychology for that—but may I point out that there are only ten known specimens, including Squeak?"

"I hadn't overlooked that," said Gibson impatiently. "I simply don't believe the group I found is the only one in existence. That would be a quite incredible coincidence.

Certainly they're rather rare, but there must be hundreds, if not thousands, of them over the planet. I'm going to suggest a photo-reconnaissance of all the airweed forests—we should have no difficulty in spotting their clearings. But in any case I'm taking the long-term view. Now that they've got far more favourable living conditions, they'll start to multiply rapidly, just as the Martian plant life's already doing. Remember, even if we left it to itself the airweed would cover the equatorial regions in four hundred years—according to your own figures. With the Martians *and* us to help it spread, we might cut years off Project Dawn!"

The biologist shook his head doubtfully, but began to do some calculations on a scribbling pad. When he had finished he pursed his lips.

"Well . . . I," he said, "I can't actually prove it's impossible; there are too many unknown factors—including the most important one of all—the Martian's reproduction rate. Incidentally, I suppose you know that they're marsupials? That's just been confirmed."

"You mean like kangaroos?"

"Yes. Junior lives under cover until he's a big enough boy to go out into the cold, hard world. We think several of the females are carrying babies, so they may reproduce yearly. And since Squeak was the only infant we found, that means they must have a terrifically high death-rate—which isn't surprising in this climate."

"Just the conditions we want!" exclaimed Gibson. "Now there'll be nothing to stop them multiplying, providing we see they get all the food they need."

"Do you want to breed Martians or cultivate airweed?" challenged the biologist.

"Both," grinned Gibson. "They go together like fish and chips, or ham and eggs."

"Don't!" pleaded the other, with such a depth of feeling that Gibson apologised at once for his lack of tact. He had forgotten that no one on Mars had tasted such things for years.

The more Gibson thought about his new idea, the more it appealed to him. Despite the pressure of his personal affairs, he found time to write a memorandum to Hadfield on the subject, and hoped that the C.E. would be able to discuss it with him before returning to Earth. There was something inspiring in the thought of regenerating not only a world, but also a race which might be older than Man.

Gibson wondered how the changed climatic conditions of a hundred years hence would affect the Martians. If it became too warm for them, they could easily migrate north or south—if necessary into the sub-polar regions where Phobos was never visible. As for the oxygenated atmosphere—they had been used to that in the past and might adapt themselves to it again. There was considerable evidence that Squeak now obtained much of his oxygen from the air in Port Lowell, and seemed to be thriving on it.

There was still no answer to the great question which the discovery of the Martians had raised. Were they the degenerate survivors of a race which had achieved civilisation long ago, and let it slip from its grasp when conditions became too severe? This was the romantic view, for which there was no evidence at all. The scientists were unanimous in believing that there had never been any advanced culture on Mars—but they had been proved wrong once and might be so again. In any case, it would be an extremely interesting experiment to see how far up the evolutionary ladder the Martians would climb, now that their world was blossoming again.

For it was their world, not Man's. However he might shape it for his own purposes, it would be his duty always to safeguard the interests of its rightful owners. No one could tell what part they might have to play in the history of the universe. And when, as was one day inevitable, Man himself came to the notice of yet higher races, he might well be judged by his behaviour here on Mars.

17

"I'm sorry you're not coming back with us, Martin," said Norden as they approached Lock One West, "but I'm sure you're doing the right thing, and we all respect you for it."

"Thanks," said Gibson sincerely. "I'd like to have made the return trip with you all—still, there'll be plenty of chances later! Whatever happens, I'm not going to be on Mars *all* my life!" He chuckled. "I guess you never thought you'd be swapping passengers in this way."

"I certainly didn't. It's going to be a bit embarrassing in some respects. I'll feel like the captain of the ship who had to carry Napoleon to Elba. How's the Chief taking it?"

"I've not spoken to him since the recall came through, though I'll be seeing him tomorrow before he goes up to Deimos. But Whittaker says he seems confident enough, and doesn't appear to be worrying in the slightest."

"What do *you* think's going to happen?"

"On the official level, he's bound to be reprimanded for misappropriation of funds, equipment, personnel—oh, enough things to land him in jail for the rest of his life. But as half the executives and all the scientists on Mars are involved, what can Earth do about it? It's really a very amusing situation. The C.E.'s a public hero on two worlds, and the Interplanetary Development Board will have to handle him with kid gloves. I think the verdict will be: 'You shouldn't have done it, but we're rather glad you did.' "

"And then they'll let him come back to Mars?"

"They're bound to. No one else can do his job."

"Someone will have to, one day."

"True enough, but it would be madness to waste Hadfield when he's still got years of work in him. And heaven help anyone who was sent here to replace him!"

"It certainly *is* a peculiar position. I think a lot's been going on that we don't know about. Why did Earth turn down Project Dawn when it was first suggested?"

"I've been wondering about that, and intend to get to the bottom of it some day. Meanwhile my theory is this—I think a lot of people on Earth don't want Mars to become too powerful, still less completely independent. Not for any sinister reason, mark you, but simply because they don't like the idea. It's too wounding to their pride. They want the Earth to remain the centre of the universe."

"You know," said Norden, "it's funny how you talk about 'Earth' as if it were some combination of miser and bully, preventing all progress here. After all, it's hardly fair! What you're actually grumbling at are the administrators in the Interplanetary Development Board and all its allied organisations—and they're really trying to do their best. Don't forget that everything you've got here is due to the enterprise and initiative of Earth. I'm afraid you colonists"—he gave a wry grin as he spoke—"take a very self-centred view of things. I can see both sides of the question. When I'm here I get your point of view and can sympathise with it. But in three months' time I'll be on the other side and will probably think you're a lot of grumbling, ungrateful nuisances here on Mars!"

Gibson laughed, not altogether comfortably. There was a good deal of truth in what Norden had said. The sheer difficulty and expense of interplanetary travel, and the time it took to get from world to world, made inevitable some lack of understanding, even intolerance, between Earth and Mars. He hoped that as the speed of transport increased these psychological barriers would be broken down and the two planets would come closer together in spirit as well as in time.

They had now reached the lock and were waiting for the transport to take Norden out to the airstrip. The rest of the crew had already said good-bye and were now on their way up to Deimos. Only Jimmy had received special dispensation to fly up with Hadfield and Irene when they left tomorrow. Jimmy had certainly changed his status, thought Gibson with some amusement, since the *Ares* had left Earth. He wondered just how much work Norden was going to get out of him on the homeward voyage.

"Well, John, I hope you have a good trip back," said Gibson, holding out his hand as the airlock door opened. "When will I be seeing you again?"

"In about eighteen months—I've got a trip to Venus to

put in first. When I get back here, I expect to find quite a difference—airweed and Martians everywhere!"

"I don't promise much in that time," laughed Gibson. "But we'll do our best not to disappoint you!"

They shook hands, and Norden was gone. Gibson found it impossible not to feel a twinge of envy as he thought of all the things to which the other was returning—all the unconsidered beauties of Earth which he had once taken for granted, and now might not see again for many years.

He still had two farewells to make, and they would be the most difficult of all. His last meeting with Hadfield would requite considerable delicacy and tact. Norden's analogy, he thought, had been a good one: it would be rather like an interview with a dethroned monarch about to sail into exile.

In actual fact it proved to be like nothing of the sort. Hadfield was still master of the situation, and seemed quite unperturbed by his future. When Gibson entered he had just finished sorting out his papers; the room looked bare and bleak and three wastepaper baskets were piled high with discarded forms and memoranda. Whittaker, as acting Chief Executive, would be moving in tomorrow.

"I've run through your note on the Martians and the airweed," said Hadfield, exploring the deeper recesses of his desk. "It's a very interesting idea, but no one can tell me whether it will work or not. The position's extremely complicated and we haven't enough information. It really comes down to this—would we get a better return for our efforts if we teach Martians to plant airweed, or if we do the job ourselves? Anyway, we'll set up a small research group to look into the idea, though there's not much we can do until we've got some more Martians! I've asked Dr. Petersen to handle the scientific side, and I'd like you to deal with the administrative problems as they arise—leaving any major decisions to Whittaker, of course. Petersen's a very sound fellow, but he lacks imagination. Between the two of you, we should get the right balance."

"I'll be very glad to do all I can," said Gibson, quite pleased with the prospect, though wondering a little nervously how he would cope with his increasing responsibilities. However, the fact that the Chief had given him the job was encouraging: it meant that Hadfield, at any rate, was sure that he could handle it.

As they discussed administrative details, it became clear

to Gibson that Hadfield did not expect to be away from Mars for more than a year. He even seemed to be looking forward to his trip to Earth, regarding it almost in the light of an overdue holiday. Gibson hoped that this optimism would be justified by the outcome.

Towards the end of their interview, the conversation turned inevitably to Irene and Jimmy. The long voyage back to Earth would provide Hadfield with all the opportunities he needed to study his prospective son-in-law, and Gibson hoped that Jimmy would be on his best behaviour. It was obvious that Hadfield was contemplating this aspect of the trip with quiet amusement. As he remarked to Gibson, if Irene and Jimmy could put up with each other in such close quarters for three months, their marriage was bound to be a success. If they couldn't—then the sooner they found out, the better.

As he left Hadfield's office, Gibson hoped that he had made his own sympathy clear. The C.E. knew that he had all Mars behind him, and Gibson would do his best to gain him the support of Earth as well. He looked back at the unobtrusive lettering on the door. There would be no need to change that, whatever happened, since the words designated the position and not the man. For twelve months or so Whittaker would be working behind that door, the democratic ruler of Mars and the—within reasonable limits—conscientious servant of Earth. Whoever came and went, the lettering on the door would remain. That was another of Hadfield's ideas—the tradition that the post was more important than the man. He had not, Gibson thought, given it a very good start, for anonymity was scarcely one of Hadfield's personal characteristics.

The last rocket to Deimos left three hours later with Hadfield, Irene, and Jimmy aboard. Irene had come round to the Grand Martian Hotel to help Jimmy pack and to say good-bye to Gibson. She was bubbling over with excitement and so radiant with happiness that it was a pleasure simply to sit and watch her. Both her dreams had come true at once: she was going back to Earth, and she was going with Jimmy. Gibson hoped that neither experience would disappoint her; he did not believe it would.

Jimmy's packing was complicated by the number of souvenirs he had gathered on Mars—chiefly plant and mineral specimens collected on various trips outside the Dome. All these had to be carefully weighed, and some heartrending decisions were involved when it was discovered that he had exceeded his personal allowance by two kilogrammes. But finally the last suitcase was packed and on its way to the airport.

"Now don't forget," said Gibson, "to contact Mrs. Goldstein as soon as you arrive; she'll be expecting to hear from you."

"I won't," Jimmy replied. "It's good of you to take all this trouble. We really do appreciate everything you've done—don't we, Irene?"

"Yes," she answered, "we certainly do. I don't know how we'd have got on without you."

Gibson smiled, a little wistfully.

"Somehow," he said, "I think you'd still have managed in one way or another! But I'm glad everything's turned out so well for you, and I'm sure you're going to be very happy. And—I hope it won't be too long before you're both back on Mars."

As he gripped Jimmy's hand in farewell, Gibson felt once again that almost overwhelming desire to reveal his identity and, whatever the consequences, to greet Jimmy as his son. But if he did so, he knew now, the dominant motive would be pure egotism. It would be an act of possessiveness, of inexcusable self-assertion, and it would undo all the good he had wrought in these past months. Yet as he dropped Jimmy's hand, he glimpsed something in the other's expression that he had never seen before. It could have been the dawn of the first puzzled surmise, the birth of the still half-conscious thought that might grow at last to fully fledged understanding and recognition. Gibson hoped it was so; it would make his task easier when the time came.

He watched them go hand-in-hand down the narrow street, oblivious to all around them, their thoughts even now winging outwards into space. Already they had forgotten him; but, later, they would remember.

It was just before dawn when Gibson left the main airlock and walked away from the still sleeping city. Phobos had set an hour ago; the only light was that of the stars and Deimos, now high in the west. He looked at his watch—ten minutes to go if there had been no hitch.

"Come on, Squeak," he said. "Let's take a nice brisk walk to keep warm." Though the temperature around them was at least fifty below, Squeak did not seem unduly worried. However, Gibson thought it best to keep his pet on the move. He was, of course, perfectly comfortable himself, as he was wearing his full protective clothing.

How these plants had grown in the past few weeks! They were now taller than a man, and though some of this increase might be normal, Gibson was sure that much of it was due to Phobos. Project Dawn was already leaving its mark on the planet. Even the North Polar Cap, which should now be approaching its midwinter maximum, had halted in its advance over the opposite hemisphere—and the remnants of the southern cap had vanished completely.

They came to a stop about a kilometre from the city, far enough away for its lights not to hinder observation. Gibson glanced again at his watch. Less than a minute left; he knew what his friends were feeling now. He stared at the tiny, barely visible gibbous disc of Deimos, and waited.

Quite suddenly, Deimos became conspicuously brighter. A moment later it seemed to split into two fragments as a tiny, incredibly bright star detached itself from its edge and began to creep slowly westwards. Even across these thousands of kilometres of space, the glare of the atomic rockets was so dazzling that it almost hurt the eye.

He did not doubt that they were watching him. Up there in the *Ares*, they would be at the observation windows, looking down upon the great crescent world which they were leaving now, as a lifetime ago, it seemed, he had bade farewell to Earth.

What was Hadfield thinking now? Was he wondering if he would ever see Mars again? Gibson no longer had any real doubts on this score. Whatever battles Hadfield might have to face, he would win through as he had done in the past. He was returning to Earth in triumph, not in disgrace

That dazzling blue-white star was several degrees from Deimos now, falling behind as it lost speed to drop Sunwards—and Earthwards.

The rim of the Sun came up over the eastern horizon; all around him, the tall green plants were stirring in their sleep—a sleep already interrupted once by the meteoric passage of Phobos across the sky. Gibson looked once more at the two stars descending in the west, and raised his hand in a silent farewell.

"Come along, Squeak," he said. "Time to get back—I've got work to do." He tweaked the little Martian's ears with his gloved fingers.

"And that goes for you too," he added. "Though you don't know it yet, we've both got a pretty big job ahead of us."

They walked together towards the great domes, now glistening faintly in the first morning light. It would be strange in Port Lowell, now that Hadfield had gone and another man was sitting behind the door marked "Chief Executive."

Gibson suddenly paused. For a fleeting moment, it seemed, he saw into the future, fifteen or twenty years ahead. Who would be Chief then, when Project Dawn was entering its middle phase and its end could already be foreseen?

The question and the answer came almost simultaneously. For the first time, Gibson knew what lay at the end of the road on which he had now set his feet. One day, perhaps, it would be his duty, and his privilege, to take over the work which Hadfield had begun. It might have been sheer self-deception, or it might have been the first consciousness of his own still hidden powers—but whichever it was, he meant to know.

With a new briskness in his step, Martin Gibson, writer, late of Earth, resumed his walk towards the city. His shadow merged with Squeak's as the little Martian hopped beside him; while overhead the last hues of night drained from the sky, and all around, the tall, flowerless plants were unfolding to face the sun.